TREASURED SECRETS

Book One in the Treasure Hunters Series

KENDALL TALBOT

Published 2018

Treasured Secrets

Book One in the Treasure Hunter Series

© 2018 by Kendall Talbot

ISBN: 9781072439981

v.2022.7

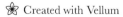 Created with Vellum

Contents

About the Author

Romantic Book of the Year author, Kendall Talbot, writes action-packed romantic suspense loaded with sizzling heat and intriguing mysteries set in exotic locations. She hates cheating, loves a good happily ever after, and thrives on exciting adventures with kick-ass heroines and heroes with rippling abs and broken hearts.

Kendall has sought thrills in all 44 countries she's visited. She's rappelled down freezing waterfalls, catapulted out of a white-water raft, jumped off a mountain with a man who spoke little English, and got way too close to a sixteen-foot shark.

She lives in Brisbane, Australia with her very own hero and a fluffy little dog who specializes in hijacking her writing time. When she isn't writing or reading, she's enjoying wine and cheese with her crazy friends and planning her next international escape.

She loves to hear from her readers!

Find her books and chat with her via any of the contacts below:

www.kendalltalbot.com
Email: kendall@universe.com.au

Or you can find her on any of the following channels:

Amazon
Bookbub
Goodreads

Books by Kendall Talbot

Treasure Hunter Series:

Treasured Secrets

Treasured Lies

Treasured Dreams

Treasured Whispers

Treasured Hopes

Treasured Tears

Waves of Fate Series

First Fate

Feral Fate

Final Fate

Waves of Fate

Alpha Tactical Ops Series

Escape Mission

Hostile Mission

Rescue Mission

Maximum Exposure Series:

(These stand-alone books can be read in any order):

Extreme Limit

Deadly Twist (Finalist: Wilbur Smith Adventure Writing Prize 2021)

Zero Escape

Stand-Alone books:

Lost in Kakadu (Winner: Romantic Book of the year 2014)

Jagged Edge

Double Take

If you sign up to my newsletter you can help with fun things like naming characters and giving characters quirky traits and interesting jobs. You'll also get my book, Treasured Kisses which is exclusive to my newsletter followers only, for free.

Here's my newsletter signup link if you're interested:

http://www.kendalltalbot.com.au/newsletter.html

Chapter One

Archer bolted upright. A scream burned his throat, and sweat-soaked sheets strangled his body. Determined to shake the horror, he covered his face with his hands and inhaled sharply.

But it was useless.

The nightmares were parasites, every night nibbling at his sanity, piece by piece.

Rosalina switched on the bedside lamp. "Oh babe, another nightmare?"

Archer squinted against the glare.

"Want some water?" Her warm hand was of little comfort on his shoulder.

Archer nodded, not trusting his voice.

He focused on her well-toned bottom as she walked towards the bedroom door. She wore only white underpants that hugged her athletic curves. And yet even her spectacular body couldn't settle the horror in his mind.

The night outside was his enemy, mocking him with its soothing darkness, but at the same time declaring many more hours until morning.

He wouldn't get back to sleep. He never did.

Rosalina returned with a glass of water, and he gulped down the cool liquid.

"That was a bad one." She sat on the edge of the bed. "Do you want to talk about it?"

"No."

"It might help."

"I said no." He threw off the sheets and strode to the window.

How many times had he done this?

When Rosalina wrapped her arms around him, he wondered how many times she had, too.

And how many more would the future hold? What kind of life is this?

Her warm breasts pressed into his back as she planted kisses across his shoulders. The nightmares were his punishment, and his alone. Not one that he needed to share, let alone with the woman he loved. Her suffering like this was selfish.

It had to stop.

She ran her hands over his chest, and he melted into her embrace. The hairs on his neck bristled with desire as he softened under her caress. Rosalina knew how to bring back his sanity. He had no idea how he could live without her.

But he had to. Somehow.

He turned to her. The wetness of her eyes glistened in the glow through the window. Seeing her like this, hurting for him, suffering through the nightmares as much as he did, convinced him it was time to step back.

They'd become too close.

He could never give her what she deserved. His heart clenched like a fist at what he had to do. He had to let her go. It was best for Rosalina, and although it would hurt her in the short term, it was the right thing to do.

If he didn't, she'd suffer alongside him forever.

And that was worse than some temporary heartache.

He kissed the salty tears from her lips. When she opened her mouth, their tongues danced. It took all his willpower to withdraw. He wove his fingers into her long hair and, as he clutched her to his chest, he stared across the marina.

His mind twisted and bucked.

Despite his want for her, Rosalina could no longer be part of his life.

Today would be their last day together. The inevitable decision, long overdue, smothered his heart like a dark stain.

He kissed her forehead, led her back to bed and tucked her under the sheet. Once he slipped into bed beside her, she rolled onto her side and turned off the lamp. The marina lights once again gave the room a warm glow.

"I love you," she said.

"You too, babe." He couldn't say he loved her.

He never had.

And now I never will.

Chapter Two

Rosalina breathed in the crisp, salty air, trying to eradicate the torment racing through her mind. During her short walk to the marina, she usually planned her meals for the day.

Not today, though.

Not when she'd laid awake most of the night worrying about Archer. She'd tried to talk to him many times about his nightmares. But he refused to open up.

How much longer could they do this for? Months? Decades?

The smell of frying bacon wafting in the breeze snapped her free of the impossible questions and she turned her attention to planning today's menu.

Heavy ropes clanged against towering masts of the surrounding boats in a creative staccato and she waved to familiar faces as she walked along the pontoon to Archer's luxury, multi-million-dollar yacht.

Evangeline's sleek lines showed off her power and shiny chrome railings proved she was loved.

Rosalina headed straight to her favorite place on the yacht. . . the galley. Archer would seek her out when his stomach rumbled enough. He always did.

Within minutes of putting on her apron, she was whizzing around the kitchen with the skills she'd mastered at one of Italy's most prestigious culinary schools. Although her love of cooking came from her beloved Nonna, the woman who'd raised her and her five siblings.

Nonna's constant mantra had been. . . 'eat, then we talk'.

Food solved everything.

Although Rosalina knew first hand, that wasn't always true.

Glancing at the time, she opened the oven door to check on her pastries, and the sweet aroma of apples dusted with cinnamon sugar filled the galley.

She nibbled on the buttery pastry, hoping it would ease her apprehension, like it usually did. Not this time. As a full-blooded Italian and a chef, that rarely happened.

But she was not one to procrastinate and at the sound of footsteps, she made up her mind to discuss the nightmares. *Again.*

She lost her appetite at that decision and put the half-eaten pastry aside.

Archer strolled into the kitchen. His white singlet showed off his healthy tan. Rosalina drank in the lines of his nicely toned shoulders, just enough muscle to make her feel safe in his arms, but not too much to throw his figure out of proportion. She inhaled his musk-scented cologne as he kissed her cheek and reached for a still steaming pastry.

"Looks like it's going to be a nice day." She leaned against the counter, hugged her mug to her chest, and breathed in the full-bodied aroma, but her favorite coffee blend did little to settle her nerves.

His quick smile drilled a dimple into each cheek. "Sure is. There's a nice breeze coming in, but it'll be a hot one." He bit into the pastry, but the heat had him sucking in air.

She giggled. He never waited for her pastries to cool. Yet it didn't stop him from devouring it in three more mouthfuls.

"Mmm, yummy."

She smiled. "You're the one that's yummy."

He picked her up, sat her on the marble counter, and parted her knees to ease his hips between her thighs. She wrapped her legs around him and hooked her ankles together, trapping him.

His eyes softened, and subtle creases curled at their corners when he smiled. "I'm sorry about last night."

"That damn nightmare…" She let the sentence hang, hoping he'd respond.

But he didn't. "Did you get back to sleep?"

"Yes." He drove his fingers through his blond curls.

She regarded him for a moment, trying to read his mind. It was impossible. "I know you didn't."

The halo of gold flecks around his dark irises vanished in a flash. He released her ankles and stepped back; his jaw clenched.

She persisted anyway. "Honey, I really think you should see someone about what's haunting you."

"Not this again."

"But it's always the same dream. Right?" It was a trick question. She had no idea what the nightmares were about.

"Yes."

"Are you being attacked or something?" She held her breath; her heart thumping as she waited for his answer.

He narrowed his eyes. "I know what you're doing. But forget it. I'm not talking about it."

"This is ridiculous, Arch." She jumped down from the counter and tilted her face at him. "For three years you've been waking up beside me screaming, and I don't know how to help."

He grinned. "Lying next to your naked body helps."

She cupped her coffee mug in one hand, placed her other hand on his chest, and stared into eyes that'd lost a fraction of their usual glimmer. "Let me in, Arch."

"I told you, no." He took another step back, shaking his head.

"Just tell me what it's about. Are you being murdered?"

"No." His tone implied she was being ridiculous.

"It's frightening to see you like that." She hesitated, her mind scrambling for the best way to make him open up. "You always seem so scared. If I knew a little, I could help."

"It's nothing like that. Just a shark attack."

She searched him for signs of truth. Although this admission was huge, it struck her as strange. When they scuba-dived together, she'd seen him try to touch sharks many times. He was obsessed with getting close to them. Him having nightmares about sharks made little sense. "But you're not scared of sharks," she stated the obvious.

"Nope. It's a stupid dream." He reached for the necklace that never left his neck, wrapping his fingers around the unusual pendant. The heavy, gold piece was curved in shape and about the same size as his thumb.

As she'd done a hundred times before, she pondered its significance. It was another secret that frustrated her. *Why won't he talk about them?*

She decided to push her luck. "Does the pendant have anything to do with it?"

Simmering distrust flashed across his eyes, and she instantly regretted the question.

"I'm not talking about it, so drop it."

Rosalina sighed and placed her coffee mug on the marble countertop. The morning elixir had become bitter. Archer's stubborn reluctance to trust her with the details of the nightmares and the pendant had her heart crumbling.

What could make them such guarded secrets?

The two things were linked somehow. . . the way he clammed up when she mentioned either of them was testament to that.

"We can't go on like this, Arch." Their love would never be whole if he couldn't tell her everything. "You refuse to talk about two significant things in your life, and I go crazy thinking about them."

"You don't need to know. They mean nothing."

Her heart jumped. "They mean everything to you, and that affects me. Your nightmares have us both crying in the middle of the night, and that damn pendant you refuse to take off just about knocks my teeth out every time we have sex."

His eyes drilled into her. Rosalina had crossed a line.

But this was the argument they had to have.

"This is who I am. I can't change. Maybe it's time. . ." He hesitated, the muscles in his jaw tightened, "for you to leave."

Her stomach twisted. He'd said that so easily. As if he'd been searching for a reason to say them. "Is that what you want? You'd rather lose me than share your secrets? What the hell, Archer? Do you even love me?"

He folded his arms across his chest. "Right now, I don't know."

Her heart launched into her throat. "Love isn't something you can switch off. Either you love me or you don't."

The coldness in his eyes scared her. Her chin quivered, but she fought her emotions. She wanted the truth and didn't want her tears affecting his reaction.

She walked to the window, turning her back to him, steeling herself. "Answer me. Do you love me?" She held her breath as she stared out at the marina. His stony silence was sickening.

She spun towards him. "Will you ever let me into your heart?" She waited for a reaction, any reaction.

Archer appeared frozen, trapped in confusion. His usual smiling eyes darkened, and in that moment, Rosalina had her truth.

She tore off her apron and stomped from the galley. Tears spilled down her cheeks. By the time she reached the pontoon, her throat had constricted so much she could barely breathe. The smell of frying bacon made her nauseous.

Archer called after her, but she sprinted away, ignoring the stares from people along the marina.

Rosalina kept her pace until she reached the door to Archer's apartment. Once inside, she jabbed the combination into the alarm panel and raced to the upstairs bedroom.

Resisting the urge to throw herself onto the bed and cry the day away, she went into the restroom to splash water on her face. The mirror reflected her bloodshot eyes and fighting back tears had brought out the small scattering of freckles across her cheeks. Eleven freckles in total. They weren't there when she'd left Italy nearly five years ago.

It was over.

Everything was over. . . her relationship with Archer and her dream of living in Australia forever. She couldn't live in the country she'd grown to love without him. It would never be the same.

Anguish burned a hole in her heart. It was time to return home to Italy.

Archer would stay with the real love of his life, his luxury super yacht, *Evangeline*. And Archer did love her. He spent every spare moment refining the multi-million-dollar yacht, preparing her for clients with fistfuls of money and a sense of adventure. He'd be trapped there for the rest of the day.

That gave her seven hours to get out of his life.

Flicking away tears, she packed her belongings into boxes, addressed them to her Nonna in Tuscany, and carted them to the post office. Then she made the difficult calls to her friends to say goodbye, knowing full well she might never see them again.

Within six hours, she was at Cairns airport, waiting for her flight to Rome.

Chapter Three

A rcher dreaded every step he took towards home. All day he'd stewed over his argument with Rosalina, and no matter which way he replayed it, it wasn't good.

His head pounded with an ache that started at the base of his neck and ended as a deep thump behind his eyelids. After a long, frustrating day with his Japanese guests, the last thing he wanted to do was continue his fight with Rosalina. He tried to picture how she'd greet him.

There were two options. One would be the forgiving Rosalina, keen on working through their problems. The other would be the cold-shouldered Rosalina, where she'd want him to make the first move. A move he usually did.

Not this time, though.

This time, he had to continue what he'd started.

He was in for a long night.

Archer pressed the code into the door lock and stepped over the threshold. Her name formed on his lips but stayed trapped in his throat when he saw the lounge room. Every one of her little knick-knacks, the ones she'd insisted on buying to make the apartment look more homely, were gone.

With his heart in his throat, he raced upstairs. "Rosa!" One look around their bedroom confirmed she'd gone. He checked the restroom. Even her pink toothbrush was no longer there.

Archer sat on the bed, heaved a massive breath and covered his eyes with his palms.

She's gone.

He never pictured her leaving like this.

His first instinct was to go after her and explain his reasons for acting the way he had. But he'd only be drawing out the inevitable. As shocking as this was, the result was what he'd hoped for her.

His brain and his heart were both a scrambled mess as he returned downstairs. With no idea what to do, he grabbed a six-pack of beer from the fridge and carried it out to the deck. As he sat looking out to the marina, a sea eagle soared with all the grace and freedom in the world over the dozens of boats moored in the calm water.

It was a sign.

Setting Rosalina free was the best decision he'd ever made. But with each bottle of beer he downed, the conclusion didn't get any easier.

By the time he crawled into bed hours later, he still felt like crap.

His head kept pounding and the empty bed beside him didn't help one bit.

Archer switched off the lamp and, as the yellow marina lights fought the darkness, he slipped into both a restless sleep and the watery purgatory that dominated his life.

Bubbles, lots of bubbles, large and small, rumbled from his mouthpiece and floated upward until they vanished into the sunlit surface. The color of the water gradually morphed from turquoise to blue.

Maybe the clouds had covered the sun.

His shadow shifted across the seafloor as a school of small, silvery fish swirled around him like windblown leaves. Something shiny glowed from within a small hole in the colorful coral, and, with a kick of his fins, he glided towards *it. He reached into the hole, feeling with his fingers, and the golden trinket slotted into his palm as if it was meant to be there.*

A shadow, more solid and definite than shifting cloud cover, slid over him and he looked up. The shape materialized through the sun-filtered haze, slicing through the water like a demon.

A shark as big as a surfboard swam past him, slow and steady, as if sizing him for dinner.

Its eyes were flat and unblinking, as black as onyx.

Messengers of death.

A figure appeared through the haze. He couldn't make out the person's face through his dive mask, but somehow, he knew it was his father.

Water wrapped around his body grew heavy; squeezing the air out of him. The bubbles rose more slowly, as if taking in every second of the show. With each forced breath, his father gradually disappeared, like he'd been an illusion.

The shark came close. Too close.

It opened its mouth, exposing its teeth. So many razor-sharp teeth.

Archer screamed and kicked backwards. Blood swirled, coloring the water crimson. Pain blazed down his leg. Churning bubbles clouded his vision. He thrashed around, fighting for the surface.

He looked down.

A ten-foot, solid killing machine charged through the water.

Straight at him.

ARCHER JOLTED AWAKE.

He sat, gasping for air. Adrenaline surged through him like a lit firecracker.

He reached for the glass of water he'd put on his nightstand before he'd gone to bed, and gulped it down, hoping the liquid would cool his boiling insides.

His heart sank at the emptiness in the bed beside him. It sank even further when he glanced at the clock. Two a.m. Always two a.m.

Archer untangled himself from the sheets and strolled to the open window. He eased into the comfy chair he'd placed there for this very purpose and let the ocean breeze lick the sweat from his body.

Hundreds of flickering lights from the marina lit up the view like a busy cityscape. The sight usually brightened him, reassured him he was living his dream.

But his dream would never be perfect.

Not when it was constantly hijacked by recurring nightmares.

It was not up to Rosalina to save him from his living hell.

They were his burden. His guilt. His fucking mess.

Chapter Four

Rosalina wrapped her fingers around her grandmother's frail hand and followed her to the dining table. A dozen family members sat around a mountain of home-cooked meals, but their smiling faces and infectious laughter did little to lift her spirits.

They were there to celebrate her birthday, yet she saw the disappointment in their eyes. A woman her age should be married and have a family of her own, not starting over.

"Happy birthday, Aunty Rosa." Her little nephew was missing his two front teeth and his innocent smile almost crushed her heart. *Almost.*

For eight months she'd been a sponge, absorbing everyone's well-meaning advice, to the point where she was emotionally numb. She was working again, but it was only out of sheer desperation that she'd accepted the waitressing job.

Her wonderful days spent creating amazing meals in *Evangeline's* galley were already a world away. But her current situation only made her more determined to keep searching for the job of her dreams, which she did every single day.

Nonna leaned into her ear. "Do not worry, Rosalina. You will find a good man soon. Now eat." Her eyes were a mixture of conviction and sadness.

"I have plenty of them, Nonna." She winked at her grandmother, and as she tugged on the dangling pearl earrings Nonna had given her for her birthday, she forced a smile.

It was true. There'd been no shortage of men knocking on her door since she'd returned home. And although she'd been on a few dates, she couldn't get Archer out of her thoughts.

Despite being halfway around the world, everywhere she looked, she was reminded of him. A bottle of wine would bring back a memory of a romantic dinner. A painting of a beautiful beach would place her with him. A cross on a man's chest would allude to that damn pendant Archer never removed.

At Villa Pandolfini, mealtimes were always a feast. But the extended Calucci family took that a step further, with friendly food rivalry practically a tradition. Rosalina was already full, but there was still so much she hadn't sampled.

As this party was for her, she was expected to taste everything, and all the women around the table would wait for her approval of their dishes.

As she smiled at her family and forced down each mouthful, she replayed that final argument with Archer over in her mind. Archer's reluctance to talk about his nightmares, or the pendant, made her believe something horrific had happened to him, or he'd done something terribly wrong.

All manner of scenarios had entered her overactive mind, everything from theft to murder. She wanted to believe he was incapable of any of them.

His reluctance to trust her, though, had her thinking otherwise.

It was a dart through her heart.

A dart that turned fatal when, after three years together, he still hadn't been able to say he loved her.

How could I have been so stupid?

Her oldest brother whispered something into her sister-in-law's ear. Rosalina smiled at how comfortable they were together. She longed for that. She wanted love and lust, a soul mate to share life with. All of which she was determined to find, no matter how long it took.

The afternoon rolled on like a perfect scene from a wholesome family movie. Wine was poured freely and complaints of being too full were only brief when desserts arrived.

Her birthday cake was placed before her. The number twenty-eight, written in dark cherry frosting, dominated the cake like a blazing hazard symbol. She took a large gulp of Chianti and the smooth liquid slid down her throat as she pulled a speech together in her mind.

It took two attempts to blow out all the candles and everyone clapped as they chanted. *"Favella! Favella!"*

"Bene, bene. Quiet down, you lot." They hushed, and she felt their expectation of something brilliant. "First of all, *grazie* to Nonna for having this party for me. I bet you didn't expect me to be living under your roof again."

Nonna waved her hand. "It is *temporaneo.* The man of your dreams will come round the corner very soon. You will see."

It didn't matter what she said. Every part of her speech reminded her she was nearly thirty and single. She couldn't wait to get this long lunch over with. Thankfully, she had a legitimate reason to leave soon. Her friends were taking her out to dinner.

Not that she could eat a single thing after all the family specialties she'd been obliged to eat so far. The thought of eating even a mouthful of the cake, overloaded with cream and chocolate and laced with Frangelico, made her feel ill.

The doorbell rang and, grateful for the interruption, she raced to open it. She sighed with relief. Alessandro greeted her with a bunch of yellow roses and a kiss on each cheek.

"Thank God you're here. Quickly say hello then goodbye and get me out of here."

Alessandro was a long-time friend from university, although their relationship had never been the same since their one liquor-fueled mistake many years ago. He was handsome, considerate, generous, safe, and he'd make a great husband. Everyone in her family loved him. So that made him exactly the distraction she needed.

After the longest of goodbyes, she was finally in Alessandro's car and on the way to Florence for dinner. The combination of wine and the rush to escape had her a little dizzy, and she blinked to refocus on the road ahead.

As they drove along, their conversation lacked any real flow and she longed for the comfortable banter she'd had with Archer.

When Alessandro turned off the main highway, heading away from the city center, she frowned. "Where are we going?"

"Well, we're not meeting the others until eight, so I thought I'd show you one of my favorite little churches. It has a fascinating history. You're going to love it."

Rosalina didn't share Alessandro's love of churches. As a professor of ancient history and architecture, he could spend days exploring every building and alleyway in Florence. She wanted to show her excitement, but she'd rather crawl into bed and disappear from the world.

His gaze was heavy upon her as she lifted her handbag onto her lap and flipped open her powder compact to apply a little make-up. Sadness reflecting in her eyes was the jolt she needed.

She straightened her back, combed her hair, and told herself to snap out of it. She would no longer be a victim. Wallowing in self-pity would not find her love. To find a soul mate, she needed to get back to the fun-loving Rosalina who craved adventure, cooked amazing meals and laughed freely.

But most of all, she needed to love herself again.

She glanced at Alessandro. He was the archetypal Italian man. . . square jaw, swarthy complexion, hair that was closer to black than chocolate, and dark almond-shaped eyes framed with long eyelashes. He'd barely changed in the twelve years she'd known him and she was certain he was still wearing the same aftershave he'd worn that fateful night she'd rather forget.

But he was there for her then, and he was here for her now. She might as well try to enjoy herself. "Tell me about this church."

His eyes gleamed. "It was built in the eleventh century and is situated in a medieval section of Florence. The church has some of the most elegant and well-preserved Romanesque stonework façades in Florence." He spoke with flamboyant animation, like a professor before a crowd of interested students. Despite her initial reluctance for his history lesson, she was soon wrapped up in his passion.

Finding a parking space in Florence was normally impossible, however, one presented itself as if they were destined to have it. They locked the car and Alessandro's hand warmed the small of her back as he guided her through a large concrete plaza.

"This is the Piazza del Limbo. Hundreds of years ago, it was a cemetery where unbaptized babies were buried."

She looked around the unremarkable area that was devoid of any hint of its original purpose.

This is exactly the distraction I need.

There was no chance anything in a church would provoke memories of Archer.

The church itself was simple in its construction, lacking the usual flamboyance prevalent amongst the more famous Florence churches.

"See this beautiful brickwork?" His fingers floated over the bricks and his expression was one of awe.

"Yes, I see it." It looked like every other brick wall, but she was determined not to spoil it for him.

They stepped over the main threshold, and the sense of complete tranquility dominated her first impression of the little church.

Alessandro leaned in to whisper. "The first church on this site was said to have been built in the time of Pope Pelagius, in the years 556 to 561."

Rosalina tried to do the math on how long ago that was, but gave up. Numbers were not her friend.

She studied the richly decorated wooden ceiling, held up by enormous marble columns. They reminded her of the columns outside the Pantheon in Rome.

He pointed at the first two. "These two columns are from an ancient Roman bath."

Ha! I was close.

The floor was incredible, too. Black and white mosaic tiles, set in a checkerboard pattern, stretched the full length of the church, with an oval decoration in the middle of the aisle.

"See that oval?" Alessandro whispered in her ear. "That's where they discarded the bodies during the plague. There were so many deaths they didn't have time for decent burials."

"That's awful."

"Sadly, although they saved time, they were actually contributing to the disease."

She cupped her mouth in horror. "Of course. The rats." She kept her distance from the oval as Alessandro led her further into the church.

Remnants of the setting sun illuminated red and blue glass fragments in a large stained-glass window. She was drawn to it. Its ethereal glow was mesmerizing. Depicted in the masterpiece was a cloaked priest holding a scale with a flat dish at either end containing a variety of objects. Its beauty captured her.

There was something alluring about it.

She leaned in to study it more closely and her breath caught in her throat. A knot turned in her stomach as she stared at the item featured in the higher dish.

It was identical to Archer's pendant. There was no mistaking it.

The curved object was a plaque with the letters APOSTOLI embossed in distinct decorative text. Archer's pendant, however, was not complete and only had the letters *OSTOL*, and even then, half of the *L* was missing. All this time she'd thought it was an *I*. The shape of the letter *S* convinced her of the match. It was like no other style of writing she'd ever seen.

"Are you okay, *mio dolce*? You look like you've seen a ghost." Alessandro placed his hand on her arm.

Rosalina swallowed her shock, determined to keep it from him. "Tell me about this." She pointed at the scale.

"This masterpiece commemorates a victory Pope Pelagius had over the Goths and their expulsion to the Apostles, St. James and St. Philip. That's why it's called the Church of the Apostles. See the balance of the scale is tilted in favor of the Apostles: The Goths have been conquered."

Her mind raced as she stewed over how a part of this commemorative piece ended up around Archer's neck. None of it made sense.

Archer had never told her he'd been to Italy. Although he could have found the pendant anywhere, a fire raged within her as she dreaded that this was yet another secret.

With clenched teeth, she removed her phone from her pocket, keyed her pin to select the camera and held it towards the stained glass. She zoomed in on the plaque to get a better picture.

Rough fingers clutched her arm. Gasping, her phone tumbled to the floor.

She twisted to see her attacker, but a heavy hood shrouded most of his face. What she did see—dry, flaky lips and a stubbled chin, pockmarked with scars, was scary enough.

"Hey!" She tried to shake her arm free. "Let go of me!"

The man's fingers bit further into her wrist.

"Let her go." Alessandro shoved at the man's shoulder.

The man's insipid lips drew into a thin line as he released her. *"Non le è permesso di fare foto!"*

Rosalina cowered from his yellow teeth, and Alessandro stepped between them. It was a brave, uncharacteristic move, and his trembling hands showed his unease.

Without another word, the man stormed away. His robe swished around his legs and he quickly vanished into a dark corner at the back of the church. His foul body odor lingered. The stench poisoned the air.

Rosalina stepped back, trying to escape it.

"What was that about?" Alessandro's chocolate eyes darkened even further.

Rosalina collected her phone from the floor. "I was about to take a photo." She pointed to the stained-glass window. "I can't believe how quick he was. He came from nowhere."

"Are you okay?" Concern engulfed his gaze.

She nodded and rubbed her wrist where the man's fingers had dug in.

"Come on, let's get out of here."

With his hand on her waist, Alessandro guided her towards the front door. She only broke his embrace to sidestep around the oval mosaic.

She couldn't wait to get out of the creepy building.

By the time she joined her friends for dinner, she was well beyond tired.

Dinner was long and draining, and although she cherished their company, Rosalina couldn't stop analyzing the significance of the plaque in the stained-glass window.

At every silent interval, another unanswered question slotted into her mind.

But two things were certain.

Archer had been lying.

And she needed answers.

Chapter Five

Archer snapped his eyes open, releasing him from the nightmare.

He didn't want to look at the other side of the bed, but even after all these months, he couldn't help it.

The plump pillow. The unused sheet. The cold emptiness.

It was a painful reminder that Rosalina wasn't there.

He missed her loving caress, her reassuring whispers, and every single thing about her.

He sat, flicked off the sheets, and wiped sweat from his forehead. Huffing out his fury, he slid out of bed and paced the floor until his heartbeat returned to normal.

Standing naked at the window, he allowed the gentle breeze to cool his burning skin. The sound of ropes clanging against hundreds of boat masts was a song to his ears, but just like the twinkling lights, it failed to lift the darkness shrouding his heart.

Evangeline was easy to see. She was the largest yacht in the marina, proudly occupying two berths. Although he'd purchased her eight years ago, he still treasured her as if they had delivered her yesterday.

He chuckled at the memory of buying the extravagant yacht.

The boat broker took some convincing that Archer was a legitimate buyer. It wasn't very often a long-haired, twenty-five-year-old in shorts and a singlet had millions of dollars to spend.

He'd encountered the same reaction when buying his apartment, but once he'd walked through the doors, he simply had to have it. The penthouse had a flawless view of the marina, and he'd been prepared to pay much more for it. Lucky for him, the agent had nearly fallen over at his first offer.

The money was the one good thing. . . the only good thing, to come out of his crappy childhood.

Although, it'd taken him nearly a decade to come to his senses and use it.

Even then, it didn't feel right spending the inheritance.

But his wealth was no longer important. Losing Rosalina had hit him harder than he'd ever believed possible. The way they broke up, a big fight like that, was not what he'd intended.

It didn't matter now, though. Nothing mattered, except that breaking up was best for Rosalina. She was young and gorgeous, and it wouldn't be long before she found someone else.

He told himself over and over again he'd done the right thing, knowing he could never offer her the love she deserved.

It didn't help, though. Not one bit.

Since the break-up, he'd tried to keep busy by reaching out to new clients and touching base with existing ones. But the loss of Rosalina had been a massive blow to his business, too. She was an amazing chef, dedicated, adventurous, and fastidious in the yacht's professional kitchen, and he hadn't realized how many clients came back just because of her delicious meals.

He'd struggled to hire her replacement. None of the candidates offered the quality of cooking or the charisma she had. His latest choice was made out of desperation. But every moment he spent with the overbearing German woman grated on his nerves, and he missed Rosalina even more.

The glow from the clock was a brutal indicator that there were at least three hours until sunrise. He was tempted to crawl back into the crumpled bed sheets, but knowing it was pointless, he made his way to the kitchen, turned on the coffee machine, and flicked the television to the sports channel.

Archer jumped when the phone rang. His eyes darted to the clock first and then to the marina. A call at two in the morning could only mean disaster, and his thoughts went straight to his yacht. But the marina was as tranquil as ever.

He snatched up the phone. "Archer here."

"*Bastardo marcio, hai mentito ancora una volta.*" Torrents of angry Italian words fired at him, and yet he smiled. Hearing Rosalina's seductive voice appeased him, despite her obvious outrage.

"Whoa. Slow down, honey, I don't speak Italian."

"I'm not your honey."

"Have you been drinking? It's the middle of the night here."

"Yeah? Well, I bet you were up. Still having those nightmares?"

Archer winced. She knew him well, even from six thousand miles away. The nightmares had almost become a nightly occurrence since she'd left, and he now prepared for his expected awakening before he even went to bed.

The glass of water on the nightstand was a testament to that.

"You're right. I was awake."

"Let me guess. Staring out over the marina and playing with that stupid pendant."

Archer dropped the necklace. "Rosa, if you rang to abuse me —"

"I rang to say I have proof you're a lying, stinking *bastardo*. You told me you'd never been to Italy."

"That's the truth." It was one of the few countries in the world he'd never been to.

"Oh yeah? Well, I know where you got your damn pendant from."

Archer stiffened. He reached for the necklace again. His mind thrust back to where he'd found it, but he shook the horrific memory free. "What're you talking about?"

"The Church of St Apostoli."

Archer tried to comprehend what she was saying, but he had nothing. "The Church of what?"

"Saint Apostoli!" She said it like he was a complete fool.

"What about it?"

"Your pendant is pictured in the stained-glass window."

His mind raced.

Was this the clue I've waited nearly two decades for?

He couldn't let this information go untouched, even if it took him back to his horrific past. "Where? What does it look like? Tell me everything."

"No." Her voice was drunken defiance.

"Please." Archer put on his sweetest voice, hoping to persuade her past the anger.

"You don't deserve any sympathy from me. I tried to help you, but you cast me aside like a snotty tissue."

She was right, but hearing those words was a spear piercing his heart. She was hurt and had every right to be. However, with this new lead, he had to see that stained-glass window for himself. It'd be easier with her help, though; he didn't speak a word of Italian.

"Please, Rosa, I never meant to hurt you."

Would she ever forgive me?

"*Sei un bugiardo*! You knew what you were doing."

Her tone was fierce. "Please. . . I want to make it up to you."

"You can *never* replace the years you stole from me. I loved you and would've done anything for you." Rosalina sobbed into the phone.

He wanted to put his arms around her, to feel her golden skin against his and kiss the tears from her eyes. But it could never be. He'd destroyed the most important person in his life and was powerless to fix it. "I'm sorry —"

"Don't say it again!"

A click resonated down the phone, then nothing.

As he stared out over the marina, a sense of fear, as familiar as it was unwanted, crawled through his body.

I need to return to where the nightmare began.

Chapter Six

Pure determination drove Archer through the night, and by the time the sun glowed on the horizon, he had a list of everything that needed to be done to get *Evangeline* looked after so he could get to Italy ASAP.

It was too early to wake Jimmy, and with adrenaline wasted on him pacing his apartment, he threw on his jogging gear and dashed out the front door.

His pounding feet on the pavement matched the rhythm of his heartbeat. He blocked out the pain in his left knee and picked up his pace along the path that snaked up the headland.

Waves crashed into the rocks below and seagulls squawked above as they fought over breakfast. Leaning into the slope, he accelerated even more and as he powered his arms, his surroundings morphed into visions of Rosalina.

Since she'd left, he'd lost all focus on life. Nothing was important anymore.

But her call last night had thrown him a lifeline.

It gave him a glimmer of hope, and maybe, just maybe, he could salvage his life amongst the ruins.

Endorphins kicked in, barely softening the ache in his knee, yet he raced towards the top, forging through the pain.

The cresting sun gave the peeling white paint on the wooden bench seat at the hilltop an unearthly glow. He arrived at the chair, panting with exhaustion. Groaning, he plonked himself down and rubbed above his kneecap, trying to release the fierce throbbing.

Sunrise glistened across a dark-blue ocean that stretched as far as he could see. The scene presented like a dazzling oasis in a desert of uncertainty. Colorful sailing boats skipped along the small waves and several couples walked hand-in-hand along the beach down below.

It was a perfect scene. No. It would be a perfect scene, but without Rosalina, it was far from complete.

Was this clue in the stained-glass window the beginning to the end of my nightmares?

He'd tried everything — hypnosis, acupuncture, herbal and medicated drugs, and nearly everything else in between. Fast cars. Fast women. Fast drugs that took him to nosebleed highs but always ended in soul-shattering lows.

He was miserable in isolation and pissed-off in crowds.

Years of therapy had been nothing but a waste of time and a bucket-load of money.

Turning his angst towards his business proved to be the only positive from his restlessness. The success of his crazy treasure-hunting concept had surprised the crap out of him. It didn't just plod along, though. It thrived.

When a customer suggested he add a quality culinary angle to his treasure tours, it literally changed his life.

Rosalina had been a breath of fresh air. She'd put fresh blood in his veins, a new purpose into his life, and brought new clients by the truckload.

She'd brought out the best in him, too.

In the first year they were together, life had been normal.

No, it was better than normal; it was perfect. The nightmares had eased back to just a couple each month, and he'd laughed more in that year than he'd done in a decade.

But just when he'd become comfortable, when he'd genuinely thought his penance was over, the nightmares came back, more brutal and more persistent than ever. He was a failure, and the nightly torture was proof of that.

Something the therapist said all those years ago had always stayed in his mind. "You need to find the key, Archer."

Is this clue in the stained-glass window the key?

His heartbeat raced at the hint of a resolution.

Once he regained his breath, Archer left the seat and maintained a steady jog back to the marina. He only slowed when he reached the main walkway.

Halfway along, he turned onto a narrow pontoon and strode to the fourth cabin cruiser secured alongside. He stepped onto the *Cat's Cradle* and sidestepped towards the wheelhouse doorway. "Hey Jimbo, you up yet?" Without waiting for an answer, he opened the door.

Silence greeted him as he ducked under the bulkhead to descend the steps to the lower deck. "Jimmy, I'm coming down. Make yourself decent."

Jimmy was notorious for late nights drinking and late mornings sleeping. But Archer needed him awake and sober enough to make some quick decisions. Snoring thundered from the bedroom.

Archer banged on the door. "Wake up, Jim!"

"What the hell?" Jim's ragged voice rattled through the wood paneling.

"It's me, Archer. Wake up."

"What time is it? Jesus, it's only six o'clock. You got some balls, man."

Archer pushed open the door. "Sorry, buddy, but we need to talk."

Jim was in bed. His eyelids looked like slabs of chicken meat, and his greasy hair scrambled in all directions.

Archer leaned on the doorframe. "Can I get you a coffee?"

"You can get the fuck off my boat and let me sleep."

"No can do, buddy." Archer turned and walked toward the

galley, filled the kettle and turned on the gas. "Get some clothes on. I'll meet you up top."

"Piss off."

Jim's grumbling and swearing continued from the bedroom as Archer rummaged for coffee and sugar amongst the tins of baked beans in the cupboard. Soon the kettle whistled and he filled two mugs with boiling water. "Up top, Jim. One minute."

"Jesus! Who are you. . . my ex-wife?"

Archer laughed as he carried the mugs to the table bolted to the back deck of the old timber cruiser. Jimmy had been living on this boat since his messy divorce cost him everything he owned eight years ago.

Archer and Jim had become solid friends, and they spent many evenings sharing a drink or three and some serious games of poker. Jim was a good guy with solid morals, protective instincts and a great friend; exactly the man Archer needed right now.

Cat's Cradle had been neglected over the years, and Archer picked at the table's peeling paint as he waited for Jim to appear.

His buddy finally arrived, wearing crinkled stubby shorts and scratching at his graying chest hairs. Jim was a brute of a man, not in an overweight, lost-control kind of way, but more the don't-mess-with-me warrior type. Other than rum, his love was pressing weights.

Archer often saw him working out in the midday sun, unconcerned at the further reddening of his leathery skin.

Archer allowed Jim to drink half a mug of coffee before he spoke. "Sorry about this."

"What's so damn important?"

"I need you to skipper *Evangeline* for a while."

Jim squinted. "Where you goin'?"

"I got business in Italy."

"You want an old drunk like me controlling your million-dollar yacht? You lost your marbles?"

"I know you. I trust you. And I know you'll give up the grog to do it."

"Give up the grog? That's gonna cost you. How many weeks we talking? I work, you know."

Jim's laboring job at the wharf was eternal cycles of no work one week, then eighty-plus hours the following. He'd taken the job out of desperation and his body paid for it with erratic meals and a crushing routine.

"I'll pay for one month up front and then on a weekly basis."

"I won't look after them tourists!"

Archer laughed. Jim had no patience for people who didn't speak English. "I'll cancel the tourists. It'll just be you. But I need your promise you'll stay dry and do everything by the book."

Jim sipped his coffee and his gaze confirmed he was crunching numbers. "I got a seventy-hour week coming up. That's big bucks I'll be missing."

Archer held Jim's red-eyed glare. "Start the bidding."

Jim set his poker face.

Archer was in for some tough negotiation. But he was prepared to pay more than enough.

A smile curled at Jim's lips. "Thirty thou for the first month and five *G*s each week after that."

Archer allowed Jim a moment of tense waiting while he sipped his coffee. "Done."

Jimmy smacked his mug on the table and nearly choked on his coffee. When he smiled, his gold tooth glimmered in the morning sun. He shook Archer's hand with a solid grip, and his eyes brightened.

"I would have taken ten." Jim laughed a hearty cackle.

"I would have paid fifty." Archer laughed with him.

"Ahh shit! Really?" A frown rippled across Jimmy's forehead. "What're you getting into?"

"Just some good old-fashioned treasure hunting." Archer left him with a slap on the back, and the old bugger burst into laughter as Archer made his way to *Evangeline*.

The following days were consumed with frantic phone calls to cancel reservations and refund deposits in time to hand over *Evangeline*, and with a twinge of apprehension Archer watched Jimmy cruise into the distance with his prized possession for what Jimmy called a practice run.

Archer remained at the end of the pier, unable to tear himself away until *Evangeline* was just a blip in the ocean.

The following day, he arrived at the airport with nothing but carry-on luggage and nervous determination.

Thirty-three hours later, after long and frustrating stops in both Sydney and Singapore, he landed in Rome.

He navigated his way through the bustling crowd to the car hire booth, and within an hour, he was driving up the Superstrada in his rented Alfa Spider convertible. The expressway weaved through magical landscapes with medieval hilltop cities and colorful countryside.

But the surrounding vistas whizzed by in a blur.

His mind was only occupied with visions of Rosalina.

He hadn't told her of his planned arrival. His forecasted greeting with her alternated between a savage slap across his face, and her jumping into his arms to suffocate him with hot kisses.

He'd settle for anywhere above the slap.

Hell, he'd even take the slap, if it meant seeing her again.

But if their last conversation was anything to go by, she'd most likely hurl a pot at him. Or slam the door in his face.

Armed with his GPS and the address he'd bribed from the nice lady at the post office near his home, he hoped he wouldn't have too much trouble finding her.

Several hours later, he turned off the main freeway and followed the signs to the small town of Signa. The streets were so narrow, only one direction of traffic traveled through the town's center at a time.

Pausing at the signals, he studied the buildings lining the road.

Each home had a dark wooden door with a dangling brass bell, but that was where the similarities ended. The dark brick buildings were an interesting mix of history and creative individuality. Wooden shutters were painted in a variety of colors. Vegetables and herbs grew in planter boxes that hung off first-level windows, and eclectic decorations featured on walls, fences, and in gardens.

A young woman sat at a pizzeria nearby with a small fluffy dog on her lap. She sipped a glass of red wine and seemed blissfully unaware of how close she was to the waiting traffic. An elderly woman with a scarf over her hair and a seriously bent spine dragged a shopping trolley over the uneven cobblestone crossing.

Archer had to pinch himself. *I can't believe I'm in Italy.*

With each mile he traveled he looked forward to learning more about Rosalina's home town.

A small shop, overflowing with an abundance of flowers, caught his eye. It took a full five minutes to find somewhere to park and run back to the shop. But it was worth it.

He selected an enormous bunch of pink oriental lilies, Rosalina's favorite. Their distinct scent reminded him of her. She loved receiving flowers, and although he considered them a waste of money, her delight at accepting them was worth every cent.

He returned to the car and maneuvered the Alfa through seemingly never-ending one-way streets until he was back on the main road. The light turned green and he followed the line of cars that snaked their way through the narrow streets.

Barely a mile later, he rounded a corner, and the GPS announced his arrival at *Villa Pandolfini*. He turned in and skidded to a halt, narrowly avoiding a boom gate.

The long driveway was lined with enormous cypress trees that stood as sentries to an extravagant palace centered at the top of the hill.

Is this the right place?

Archer vaguely recalled Rosalina telling him she lived in a seven-hundred-year-old villa, but he'd never envisaged anything so grand.

He heaved a heavy sigh.

He barely knew anything about Rosalina's home life in Italy.

Climbing out of the car, he ran his hands through his wind-blown hair as he searched for a way to lift the boom gate.

Conceding defeat, he hopped back in the car and moved it to the side.

He grabbed the flowers and his valuables and abandoned the vehicle to walk up the gravel driveway.

As he trudged up the path, he glimpsed vineyard-covered hills beyond the villa and arched bridges that crossed a river winding through the valley. A dog barked somewhere in the distance and dozens of butterflies fluttered around yellow flowers planted at the base of the enormous trees.

As he neared the villa, he felt like a stranger in a magical land. The building was as grand as a palace. The arched doorways were ten-feet high. An ancient bougainvillea vine, as thick as his thigh, snaked its way over a wooden trellis that looked equally ancient. The villa was three levels, and based on the size of the windows, each level must be at least twenty-feet high.

As a child, he'd explored great reaches of the globe with his parents, but he couldn't recall seeing a house this grand.

The fact that he'd never taken the time to learn of Rosalina's childhood home highlighted his selfishness.

He clenched his jaw at the confronting acknowledgement.

Three arched doorways were evenly spaced apart on the ground floor. At the middle door, he placed his pack down, raised the flowers and banged the heavy brass knocker.

His nerves were as tight as high-tensile wire as he waited for the door to open.

Chapter Seven

Rosalina dusted her flour-caked hands onto her apron and checked the Murazzano cheese rolls baking in the oven.

"Yum. They smell *magnifica*." Alessandro ran his tongue over his lips, and a sudden desire to kiss him crashed through Rosalina. The urge came from nowhere. Maybe she'd had too much wine. Maybe she was falling for him, despite all her determination not to.

Maybe I'm finally over Archer.

That would be nice.

After removing the tray from the oven and placing it onto the cork placemat, scents of aromatic spices, melted cheese, and freshly-baked pastry wafted around Nonna's tiny kitchen.

She smiled as Alessandro practically drooled over her cooking. He'd always been loyal, and that was something she needed right now. And he was always a willing guinea pig for her culinary experiments. He reached for a steaming pastry.

She slapped his hand. "Wait! You want the whole experience, don't you?"

His eyes lit up. "*Sì, mio dolce.*"

My sweet. She liked that. Especially given her love of cooking all things sugary. He was patient with her and seemed to understand her need to take everything slow.

Rosalina sliced cooled poached pear and placed a sliver onto the savory, cheese pastry. "Open up."

She popped the nibble into his mouth. His eyes did that heavenly eye-roll before he closed them and savored the treat. A low moan of approval teased from his throat.

First, he would taste the sweetness of the pear, delicately poached with cinnamon and Chinese five-spice. Next would come the multifaceted Murazzano cheese, smooth and rich in flavor. Finally, the buttery pastry would round it off. She liked to think of it as a smorgasbord in a bite.

After he swallowed, he sighed his approval.

"Now, keep your eyes closed."

A smile of pure bliss curled at his lips.

"This second sample is the same cheese pastry, but this one I've topped with my homemade fig jelly and a sprinkle of crispy prosciutto."

A fresh moan tumbled from his lips and he hadn't even tasted it yet. His eyelids fluttered as she placed the second canape into his mouth.

"Take your time. I need to know which one is better."

His eyes opened, but it was as if he'd slipped into another world. He shook his head slowly.

"You don't like that one."

He shook his head faster. "You can't make me choose one."

Rosalina put her hands on her hips. "Come on, Alessandro, you know the game."

"But I can't decide. They're both *delizioso*." He kissed the tips of his fingers.

"This is serious." She giggled. "There can only be one clear winner. So, which is it, pear or prosciutto?"

"Rosa, you torture me."

She giggled. "I tantalize you."

He flashed a devious smile and fluttered his long lashes. "Yes, you do, *il mio dolce*."

Another drink was in order. "Want to choose a bottle of wine while you decide?"

"Okay, but I can't guarantee I'll have an answer before I get back. Red or white?"

"Red tonight." The red wine would perfectly complement her cheese nibbles.

Alessandro pushed his chair back, scraping it against the terracotta tiles. As he crossed the room, she admired his physique. He was tall, dark and handsome, and although she'd never seen him do anything even remotely physical, he looked after himself.

She refrained from telling him to duck his head on the doorframe down to the cellar. Alessandro had already hit his head once, and he never had to be told anything twice; he had an amazing memory.

A knock sounded on the front door, and Rosalina frowned. Everybody who visited Villa Pandolfini came around to the much less grandiose back door.

She washed her hands and, drying them on her apron, she made her way through a maze of rooms.

She opened the door, and her heart lurched.

"Archer?" The smile fell from her face. She clutched the doorknob, fearful her weakened knees would tumble her onto the terracotta tiles. Despite the demise of their relationship and months of separation, his very presence still put her in emotional danger.

"Hi, Rosa."

Her hand went to her hair, trying to smooth the frizzy mess. She silently cursed herself with a reminder that Archer destroyed her faith in romance.

She swallowed dryness from her throat. "What are you doing here?"

"I had to see you." Despite his high-neck T-shirt, the outline of his pendant was still visible beneath.

"Liar. You're here to see that church."

"I wondered if you'd remember that phone call."

A wave of heat flooded her neck and cheeks. The day after she'd made that call, she'd gradually pieced together their conversation while nursing a crippling hangover. At first, she'd been mortified that she'd called him while in that state, but the more she thought about it, the more satisfied she grew over confronting him about the lies.

She folded her arms over her chest. "Are you ready to admit you're a liar?"

"Rosalina?" Alessandro said in a singsong manner, as if they were playing hide and seek.

Alessandro rounded the corner and her heatwave intensified. Fighting distress, she recovered by opening her arm to Alessandro. As had become his custom, Alessandro snuggled in beside her and she clutched him to her side. "Alessandro, this is Archer. Archer, this is my boyfriend, Alessandro."

Both Archer and Alessandro looked at her, and her cheeks burned even more.

"Aussie Archer?" Alessandro held his hand forward. "*Ciao*. What brings you here?"

Rosalina cleared her throat. "I was just asking him the same question."

"Rosa told me about a church with an amazing stained-glass window," Archer said.

Alessandro clicked his fingers. "The Church of St Apostoli. Did she tell you about the fright she had there?"

Archer's eyebrows jumped. "No, she didn't."

"It's quite a story. Your timing is perfect. Rosalina has made an antipasti platter. Come in, and we'll tell you all about it."

"Great, my car's down the driveway. Is —"

Rosalina groaned. "You can get it when you leave." She turned on her heel, and with their eyes drilling into her back, she stormed towards the kitchen.

Her mind was in turmoil. She never expected to see Archer again, but her feelings for him sprang to the surface the instant she did. She cringed at her lack of control over her emotions.

Archer had to get out of her home. The sooner the better.

Her reflection in the glass microwave door was ghastly. Yet although her instant reaction was to fix her hair and apply a dab of lipstick, she resisted. There was no need to impress Archer anymore, or any man, for that matter.

A man should love me for who I am, adorned or not.

She added the cheese-crusted pasties to the already overflowing antipasti board and centered it on the kitchen table. She hadn't realized she'd been holding her breath until Archer and Alessandro entered the kitchen. As she slowly exhaled, she willed her thumping heart to settle.

Archer handed her a beautiful bunch of flowers and it took all her might not to swoon over them. Oriental lilies were her favorite. At least he remembered that.

"You never told me this villa was so grand," Archer said with a glowing smile.

"You never asked." She shot him an icy glare, hoping he'd crumble.

"But you could've mentioned something." He picked up one of Nonna's cookbooks, flipped it over, then plonked it back down. It was written in Italian; he wouldn't have understood a word on the covers.

Rosalina placed the flowers on the counter, deciding against fussing over them. "Why would I? It's not like you told me everything."

Alessandro swallowed loud enough for her to hear. "Would you like me to leave you two alone?"

"No. That won't be necessary. He won't be staying." She flicked her hand at Archer, like she was shooing away an insect.

After an awkward pause, Alessandro cleared his throat. "Where *are* you staying?"

Archer shrugged. "Don't know yet. I've come straight from the Rome airport."

"There's a bed and breakfast down the road." Rosalina had no intention of offering him a room, even though there were twelve bedrooms on the property and only two were permanently occupied.

An uncomfortable silence settled between them.

She cut a sliver of local Accasciato cave-cured cheese and

topped it with a wedge of fresh fig. "I'll give Maria a call." She popped the nibble into her mouth and left the table without a glance at either of them.

Rosalina slipped into the restroom and adjusted her hair in the mirror. Despite all her effort, the frizzled mop remained untamed. Staring into her eyes, she willed her emotions to settle down. This unexpected glitch didn't deserve anywhere near the amount of turmoil she was allocating to it.

Inhaling a calming breath, she went into her bedroom and picked up the phone.

"*Ciao, Maria, è Rosalina.*" She asked Maria about a room for Archer, but when she learned there were no vacancies, she was annoyed with herself for not being disappointed.

The town clock began its hourly chime, and she checked her nightstand clock. It was already nine.

With no other accommodation in town, Archer would need to travel into Florence for a hotel room and at this time of night, he'd have little chance of success. He had to stay there. Her heart fluttered at that decision, and she scowled at herself even more.

With the decision made, she strode towards the kitchen, determined to lay down the rules to Archer. But her plan to move Archer into the guesthouse early was crushed when she saw Archer's full glass of red wine and Alessandro going through a book on Italian churches.

"Here she is. I was just showing Archer how beautiful the Duomo is. He's never been to Italy."

"So he says." She sat, plucked her glass from the table and sipped the smooth liquid. The exquisite wine was made from Villa Pandolfini's very own grapes and she never tired of the taste. She allowed the liquor to settle her as she listened to Alessandro ply Archer with trivia about the churches of Florence.

"So, what scared Rosa?" Archer drove his hand through his wavy hair.

Alessandro relayed the events with the man in the robe and how rough he was with Rosalina. He ramped up the part he'd play in protecting her, and the honey-colored halo in Archer's eyes was a shade or two darker when he looked in her direction.

Alessandro reached for her hand, and Rosalina squeezed, fully aware that Archer was watching.

She released her hand and took a large sip of wine. "Show Archer the stained-glass window." She wanted to see his reaction.

"Oh, okay." Alessandro flicked through the book until he found the page he wanted. "Here." He turned the book to Archer and Rosalina stared at him, waiting for the moment of recognition.

Archer leaned forward. His eyes widened. "It's an *L*!"

So, he too thought the letter on his pendant was an I.

"What's an *L*?" Alessandro questioned.

"Oh. Nothing." Shaking his head, Archer pushed back from the book.

Questions would be eating him up. Yet he acted like this massive revelation was nothing.

He still won't share his stupid secret!

Archer cleared his throat, curling a small smile on his cinnamon lips. "So. . . how long have you two been a couple?"

"None of your business." Rosalina pushed to her feet and turned her back on them. "Maria didn't have any vacancies, so it seems you'll have to stay here after all. Alessandro, would you mind showing Archer to the back guesthouse while I clean up?"

"Sure." Alessandro knew there were more comfortable rooms to offer, but thankfully didn't question her decision. "Bring your wine. We'll get your car first, then drive up there. It's quite a distance."

After they left through the back door, Rosalina crumbled to a chair. As Alessandro led Archer along the portico, he explained the villa's elaborate architecture and she smiled.

Archer's manly cologne lingered, bringing with it memories of him standing naked at his window that flickered across her mind like the old-fashioned home movies her Nonna was fond of viewing over and over.

She dragged herself to the sink and as she washed the dishes and put away the food, the wine warmed her insides. Her mind drifted to visions of Archer's hands on her skin, gently touching her hips and then wandering up to her breasts. She closed her eyes and pictured him gathering her up into his arms.

The back door creaked open, launching her from her wretched memories. She wiped her hands on a dishcloth, and as she pulled herself together with the last sip of her wine, Alessandro reentered the kitchen.

"He seems like a nice fellow."

Nice fellows don't dump girlfriends without explanation.

"So, ummm, did you want him as far away as possible, or did you want him to have the least appealing room on the estate?"

"Both."

Alessandro eased behind her and wrapped his arms around her waist. She leaned into his embrace.

Alessandro was a wonderful guy and the perfect gentleman, but he didn't make her heart flutter. Unlike Archer.

Her heart hit overdrive just thinking about the hunky Australian.

Until now, that hadn't seemed important. Clearly it was.

What the hell am I going to do?

Chapter Eight

Seeing the picture of the stained-glass window had given Archer a clue to a mystery that'd plagued him for decades.

He ran his thumb over the raised letters on the pendant around his neck

For twenty years, he'd been searching for clues to the word "OSTOI". But it wasn't an *I*, it was an *L*. This explained why he'd found nothing. He was searching for the wrong thing. A spike of excitement shot through him.

It was time to go treasure hunting.

Archer threw his travel case onto the bed and grumbled at the squeaking bed springs beneath the oversized mattress. He stripped off and strolled across the smooth terra-cotta tiles, searching for the restroom.

Turning on the lights revealed an enormous claw-foot bath with a shower rose hoisted above it. He fiddled with the brass faucets until the water was scalding hot, then stepped over the rim and let the red-hot needles stab his back.

Seeing Rosalina tonight had reignited the fire within him that'd been a smoldering hell since he'd let her go. As water pounded his face, his gut twisted into angry knots over what he had to do.

Solving the pendant mystery would require revealing his rotten past to Rosalina.

It was something he'd never wanted to do.

Images of his mother's gaunt frame flashed into his mind. The last time he'd seen her, she was beyond help, lost in a cloud of pain and misery and nothing could undo what he'd done to her or his father. He'd never forgiven himself.

How could he expect a woman, especially an intelligent woman like Rosalina, to love him after what he'd done?

The shower sputtered and the pipes groaned within the ancient walls. Water turned icy cold, and he leaped out of the tub. After he'd dried off, he wrapped the towel around his waist and explored the rest of the cottage.

The ceilings were at least ten feet high, elaborately decorated with large cornices and intricate paneling. Gold-framed paintings of men in tight, white pants lined the walls, and heavy velvet drapes covered most of the windows.

It wasn't his kind of decorating. Not that he didn't appreciate it. Much of his childhood was spent exploring ancient buildings.

Maybe that's why he preferred the modern look.

There wasn't much to the cottage, and he returned to the bedroom where, like in the rest of the cottage, the furnishings matched the villa's fourteenth century vintage. He hoped the mattress on the bed didn't replicate the era.

Archer sat on it and was pleased the mattress wasn't rock hard. He'd slept on some shockers in his life, but thankfully he hadn't had to suffer that kind of torture in a long while. He reached for his phone and punched in Jimmy's number.

"Archer, how ya doin', man?" Jimmy's gruff voice answered on the second ring.

"I'm good, buddy. How's my *Evangeline?*"

"She's a bit rough after the *Cat's Cradle.*" Jimmy's laugh highlighted years of liquor and cigarette abuse to his throat. "Only kidding, man. She's a dream come true. I'm treating her better than my baby."

"I've seen the way you treat your baby, so I appreciate that."

"You found that treasure yet? Is it in the form of a beautiful Italian woman?"

"I've found Rosalina, if that's who you're referring to."

"Mighta been. How is she?"

"She's still pissed at me."

"Don't blame her. A woman like that deserves the royal treatment."

"I hear ya, Jimmy, and I'm trying to fix things."

"So, are you still goin' to be a month or so?"

Archer imagined Jimmy panicking that he'd be short paid. "Actually, I need another favor."

"Christ, man, what now? I'm already sufferin'." Jimmy laughed again and then erupted into a coughing fit.

Archer waited out the barking hack. "I need you to bring *Evangeline* to the Greek Islands."

"What? Are you kidding? That'll take months."

"I need you there in one month."

Jimmy whistled. "That's some serious running. I'll need a good crew."

"I trust you to choose the crew. No bikini babes."

Jimmy clicked his tongue. "You sure know how to take the fun out of things."

"This is serious, Jimmy. I'll do the paperwork. You only need to deliver *Evangeline*."

"You gonna tell me how much ya paying me, or you makin' me guess again?"

Archer smiled, knowing he had him. Jimmy would be grinning like a man who'd found gold in his backyard. "Name your price, Jimmy."

"We're traveling some turbulent waters, weeks at sea. It's a big job. And you want me hirin'—"

"How much, Jimmy?"

"Fifty grand up front and ten grand a week." The line was so silent Jimmy must've been holding his breath.

"If you get there in a month, I'll pay you a hundred grand up front as well as ten grand a week."

"Holy shit, man. You got yourself a fuckin' deal."

They said their goodbyes and Archer hung up the phone. Knowing *Evangeline* was on her way, and Jimmy, made Archer relax a little. He couldn't do what he was planning without either of them.

Or Rosalina. But that was another situation he was yet to work through.

Archer strolled to the kitchen and checked through the cupboards. He was surprised to find several bottles of wine. Selecting a bottle of red, he thumbed the fine layer of dust off the label, and although he struggled to read the Italian script, he deciphered enough to learn the wine was produced right here at *Villa Pandolfini*.

He found a glass and corkscrew and made his way to the enormous bay window in his bedroom. Sitting on the padded seat provided him with a moonlit view of the elaborate villa and its surroundings.

Subtle breezes carried scents of herbs and garlic that reminded him of Rosalina's incredible cooking. His stomach grumbled. Her delicious meals were the culinary opposite of the toasted sandwiches he'd been eating for dinner ever since she'd left.

The cork released with an elegant pop and he breathed in the wine's subtle aromas of blackberry and oak. With a good slosh in his glass, he marveled at its deep pomegranate color as he swirled it around.

His view covered all fifteen windows on the upper side of the villa, five on each level. All the windows were dark except for a faint glow filtering from somewhere beyond the upper floor windows.

A light flickered on in the top left-hand corner and he stared at it, visualizing Rosalina preparing for sleep. If he closed his eyes and inhaled deeply, he could still smell her skin. Her bedtime ritual always resulted in intoxicating scents of vanilla and citrus.

Soon after the town clock chimed eleven, her light switched off and Archer drained his wine glass. He wasn't sure if he was resisting sleep because of jet lag or his fear of dreaming.

Unable to procrastinate any longer, he pulled back the heavy quilt, slipped into bed, and punched the pillow into shape. A lump under his shoulder blade had him shuffle over to the other side of the double bed.

Scanning the room to memorize the layout, he decided the bay window would be his welcome seat when the nightmare came calling.

And it would come calling.

It'd plagued him every fucking night since he'd pushed Rosalina away.

He just hoped he was closer to solving this mystery of where he found his pendant.

Because if he didn't, he wasn't sure he could carry on without resolution.

Or without Rosalina.

Chapter Nine

Unable to sleep, Rosalina stared at the decorated ceiling. Every little sound seemed amplified— a car skirting its way up the narrow hillside, distant music, and a neighbor's dog.

But she couldn't fool herself.

As every minute passed, she waited for Archer's familiar scream. It was some kind of sick satisfaction to learn that he still suffered those nightmares, and she chastised herself for reveling in his pain.

Her instinct would be to run to him and comfort him through the horror, but her common sense told her he'd brought the solitude upon himself. It was no longer her job to help him through the dark moments.

The town clock chimed two in the morning and, with each passing minute, expectation ate at her.

This is ridiculous.

Stewing over her resolve, she rolled to her side and tugged the sheet under her chin.

And then she heard it — the familiar gut-wrenching scream.

She sat upright and flicked on the lamp, but instantly flicked it off. She didn't want him seeing her light.

Her insides twisted at indecision over whether or not to go to him.

Going to him won the debate, and with breathless anticipation, she pulled on her silk gown and put on some house shoes. With each step down the creaking stairs, her mind was a tug of war between going and staying.

She opened the back door and admired the moon conquering the night sky with its pearl-like glow. As she inched up the pebble path, trying to remain quiet, she envisaged Archer waiting for her with his olive skin glistening with a fine layer of sweat.

She wrapped her long hair into a thick knot over her shoulder and moistened her lips with her tongue.

As she rounded the corner of the pool house, her breath caught.

Archer was silhouetted in the bay window. Only an artist could paint a more solemn picture. He sat with his back against the window frame, his head tilted to accentuate his strong jawline. His shoulders sagged, as if heavy with the weight of burden.

Rosalina inhaled a calming breath before she continued on the path. She was nearly upon the cottage before he moved. His instant reaction was to drape something across his lap.

He's naked! She shouldn't have been surprised. He always slept without clothes on.

"Rosa?"

She froze, but then realizing how silly it was not to respond, she cleared her throat. "I…um, I heard you scream and wanted to check you were okay?"

He groaned. "I didn't know I was that loud. Sorry if I woke you."

She probably wouldn't have heard it if she hadn't been wide awake, waiting. "Sound carries down the hill. That's why we never put newlyweds up here." She cringed at the lame statement.

"Do you want to come in?"

"No. As long as you're okay, I'll —"

"Rosalina, please. I've missed you."

Hearing those words took a chunk from her heart. She missed

him too, more than she wanted to admit. Before she even considered the consequences, she stepped towards his doorway.

Archer had wrapped a towel around his waist to greet her at the door, but the way it hung low on his hips only served as a magnet to the line of dark hair trailing down from his navel. His very sexy navel. She dragged her eyes away.

But despite her resolve, Rosalina fell into his arms with tears pooling in her eyes. Archer cupped the back of her neck, drawing her face to his. Their eyes locked, and in the dim light, the concern in his expression was heartbreaking.

"Oh, Rosa." He caught a tear with his thumb, wiping it from her cheek. "I'm sorry for what I did."

She couldn't speak. Her chin quivered, and the knot in her throat hurt as much as the ache in her heart.

Go...now.

Leave before it's too late.

Her love for him hadn't diminished, however, for her own sanity, she had to resist until he told her everything. It took all her might to place her hand on his chest and ease away. "No, Archer. I can't do this. I won't fall for you again."

His shoulders deflated, but a sense of defeat crossed his features.

She tightened the belt on her gown and stepped out the door. "Put some shorts on. I want to show you something."

With shorts and T-shirt on, he stepped into the moonlight, and she reached for his hand, interlocking their fingers as they'd done many times before.

Following the moonlit path, trimmed with miniature hedges, she led him to a small stream, fed by a man-made waterfall and decorated with lush vines. The sound of water cascading over the strategically positioned rocks was a soothing lullaby.

Rosalina led him around the side, where they could access beneath the waterfall without getting wet. She ducked under the rocks and strolled to the darkest corner of a cave beneath the overhang. Out of the moonlight, the surroundings became a black space but, as her eyes adjusted, hundreds of tiny lights appeared.

"They're fireflies," she whispered.

His breathing was steady in her ear.

"I spent many nights up here as a kid, watching them. With seven siblings, it was nearly impossible to get peace anywhere else."

She reached for the wooden seat and guided Archer to sit. He draped his arm across her shoulder and she snuggled into him. The moment was special, as calming and natural as if their relationship had returned to the way it once was.

His breath tickled her ear. "Why do they light up?"

"They communicate with each other that way. The males show off their special light dance and if the female's impressed, she'll answer with her best flash."

"It's cool."

"I guess you and I are much the same. I recognized your scream and found you."

"Ha. Very funny."

"The males also use the flashing to lure in their prey. The poor guy thinks he's going to mate, but instead he gets eaten."

"Nasty."

They remained in silence for a long time, but the weight of exhaustion soon became too much, and Rosalina shifted in her seat to stand.

Archer reached for her, placing his hand over her arm. "I've missed you so much, Rosa."

She wanted to see his eyes, to see the desperation she heard in his voice. Although crumbling under his words, she had to remain strong to save herself. "It's not enough, Archer. Not anymore."

"I know." He said it like a man defeated. It wasn't the Archer she knew.

Rosalina waited. The anticipation of the moment hung heavily in the air. She could almost hear him searching for the right words.

"I was eleven years old when it all happened."

Rosalina slipped back into the chair and leaned into him. While she dreaded what he was about to say, she didn't want him to stop. When he draped his arm around her shoulder again, the rigidness she'd originally felt in his torso softened.

Maybe he's relieved to finally be telling me.

52

She let out a slow breath, attempting to calm her racing heart.

Archer released a long sigh. "Dad dragged Mom and I all over the world's oceans, treasure hunting. He was good at it, too. It was very lucrative; he earned a good living, and we lived like royalty aboard his boat."

Rosalina placed her hand on his knee, just above his scar.

"We weren't always at sea. Often there were long periods between dives that Dad spent trolling libraries and museums, searching for clues. So, I grew up hopping from country to country. It was the best childhood. . . then again, I guess I didn't know any different. As a result, I didn't make friends my age. Mom and Dad were my best friends. I loved them more than anything in the world."

He paused and sucked in a shaky breath. "But then. . . then they died. . . because of me."

Rosalina gasped and sat up straight. "Archer!"

He slipped his arm off her shoulder and clutched her hand. "Dad had been searching for a missing treasure for nearly four years. And one day when we were preparing to dive, he had this glint in his eye. You know, like he was destined to find it, or it was destined to be found by him. I'd grown to trust that look; he was rarely wrong."

Rosalina eased back against his chest again, and his thundering heartbeat echoed her foreboding.

"The water was crystal clear, visibility about fifty yards. We dropped in and followed a coral shelf down to fifty feet. As clear as it was, you'd think the shipwreck would stand out like the Titanic. But hundreds of years of coral growth had completely camouflaged it. We didn't know we were right on top of it until I broke off a chunk of coral. It was stuck to a piece of wood."

"Oh, wow." Rosalina wondered where this was going.

"You should've seen Dad; he was so excited. But we'd been down there for sixty minutes and he signaled to me to surface, but I. . . I deliberately—"

Archer swallowed loudly. The lump in his throat must've been as big as a pot roast.

Rosalina squeezed his hand. "It's okay."

He sniffed before he continued. "I swam away. . . forcing him to follow. I couldn't help it. I just wanted to find a piece of treasure. The ship was right below us, but we couldn't see it. I kept thinking every lump and bump could be gold."

He changed his grip to intertwine his fingers with hers. "Anyway, a small hole about the width of a coffee cup appeared right below me and I saw something shiny. Without any thought about what could be in the hole, I stuck my arm into it, right up to my shoulder. Dad still hadn't caught up and was banging on his tank to get my attention. But I didn't care; I was onto something. Then a chunk of the coral gave way and a big cloud of crap blossomed around me so I couldn't see. I grabbed onto something and when the water cleared, I had this pendant in my hand."

His hand went to his neck, and he paused, no doubt toying with that necklace.

That's it? "But Archer. That's a great story. Why didn't you tell me before?"

"I'm not finished." His voice croaked like he was having trouble speaking over the lump in his throat.

"Oh." Rosalina eased back again, waiting for him to continue.

"Dad was so excited. We messed around in the water for ages, checking out the pendant and examining that hole in the wreck. We lost track of time." He fiddled with the necklace as he shifted in the seat.

"We'd gone way over our dive time limit. Dad squeezed my arm until it hurt, so I knew how serious it was. We had to surface where we were because we'd run out of time to swim back to the anchor line." He sucked in a shaky breath, and let it out in a forceful gush.

"We were at the five-yard safety stop, and I was replaying in my mind the way I found the pendant, so I could tell Mom every detail. But then I sensed something was wrong. I felt it before I saw it."

Her stomach twisted, and she reached for his hand again.

"A great white, at least twelve feet long, started circling us." He sucked air in through his teeth. "I've never been so scared in my life. Its eyes were pure evil, black as coal. Lifeless. And it was fast. One minute it was in front of us, then it was behind. No matter how fast we spun around, we struggled to keep track of it. The damn thing kept circling. Over and over. I remember seeing icy terror in dad's eyes. Nothing scared him. Until that shark."

She shuddered at how terrifying that would've been.

"Dad jabbed at the shark with the dive knife from his ankle holster. But it was one of those ones with the flat top, you know, for cutting away fishing line, or trawler netting." He huffed. "Just three inches of steel. It was like attacking a monster with a toothpick."

Rosalina had a knife similar to that in her dive kit. The stubby blade was designed to stop a diver from accidentally stabbing themselves. But it was totally useless when fighting off a man-eater.

"It was the first time in months that I'd wished I'd worn a wetsuit." Archer scratched his beard stubble, and the sound was like sandpaper on wood. "I had on a pair of yellow board shorts. They were like a friggin red flag to a bull. We hovered at the decompression stop for what seemed like forever. The worst part was when we couldn't *see* the shark. To know that monster was there, but not be able to follow it, that was terrifying. We couldn't see the anchor line either because we'd drifted so far from the boat."

Terror quivered Archer's voice.

She wasn't scared of sharks, but she'd never had one circling her like that.

"It was my fault. I should never have tricked him into carrying on the dive."

"Oh Archer, you can't—"

"Yes! I can, and I do, Rosa. If I hadn't swum away from dad, none of it would have happened."

They sat in silence and from his rigid stance, she could feel the horror going through Archer's mind.

"The shark appeared out of nowhere. Tracking toward me like a demon. Dad yanked me back, but it got me."

He reached down his left leg, probably to touch the jagged pink scar Rosalina had seen dozens of times but had never questioned him about. He was guarded about so many aspects of his life that it'd seemed pointless to ask.

"It tore off a chunk of my skin, just above my knee." He reached for her hand again and squeezed. Hard. "Blood was everywhere."

"Jesus! What'd you do?"

"The shark disappeared over a coral outcrop. But that was worse. The fear in Dad's eyes. . ." Archer strangled her hand.

But she didn't let go. She didn't want to move.

"Dad shoved me upwards, and I swam like crazy. But when I got to the surface, I couldn't see the boat anywhere. I thought Dad had followed me, but —" His voice trembled.

Rosalina's chest squeezed so tight she could barely breathe.

"He didn't make it. . . the shark, I saw it. . . there was so much blood." Archer inhaled a sharp breath.

"Oh no, Arch."

"I spent ages in the water. Screaming. Crying. Waiting. Waiting for Mom. Waiting for the shark to get me, too."

"Where was the boat?"

"Mom looked everywhere for us. She eventually heard my screams. I don't know how long she took, but I was almost unconscious by the time she found me. I got the bends."

"Oh, Jesus." Rosalina's heart was in her throat. As a diver, she understood how deadly decompression sickness was. It was one of her greatest fears.

"While I was in a pressure chamber recovering, Mom was trying to find what was left of Dad. They found part of his buoyancy vest and this pendant was in it." He reached for the necklace again. "I couldn't face her. How could I tell Mom it was my fault we exceeded our dive limits? But she knew it was me. I saw it in her eyes."

"It wasn't your fault. How can you blame yourself?"

"If we'd stuck to the dive times, we would've returned to the anchor line and been back on the boat well before that shark showed up." Archer stood and his heavy footfalls crunched on the gravel as he paced backward and forward.

"You're wrong, Archer! You didn't know that would happen."

"Mom began dying that day. She couldn't live without him. She stopped eating, stopped living, and two months later she stopped breathing. I killed them both."

She strode to him, wrapped her arms around his heaving chest, and listened to his pounding heart.

It wasn't Archer's fault.

But it doesn't matter what I say.

Archer needed to forgive himself.

But he'd been swallowing the guilt for so long, his nightmares could plague him forever.

Chapter Ten

Archer tugged Rosalina to his chest and a sense of weightlessness took over, as if a brick had been removed from his heart.

Yet he was thankful she couldn't see him in the blackness because the burden of guilt was still there. Eating at his sanity.

She squeezed, and he hugged her closer, never wanting to let go.

But that's exactly what he had to do. He could never love anyone the way his parents had loved each other, where one couldn't live without the other. Rosalina deserved that kind of love.

Releasing her, he reached for her hand. "Come on, I'll walk you to the villa."

They stepped out of the cave and strolled along the path.

"I've decided to go after the treasure."

"Really?" Rosalina turned her face up to him. "That's a great idea."

"Will you come with me?" His heart pounded as he willed her to say yes.

"I can't, Arch. I need my job."

"You could come back to *Evangeline*. I've asked Jimmy to bring her."

"Jimmy? When did you organize that?"

"When Alessandro showed me that picture of the stained-glass window. I knew straight away it was a clue to finding the treasure."

"Really? You're serious?"

"I need to do this. I owe it to Dad."

She was silent for a long time and his insides churned with the wait.

"I don't know." She shook her head. "I just don't know."

They arrived at a fork in the path. "I'll take you down to the villa," he said.

She faced him, pressing her hand to his chest. The moonlight gave her a heavenly glow. Her parted lips were a delicious shade of fuchsia and it took all his resolve not to kiss her.

"Thank you for telling me."

He wrapped his arms around her and held her body against him. Her smell, a subtle blend of vanilla and citrus, was so damn sexy. Her warm breath on his neck set his thoughts into erotic over-drive and every ounce of him wanted her. But Rosalina deserved the best.

However, he could only offer her half a man.

He could never love unconditionally and he couldn't live every day wondering if it was going to be their last day together. He'd resist his desires, and once the mystery of the pendant was solved, he'd let her go.

She deserved her freedom.

Archer kissed her, almost melted into her being, but before he tipped over that edge, he pulled back. "Come on, it's late."

He led her to the villa's back door. His breath hitched when she looked up at him. Her eyes twinkled in the moonlight, and when she blinked, it was like it was in slow motion.

Or maybe he was just savoring every millisecond he had with her again.

On her tippy toes, she kissed him. Just a brief touch of her lips.

"Goodnight, Archer." She turned, and as she walked from him, her gown did little to hide the luscious curves beneath that fine silk.

THE NEXT DAY, ARCHER WOKE WITH THE SUN ON HIS LEGS AND THE warmth gave him a good feeling about the day ahead. Last night played through his mind on repeat. He still couldn't believe he'd told Rosalina about his past. But now that she's had time to process his admission, dread crept into his mind, and the good vibes he'd had just moments ago evaporated.

He showered with water at piping hot, and as he toweled himself off, he scowled at his bloodshot eyes unsure if that was from all those rotten hours flying to Rome, or from the twisted emotion that'd been tearing him up since he saw Rosalina again.

The smell of bacon had him dressed in a flash, then he strolled down the gravel path to the villa. He peeked through the window. Rosalina was at the kitchen table, nursing her coffee mug. It was her standard morning pose, and, until now, he hadn't realized how much he'd missed it.

He could admire her morning routine for hours. So damn sexy.

Reluctantly, he tapped on the window. Her smile lit up her face, and it was the greeting he hoped for. No, it was better than that, a thousand times better.

She opened the door and her intense cornflower-blue eyes struck him. He'd missed them. Hell, he'd missed every incredible facet of this exotic beauty. It took all his might not to pull her into his arms and kiss her.

"Did you get back to sleep?" She went straight to the coffee machine to prepare a fresh brew of coffee.

"Slept right through till just now."

"Great. I've made a batch of corn fritters. Would you like some?"

He chuckled. Just the sound of corn fritters had his mouth salivating. "Yes, please."

She would cringe if she found out what he'd been eating for the past eight months. A simple boiled egg would be a step up in comparison. He tugged out one of the heavy chairs and sat so he could watch her work her magic. The flowers he'd given her were arranged in a large crystal vase at the end of the table. He was glad she hadn't thrown them in the bin.

It was a good sign.

The fritters looked as perfect as the meals on the front cover of one of those fancy *Gourmet* magazines Rosalina used to leave lying around. She'd topped the fritters with bacon and a fried egg. She added a dollop of tomato relish—no doubt homemade—a healthy serving of sliced avocado and a scattering of herbs she'd twisted off the plants in the kitchen window. Archer had woken up in heaven.

They ate the meal in relative silence. Neither of them brought up last night.

"What are you doing today?" Standing, she reached for her empty plate. "I'm off to work in half an hour. I can walk you at the train station, if you wish."

He stood and reached for her arm. "Can't you take the day off?"

She shook her head. "It took too long to get this job. I can't afford to lose it."

"I was hoping you'd take me to the church."

She slipped out of his grasp. "Maybe later."

She curled her lip through her teeth, as if contemplating her next move. Finally, she huffed. "Meet me at Café Acquacotta at three."

She scribbled the address on a slip of paper. "Here." She shoved the paper in his hand, then turned his shoulders and shoved him out the kitchen's back door.

Archer made his way back to his cottage, fell onto the bed, and stared at the ceiling. Rosalina's delicious breakfast sat heavy in his stomach. It was the biggest and definitely the most enjoyable meal he'd had since she'd last cooked for him.

He'd eaten more than he needed, though, and it took all his might to get out of the bed again. Archer threw his phone into his pocket and headed to the car. With the key in the ignition, he pressed the button to roll the top down. Slipping on his glasses, he cruised down the driveway.

Three roads led out of Signa. He chose one at random. Soon he was winding his way through Tuscany's checkerboard pastures, yet, despite the wind in his hair and the relaxing drive, he struggled to drag his mind away from Rosalina.

She was a fascinating woman, but being with her was dangerous.

He needed to be strong, for her sake.

With carefree meandering, he found himself in the medieval town of Siena. He parked the car at the base of the cliff, and rather than using the crowded elevator to reach the top, he tackled the stairs. It was a decision that had his knee in throbbing agony by the time he reached the piazza.

While he admired the medieval character of the surrounding buildings, he refrained from visiting any of them. Instead, he chose the nearest restaurant, sat at a small round table and ordered Bistecca alla Fiorentina with a glass of local red wine.

Crowds of tourists explored the hilltop village around him, and he prayed he'd never look as ludicrous as some of them did. The rare T-Bone steak was delightfully rich, and so tender he barely needed his knife to cut it.

Whilst it was excellent, the dish still didn't compare to the one Rosalina had made him once.

The hours slipped by quickly, and when it was time to go, he was once again consumed with the prospect of meeting Rosalina.

As per her earlier suggestion, he parked his car at Villa Pandolfini and walked to the train station. The train ride into Florence was just fifteen minutes and Archer merged with the crowds to follow Rosalina's hand drawn lines on the map through the bustling streets of the ancient city.

A few minutes before three o'clock, he chose a wrought-iron chair at the front of Café Acquacotta, and within seconds Rosalina served him a basket of bread and a beer. Her hair was in a high ponytail that swung as she walked away. She looked gorgeous without even trying.

The crowds passing by were a crazy mix of tourists and locals who were worlds apart. Locals took strides of purpose, apparently no longer seeing their historical surroundings. Tourists, laden with cameras and packs, strolled along taking photos of random things and checking out the stalls lining the narrow-paved street.

Alessandro walked towards the café and Archer readied to say hello. But the Italian bypassed him without a glance and went straight inside. Archer's eyes burned a hole in Alessandro's back as he the Italian kissed and hugged Rosalina as a girlfriend and boyfriend should.

Rosalina blushed and cast a quick glance in his direction. She offered Alessandro a basket of bread and pointed out Archer.

Alessandro turned and smiled like he was pleased to see Archer and shook Archer's hand. "Ah, Archer. *Va bene?*" He seemed oblivious to the awkward situation he was in. It was strange that a man would be comfortable with an ex-boyfriend being back on the scene.

Either Alessandro was very confident in his relationship with Rosalina, or he had no idea how serious they'd been.

"How was your day?" Alessandro raised one dark, bushy eyebrow. "Where'd you go?"

Archer took a gulp of his beer and shrugged. "I took a drive. Ended up in one of those, what do you call them. . . fortified towns."

"Oh, lovely. Which one, Monteriggioni? San Gimignano? Siena?"

Archer clicked his fingers. "Siena."

Alessandro gaped at him with a how-the-hell-do-you-not-know look. "So, what did you do there? Sightseeing?"

"Not much." He shrugged. "Sat at a table in the city center, ordered a meal, watched tourists walk by."

Alessandro's jaw dropped. "You mean the piazza? It's one of Tuscany's tourism highlights. Did you visit the Duomo?"

Archer felt like a student being grilled by a frustrated teacher. "Ahhh, no. Sorry."

"Sienna's Duomo is considered to be one of Italy's most impressive cathedrals."

Archer searched for Rosalina. He needed saving. "Yeah. But I didn't want to do any sightseeing."

"But you would've passed it to get to the piazza. The entire façade looks like it's decorated with marble frosting?" Alessandro raised both his eyebrows this time. If he raised them any higher, his eyes might pop out of their sockets.

Archer shrugged. "I didn't really look around much. I was just killing time."

"You should look around." Alessandro shook his head. "Some of the most beautiful things in the world are often right in front of you."

With perfect timing, Rosalina slipped into the chair between them. The coincidence of her arrival was obviously not lost on Alessandro as he locked eyes with Archer. A silent battle brewed between them, but it was Alessandro who was the ultimate winner when he placed his palm over Rosalina's hand.

When she squeezed his hand, Archer fought his seething by gulping his beer.

"So, what have you boys been talking about?" Rosalina shared her gaze evenly between the two men, like watching a ball in a tennis match.

"Archer was telling me about his visit to Siena."

"Oh, lovely," she said.

"Well, it would've been lovely, except he failed to partake in any sightseeing."

"Don't worry. I'll do plenty of sightseeing. Rosalina's showing me around now." Her eyes shot to him and Archer instantly wanted to retract his statement.

"*Per favore*, allow me to be your guide." Alessandro's eyes were alight as he leaned forward. "I know practically every brick and piece of artwork in the entire city."

"Well, um, we're only going to the Church of St Apostoli." There was no backing out now. Rosalina's clenched jaw and rolling eyes suggested she was as disappointed as he was that Alessandro would be joining them.

But it was too late. They were stuck with him now.

Their stroll from the café took them through the Piazza della Signoria, a bustling L-shaped square surrounded by ancient buildings and cafés, all overflowing and, no doubt, overpriced.

"This is one of the most significant public places in Florence." Alessandro's hands flicked like an air traffic controller as he pointed out various buildings. With an obvious photographic memory, he detailed the years the building construction began and ended, along with a pile of other trivia that had Archer's head spinning.

"Here's the Palazzo Vecchio, or in other terms, the Town Hall. See the crenelated roof line?"

Archer looked at the roof; not a view he would've remotely considered if Alessandro hadn't insisted.

"Impressive, *si*?"

Archer smiled, but he wasn't anywhere near as excited as the grinning Italian.

Alessandro pointed out an endless array of buildings, places that apparently Archer had to see while he was in Florence. "Hey, let's go via Ponte Vecchio; you'll love it. It's one of the oldest bridges in Firenze. It's an amazing—"

"Alex. Please, could you just take us to that church?"

Alessandro frowned. "But there are many, many other *affascinante* buildings worthy of a mention."

"Maybe later." Archer held Alessandro's gaze until the Italian shrugged and as his stature shrunk, he indicated the new direction they should travel.

They strolled along Florence's narrow cobblestone streets, and Alessandro continued to bombard them with the history. *The bricks were shipped in from such-and-such. So and so died here.*

Rosalina was quiet and reserved, two qualities she rarely displayed. Occasionally, she glanced sideways at Archer and her gaze suggested she was uncomfortable being sandwiched between her current boyfriend and her ex.

They arrived at the Piazza Del Limbo and Alessandro explained the significance of the cemetery as they approached the church.

"Oh, Rosa, I didn't mention that an earthquake severely damaged the church in 1348. See this brickwork?"

He pointed to a jagged row of bricks at the side of the building. "These are the original bricks and these. . ." He indicated further along. "These are the new ones. . . see?"

Rosalina followed Alessandro's finger. He couldn't decide if she was interested or not, but when she turned towards him and rolled her eyes, he stifled a laugh.

Alessandro continued the tour with Rosalina and Archer following him through the doorway into the Church of St Apostoli.

Archer couldn't pinpoint why, but his apprehension escalated with each step along the central aisle. Fading sun speared through a high window, casting a strip of light along the opposite wall.

Silence engulfed him, and Archer felt a presence. Yet the church was vacant.

He scanned the dark corners, hoping to find the reason for his unease.

Weighted drapes hung along sections of the walls, and Archer couldn't believe he was actually looking for eyes peering out from behind the black velvet. Alessandro pointed out the oval floor decoration and explained its original purpose.

How deep is that pit?

Up to fifty percent of the population in Europe died as a result of the Great Plague. If the pit was where the bodies were thrown, then it would have to be a damn enormous area down there.

A few more steps forward revealed the stained-glass window Rosalina had talked about. His hand went to his pendant, still concealed beneath his T-shirt, and he sensed her staring at him as he took another step towards the artwork.

She was right—my pendant is a replica of the plaque in the picture.

"Tell me about the man in the picture." Archer looked at Alessandro.

Alessandro approached, grinning. He pointed at aspects of the artwork as he spoke. "It was designed in 1288 by Duccio di Buonin-segna. He was a master artist but is remembered more for his fresco artwork than this stained-glass window. This piece symbolizes Pope

Pelagius' victory over and expulsion of the Goths, as conveyed to the Apostles, St. James and St. Philip."

Archer rolled his shoulders, trying to remain patient. "Tell me about this bit." He pointed to the plaque.

"The scales represent the victory. The lower plate is the Goths and the higher plate has a plaque inscribed with the Apostle, showing they were victorious."

"Is this reproduced anywhere else in the church?"

Alessandro's brows thumped together. "Yes, as a matter of fact. The tomb of Roberto D'Angio is in the crypt. I believe this picture is carved into his stone effigy."

"I need to see it."

Alessandro chuckled. "Well, unless you're a man of the faith and forgot to tell—"

Archer grabbed Alessandro's arm. "I have to see it."

"Excuse me." Alessandro pulled back. "What's wrong with you?"

Rosalina stepped in. "Is there another way to see it?"

A frown rippled Alessandro's forehead. "What's going on?"

With Rosalina's glare drilling into him, he debated over how much Alessandro should know. Finally, he reached for the pendant and let it fall atop his shirt.

Alessandro studied it, and when recognition crossed his face, he spun to the stained-glass window. "Where'd you get—"

A man in a dark robe shoved Alessandro aside.

Shit! Where'd he come from?

Archer stepped in front of Rosalina as the man lunged for the pendant.

Archer smacked his hand away.

"*Dove hai preso questo?*" His hood covered his eyes.

"What'd he say?" Archer demanded.

"He wants to know where you found it," Alessandro said.

"Tell him it's none of his fucking business." Archer wanted to see the man's eyes, but it was impossible.

Alessandro's frown framed terrified eyes. "I can't say that."

The man took another step, but Archer stood his ground,

warning him with an outstretched arm. "Hey, man, you need to back off. Tell him, Alex."

"Let's leave. Come on, Rosalina." Alessandro clutched her hand.

If Archer was alone, he would've done anything but that. But when Rosalina placed her hand on his waist and guided him sideways, he had no choice.

He wouldn't be able to look around the church with that asshole there, anyway. Reluctantly, he backed off and the threesome strode towards the front door.

Outside, Archer paced the concrete piazza with both Alessandro and Rosalina following his every move. His pendant and the stained-glass window were absolutely connected. But for the life of him, he couldn't figure out how. He had to get back into that church.

"What time does the church close?"

Alessandro chuckled. "This is Florence. Churches don't close."

Archer huffed. "Let's go get a drink. We'll come back a bit later. Maybe that guy will've gone by then."

Rosalina nodded, but didn't move, probably trying to anticipate his actions.

"Where's the closest bar? I need a beer."

"Oh, I know the perfect place. It's a local favorite. Follow me." Alessandro reached for Rosalina's hand and tugged her towards the road.

The bar, if the little hole in the wall could actually be called one, wasn't trying to win any passing traffic. Unless you knew it was there, you'd never find it. And yet it was bustling with people, not one of whom spoke English.

Within minutes of their arrival, a bar table was brought out to them, along with a basket of assorted breads and dips, and their order was taken. Their drinks arrived two minutes later.

Archer was impressed. "No wonder the locals like this joint." Archer raised his beer in a toast.

Rosalina clinked her wine glass. "So, what do you think about the window?" The way she glared at him; anyone would think she was penetrating his brain with her big blue eyes.

Archer swigged his beer, formulating a reply. "It's clearly related to my pendant, but other than that, I have no friggin idea."

"That priest couldn't take his eyes off it," Alessandro said.

Archer's thoughts spun as he took another gulp of his beer.

This new clue added more questions than answers to his mysterious pendant.

Chapter Eleven

R osalina's heartbeat thundered as they returned to the church. *Are we about to solve the mystery of the necklace?*

After what Archer had told her in the cave, she hoped so. He deserved peace. And she'd do anything to be there when he found it.

They entered the church and with Archer leading the way, she tiptoed down the main aisle behind him. Not that they were breaking any laws by being in the church that late at night, but it felt wrong creeping around looking for clues.

But it didn't stop them.

They looked behind decorated cloths, scrutinized statues and artwork, and looked behind the altar. While Alessandro's expression oozed boyish glee, Archer's was a mixture of frustration and determination.

Thankfully, the creepy man in the robe didn't show up again.

Rosalina pulled back one of the heavy velvet drapes and her heart skipped a beat. A small door was hidden behind it. Its frame was barely bigger than her body. She pushed the wood with her palm and her heart beat faster when the door popped open.

The door was heavy, as if weighted. She pushed it further and peered into the opening, but it was too dark to see anything.

Glancing over her shoulder, she searched for Archer and Alessandro. They were across the opposite end of the church, examining a large painting in a guided frame.

She pushed the door open and stepped over the threshold. As her eyes adjusted to the darkness, a sharp click echoed off the walls.

Oh shit!

She spun back around. But she was too late. The heavy door had shut behind her.

The darkness enveloped her as she groped for a handle to open the door. But there was nothing. In the silence her breathing sounded frantic. Continuing her search, her finger brushed over a small opening.

A keyhole. One that suited a very large, old-fashioned skeleton key.

But the key wasn't there.

Shit! I'm trapped.

How could I be so stupid?

She couldn't risk calling for the men on the other side. Trespassing in Florence churches was a very serious offense, one she'd like to avoid.

My phone!

She tugged it from her pocket and paused. Who to call. . . Archer or Alessandro? *Damn, this is awkward.*

Each of them was the right and wrong choice for their own reasons. She was supposed to be angry with Archer, and at the same time, she was trying not to give Alessandro any false hope that she was interested in him.

They were in this church because of Archer, but then Alessandro was the one who could probably help her out of this mess.

She released a slow breath, and for no solid reason, she scrolled to Archer's name and hit the green button.

It rang in the distance, and she pictured Archer fumbling for his phone. "Rosa?"

"I went through a doorway and now I'm stuck on the other side."

"What? Where's the doorway?"

"It's behind one of those huge velvet drapes, next to the statue of the lady with the eagle on her arm."

His footsteps pounded across the church. *So much for being discreet.*

"I'm in here." She tapped on the door, but her knuckles barely made a sound on the solid wood.

"There's no handle. How did you open it?" Archer's voice was a forced whisper on the phone.

"Is that Rosalina?" Alessandro asked.

"She went in through here and the damn door shut. She's locked in."

"It was already open," she said. "There's no handle here either. Just a keyhole, but no key."

"How do we open it, Alex?"

"Without a key, it's impossible."

"We'll have to find another way in," Archer said into the phone.

She searched her surroundings and caught a slight glow in the distance. "There's a light down the passage. It might be a way out."

"No, Rosa. Stay there," Archer instructed.

"What's she doing?" Alessandro's voice elevated a couple of notches.

"She's trying to find her own way out." Archer answered Alessandro.

"I'm stuck in here, anyway." She shifted away from the door.

"Give me the phone," Alessandro said, and she pictured Archer's squared-out jaw as he resisted handing his phone to Alessandro.

"Rosalina, *per favore* stay where you are." Alessandro sounded like a professor talking to a naughty student, and it only made her even more determined.

"I'm not waiting here and doing nothing." The thought of running into that creep in the robe scared the hell out of her, but she had to try to find a way out. The dim light in the distance beckoned.

Alessandro kept talking to her, but she ignored him.

Archer and Alessandro argued over what she should do.

"Hey, fellas," she whispered. "Keep it down? I'm trying to sneak around here."

They continued bickering in whispers that were still too loud.

She reached a set of stairs. *Go down or go back?* Nerves clamped in her stomach. But it was pointless to go back without a way to open that door.

It's up to me to find a way out.

"I'm going down some stairs," she whispered into the phone.

The uneven stones had a smooth path worn down the middle. At the bottom, she had a choice of left or right. There was nothing to indicate which way was best. She swallowed the lump in her throat and chose left.

The stone tunnels were made of sandstone blocks, fashioned into giant bricks. There were no windows. No doors. And nothing to indicate she was heading the right way. It was silent, too. Something she wasn't used to.

The word dungeon rolled around her mind as she tried to memorize where she was going, but each twist and turn of the labyrinth looked identical to the one before: nothing but cold stone walls burdened with centuries of grime.

It didn't help that the wrought-iron lamps with the bare, dangling light bulbs hung off the walls at random intervals, creating alternating dark and light shadows.

A hand darted from the darkness and latched onto her wrist.

Gasping, she spun around.

Dark shadows made it impossible to see who had hold of her.

But she smelled him. It was the creepy priest.

Rosalina forced his putrid odor into her lungs and screamed.

Chapter Twelve

Rosalina's scream clawed through Archer's heart. "Rosalina!" He yelled into the phone, but the line was dead.

"Shit." She's gone.

"Rosa!" Archer slammed his palm onto the dark wooden door. "Help me break in, Alex."

Alex shook his head. "It's pointless. That door would be six inches thick."

"Look for another way, then."

Alessandro raced up the center aisle.

Archer went after him, surprised by the Italian's speed. He didn't look athletic. They leapt over the oval floor decoration, out the door and into the piazza.

Archer followed Alessandro around the corner of the church, but they had to stop at a massive stone wall, dead-end. "Where, Alex?"

"Wait. Let me think!"

Archer threw his hands out in frustration. "Come on, man. You know these buildings. Think"

"I am!" Alessandro clenched his jaw. "Now shush!"

Somewhere below them, Rosalina screamed again. Archer looked to the concrete, searching for an access point. "Alex! You're the supposed expert."

Alessandro's eyebrows slammed together. "Try her phone again!"

Archer jabbed her speed dial number. With the phone to his ear, he stared at the cracks in the concrete as it rang. The phone clicked. "Rosalina?"

"I want the rest of it." The man's English was thick with an Italian accent, but the voice on the other end was unmistakable. That fucking creep.

A vice gripped his chest as Archer pictured that asshole clutching Rosalina. "Let her go, or we'll call the police."

"Bring me the rest."

"The rest of what? Listen, you bastard. If you touch —"

"You have twenty-four hours."

"I don't —" The phone went dead. "Damn it!"

"What happened?"

"He said I've got one day to bring *the rest*." Archer glared at the phone.

"The rest of what?"

"I don't fucking know."

"Don't swear at me." Alessandro's eyes drilled into him. "I'm calling the *polizia*."

"Okay, okay. . . I'm sorry." Archer held his palms up. "This is crazy."

Archer paced back and forward, helpless, as Alessandro spoke into his phone.

"*Ciao, la mia ragazza è appena stata rapita da un prete.*" Alessandro's rapid-fire Italian grew more aggressive with each sentence.

He cupped the phone. "They don't believe me. They even laughed." He said a few more words into the phone, then he hung up, shaking his head. "They think I'm crazy. What do we do now?"

Archer's gut twisted as he stepped back, scanning the church walls. "We figure out where he's taking her." He marched towards the other side of the church. "Tell me how to get in."

"*Va bene*, let's see." Alessandro cleared his throat. "This church was built in —"

"Jesus Christ, I don't need a history lesson."

"Do not shout at me either." Alessandro's eyes narrowed, and for the first time since he'd met the Italian, Archer saw fury in his black eyes.

Archer drove his hands through his hair. "Fine. Go ahead."

"This church was built in the eleventh century, which means a burial chamber would have been built beneath the floor. Crypts are usually found below the main apse of the church and are only accessible via an underground tunnel beneath the sanctuary."

Archer groaned *a hurry up* threat.

Alessandro glared at him. "To view the tomb, pilgrims entered through one door, passed the tomb and exited via another door. That way, they didn't interrupt the service going on above them."

"Right. So, we find those doors."

"Well. . . the tomb of Robert the Wise was once here. He was an incredibly popular man. The line of pilgrims would have been long. The doorways may not be close."

"What? You mean beyond the church?"

"Sure." Alessandro stepped back, strode to the middle of the Piazza del Limbo and shielded his eyes from the streetlights.

Archer clenched, then unfurled his fingers. "What the hell're you doing?"

"Checking for structural changes. You can tell the age of a building by several factors, such as brickwork, building height, rooftops —"

Archer balled his fists. "We don't have all night. What do you see?"

Alessandro spun to him; his jaw clenched. "The buildings on either side were built much later. Based on the architecture, I would say around the sixteenth century, which would fit, because the church was remodeled at that time. At one point, these buildings would've all had interconnecting passages. But there's no guarantee it's still like that now."

"Are you saying if we break into one of these buildings, we may get into the back areas of the church?"

"You can't break into a building!" Alessandro's eyes bulged.

"Watch me." Archer marched towards the nearest doorway.

Chapter Thirteen

The creep's fingers were iron bands around Rosalina's wrist as he dragged her down the dark passage. But the more she struggled, the tighter he squeezed. With each inhale between her terrified screams, she gagged at his foul odor.

He yanked her to his chest; his face inches from hers. "If you stop screaming, I'll leave your clothes on." His calmness was terrifying.

She shut up.

Fear coiled in her stomach. The idea of being naked in front of him set her heart to explode. "Where're you taking me?"

He carried on, dragging her behind him. "You'll be safe as long as your boyfriend cooperates."

Resistance was useless. Instead, she studied the walls, looking for something to memorize. But every wall, every passage, whether they went left or right, looked the same. It'd be impossible for Archer and Alessandro to find her.

Around yet another corner they stopped and her captor wrestled keys from his pocket. With a metal grating sound, the door opened, and he dragged her through it. The door was like something from a medieval movie, at least four inches thick and held together with parallel black iron rods.

"No one will hear you down here." He shoved her into the room and stepped back towards the door.

Rosalina dove at him. She jumped onto his back and shoved her arm around his neck.

He clawed at her arm. She squeezed even tighter.

Gagging noises oozed from his throat, but she clamped tighter still.

His hideous odor invaded her nostrils. Blocking it out, she fought harder.

He grabbed a fistful of her hair and yanked.

The pain was a thousand needles stabbing her scalp and she screamed.

Clutching her hair, he dragged her head over his shoulder.

Rosalina bit the muscle in his shoulder.

Crying out, he let go of her hair, and spun around, trying to grab her.

Her hip slammed into the open door, but still she clung on. She dodged a punch that glanced off her forehead.

But his next punch hit her square in the eye.

Pain exploded in her brain. Her body went limp. She hit the floor like a sack of potatoes.

His filthy stench poisoned her senses. The room twirled.

Everything went black.

ARCHER COULDN'T REACH THE WINDOWS HIGH ON A WALL AT THE back of the church without a ladder. He climbed a metal gate at the side of the church, but even that was three feet too short. Banging his fist on the brick wall, Archer screamed his fury.

Giving up on that idea, he jumped down and scowled at Alessandro.

What did Rosalina see in him?

The answer was obvious. Alessandro was safe and able to give love and take it equally in return.

Something I could never offer completely.

Alessandro jabbed Archer's shoulder. "See that building?" He pointed to the small stucco building with two barrel-vaulted bay windows high up the wall. "Based on the roofline and its relationship to the church, I bet it has an underground tunnel to the crypt."

"You think?"

"I'm positive."

But after ten minutes of scouring that building, Archer couldn't find a way into it either. He thumped the bricks. "How the hell did this happen?"

"Because of your pendant. Why is it *importante?*"

Archer reached for the necklace. He shook his head. "I wish I knew."

"Well, what *do* you know about it?"

"Nothing!" he snapped.

Alessandro turned his back and strode away, his arms swinging at his sides.

"Alex, stop, please. It's true. I know nothing about the damn pendant. My dad and I found it twenty years ago while scuba diving and I haven't been able to find out anything about it since. Honest."

Alessandro reached the front of the church and glared at Archer. "That man was fixated on it. What did he mean by 'get the rest'?"

"I don't know. I've been trying to figure out this fucking thing for years. But I've found nothing."

"Where'd you do your research? Google?" His tone oozed with sarcasm.

Archer shrugged. "Among other places."

"*Stupido* Aussie." He flicked his hand under his chin, demonstrating his disgust, before he marched away.

Letting him leave, Archer was torn. He needed Alessandro to figure out how to break into the church. But the church was like a fortress. He had to believe Rosalina was safe. . . for now. That bastard wanted to exchange her for 'the rest'.

Whatever that was.

He needed the Italian's help. It was a weird partnership.

They were both in love with the same woman.

Only now Archer didn't want to let her go.

ROSALINA SNAPPED HER EYES OPEN AND BLINKED AT THE COLD STONE floor. For a couple of panic-filled seconds, she couldn't recall where she was. Rolling to her knees, she fought a wave of nausea as she pushed to her feet. Pins and needles in her arm confirmed she'd been lying in the same position for a long time. Too long.

Rotten memories crashed into her mind and she shot her gaze around the dimly lit room.

Yes, I'm alone. Thank God.

The thought of that bastard watching her as she lay unconscious made her skin crawl. She scrubbed her arms, trying to rid his filth from her skin.

Her head pounded, and her eye throbbed from his punch.

She touched a large lump that had formed below her eyebrow. Thankfully, there was no blood, but by the size of the swelling, she won't be able to see out of her eye soon.

Shaking off her dizziness, she strode to the door and banged on the blackened wood until her fists hurt and her throat burned from screaming. It was useless.

She replayed the kidnap in her mind, trying to judge how far he'd dragged her.

Am I still in the church?

My phone! She searched her pockets, but it was gone.

That's right! He took my phone.

Archer or Alessandro would have called her again. Probably both.

Did he answer my phone?

She'd only seen Archer angry a couple of times, but his fury would've hit a whole new level when she didn't answer that call.

And Alessandro. He probably showed a side to him she'd never seen before.

They wouldn't give up searching for her.

But *both* of them working together?

That would be interesting.

Between Archer's impatience and Alessandro's fastidiousness, they might kill each other before they even found her.

Trying to ward off the cold, she hugged herself as she examined the room. Other than the door he'd shoved her through, there was only one other door at the far end of the room. Both doors were solid wood, possibly inches thick. Both looked as ancient as the church itself.

The room was as big as a twenty-table restaurant. There were no windows, and the walls were made of enormous stone bricks, each one probably weighed as much as a baby elephant.

A couple of ugly naked lightbulbs that'd lined the corridors dangled from the walls, casting shadows at random intervals.

The ceiling was a series of scalloped arches that were so high she couldn't touch the bottom of any arch. Six large columns, intricately decorated with carvings and mosaics, held up the arches. The expert craftsmanship wasn't lost on her. Having spent many hours listening to Alessandro drool over architecture, she recognized that this room was highly significant.

The enormous stone tomb centered in the middle would be the reason.

The floor was made of ancient cobblestones, rough and uneven, but a worn path that led from one door to the other, passed by the tomb. A lot of people had walked through here to view the tomb.

She placed her hand on the dusty sarcophagus. It was cold. Freezing. As if a frigid energy was being released from within. The ridiculous thought tumbled from nowhere and she shoved it aside.

Wiping thick dust off the carvings decorating the crypt, she read the inscription: Roberto D'Angiò, Robert the Wise, King of Naples, Count of Provence and Forcalquier, 1277 to 1343.

"You were obviously very important." Her voice sounded flat in the enclosed space.

The effigy lying atop the tomb depicted a knight holding his hands in prayer. His expression was one of deep satisfaction. At his side were his sword and shield. Examining the shield, she identified the Tuscany insignia.

"So, Robert the Wise. . . why did they stop coming to see you?"

Beneath the knight's feet, carved in the same-colored stone, was a lion, its mouth open, as if emitting an almighty roar. She leaned over to examine it and gasped.

Around the lion's neck, carved with intricate detail, was a necklace with a pendant, except half of the pendant was missing. The remaining half had raised letters identical to Archer's pendant. It was as if his gold necklace had once been positioned right there.

She jumped at the sound of keys and slammed her back against the back wall.

The robed man glided into the room with an evil presence. He was much bigger than she remembered, at least a foot taller than her.

Fear crawled up her spine. Invisible spiders scurried across her neck.

The hood that masked half his face hid his eyes. But the dark shadow it created was even more disturbing. A second man shut the door behind them but slipped into the dark recesses of the room.

The urge to run was mammoth, but useless. She was trapped.

Her courage was as fragile as bone china, yet she gritted her teeth and thrust her chin forward. Forcing her shoulders back, she tried to convey to her kidnapper, and herself, that she wasn't scared.

He stood before her: feet apart, hands balled into fists at his sides, jaw clenches, commanding attention. His eyes were still hidden.

"What do you want?" She hated that her voice quivered.

"I want answers." He waved the other man forward, and a chair was placed at her side. "Sit."

She wanted to resist, but certain her trembling legs wouldn't hold her up much longer, she did as he instructed.

The second man shuffled forward and put a small cage at her feet.

She jerked back. "What the hell is that?"

Inside the cage was an enormous black rat. Its thick tail thumped against the wooden bars as it whipped around.

"Have you heard of a rat dungeon?" The question leered off the creep's tongue.

"What? No." She couldn't drag her eyes from the cage and the hideous creature trapped inside.

"It's a form of torture. A very effective one, in my experience."

Digging her fingers into the chair, she glared at him. "Torture! What the hell? Who are you?"

He bared his yellowed teeth in a sickening grin.

Panic blazed through her veins. A metallic taste flooded her mouth. She bolted upright and raced for the door, but his fingers clutched her wrist and he dragged her to his chest.

His rotten breath made her gag.

One icy blue eye stared at her from beneath the lopsided hood.

An avalanche of terror tumbled inside her.

"There are two ways we can do this, Rosalina. One is. . . how shall I say this. . . one is a little messier than the other."

He forced her onto the chair, and a grating cackle erupted from his throat. His sick laughter echoed off the stone walls.

Rosalina sat with her back rigid against the chair and glared at the cloaked man. Everything about him was disturbing—his heavy coat, his filthy odor, his rancid breath.

Recalling Archer's description of the shark's soulless eyes, she dreaded that she, too, was looking at the devil.

He stepped back, and in one swift movement, he removed his hood. She snapped her eyes shut, petrified at what she might see.

"Open your eyes." His calm voice was more terrifying than if he'd yelled at her. "Rosalina, do you want to meet my rat?"

She squeezed her palms into her eyes until colorful dots dazzled the blackness.

"Get the cage," he said.

"No!" it took all her might to glare at him. His eyes were like vacant pits, devoid of any human emotion. She gasped at the horror.

"Now. . . tell me about the necklace."

She gripped the chair. Fear scraped up her back. "I don't know anything."

He raised his hand and, fearing he was about to hit her, she clenched her teeth, closed her eyes and braced for the pain. But it didn't come. It was several heartbeats before she looked up at him.

His eyes drilled into her. "Are you ready to tell me what you know about the treasure?"

She unclenched her jaw. "All I know is Archer found the necklace when he was eleven."

"Where?"

"I don't know. He was a kid, scuba diving with his parents. A shark killed his father." The words tumbled out, but they were useless. . . every single one of them. She knew nothing.

"Where? Tell me where!"

"I don't know!"

He was on her in an instant and slapped her cheek, fast and hard.

She flung off the chair and slammed onto the stone floor.

A stark ringing buzzed in her ears and it was a few beats before she realized it was a phone.

He plucked a phone from his robe pocket and lifted it to his ear.

Yet his soulless eyes didn't shift from Rosalina.

Clutching her cheek, she whimpered at the sting behind her eye. But that wasn't as bad as the dread crawling through her.

He's going to torture me to get answers about the treasure.

But I don't know a single thing.

Chapter Fourteen

Nox glared at Rosalina, and as she inched away from him, he answered the call he'd been expecting.

"Did they call the police?" Nox's voice was hoarse from infrequent use.

"Yes, but they didn't believe them." Brother Marcus whispered down the line.

Nox turned toward Brother Linthani and cupped the mouthpiece. "Tie her up."

Distress flared in Linthani's bulging eyes.

"Do it," Nox hissed.

Linthani helped Rosalina into the chair, and with her wrists bound by rope, she didn't struggle.

"Where are they now?" Nox spoke into the phone again.

"They're still out the front," said Brother Marcus.

What are they doing out there? "Call me when they leave."

"Yes, sir."

Nox ended the call, and satisfied the woman was secure, he exited the room. Brother Linthani would lock it behind him.

Striding with purpose, he could almost taste the victory on his tongue

This is it! Reward for decades of commitment will soon be mine.

Behind him, Linthani shuffled to catch up. "Get everyone together in the Esagonale room."

"Yes, sir." The feeble priest would do anything Nox demanded. Thanks to a series of damning videos Nox had taken of the pathetic priest, Linthani was his most devoted follower.

In the Esagonale room, Nox twisted his bulky antique ring around his middle finger. Its presence exuded sovereignty. The ring dominated his hand as he drummed his fingers on the ancient wooden table, sounding out an urgent heartbeat for the holy space.

Even after nearly thirty years, he was surprised the ring fitted him, given his large, knobby knuckles.

It was additional proof that he was the chosen one.

How and where he'd found the ring could only be accredited to pure destiny. There was no other way to explain what happened. At the time, he'd been hiding from a group of boys, his daily tormentors.

To this day, he still didn't know how the terra-cotta trumpet being played by the baby in the marble statue had fallen into his hands. He would swear on the Bible that he'd barely touched it.

Nox had been so scared when it'd happened that the fragile thing had slipped out of his hands and shattered on the floor. He'd actually thought he was going to be struck down by lightning. Nox's feet had been frozen to the floor as he waited for the wrath to come.

But the seconds ticked by. Then the minutes.

Yet nothing happened. No one came running at him with clenched fists. He didn't get another flogging. It was his lucky day. It wasn't until he'd picked up the statue's broken pieces that he saw how great that luck was. Hidden within the trumpet tube was his ring, but it was what the ring had secured that changed his life forever.

The paper-thin animal skin scroll, that was smooth and feathery to touch, had resisted his unrolling. He had attempted it only once before he'd tucked it and the ring into the pockets of his robe and, abandoning the shattered relic, ran to his room.

He'd been the only boy in the orphanage who lived alone, and it was the first time he'd considered the trappings of his disease as a blessing.

The date on the delicate parchment, inscribed in elegant cursive at the very top, indicated it had been rolled up and secured by the bulky ring for nearly seven hundred years.

He'd read the fancy handwriting and although it was brief, it'd given him enough information to piece together a secret that those he'd once looked up to had been hiding.

That secret spanned centuries.

Three of his men shuffled into the room, launching Nox from his tumbling thoughts.

He continued drumming with his ring as they sat in their seats.

Linthani and the men had little in common, except that their devotion to Nox was under duress. Some of the video leverage Nox held over them might not be considered especially heinous to a normal man; however, to a priest, it was downright sinful.

When they were all seated, Nox stopped drumming and glared at the men opposite.

For thirty years, he'd devoted himself entirely to his cause, so far with no success at finding the clues detailed in the scroll. However, the flurry of events in this past week cemented his belief that he was the chosen one.

He was destined to find the Calimala treasure. And it was only with reluctance that he admitted he needed the pathetic bunch before him.

For now, that is.

Once they've performed their duties, I'll dispose of the pathetic bastards.

Chapter Fifteen

As Archer paced the piazza concrete, a tsunami of useless ideas crashed through his mind.

He needed to get into the back of the church, or more precisely, below it.

Alessandro spun to Archer. "This is your fault."

Archer stiffened. "I'll do anything to save her. She's the most important person in the world to me."

"You have an extraordinary way of showing it."

Archer's stomach lurched. "You don't know the whole story."

"I know you will not hurt her again. I'll make sure of that."

The Italian's dark eyes burned into Archer and he conceded a niggling thought—Alessandro's protective jealousy was justified.

Clenching his teeth, Archer stared at the ground, fighting a powerful urge to bite back. "Holy shit!"

"Shush." Alessandro shot him a warning glare, then waved an apology at a couple who were walking through the Piazza hand in hand. "What now?"

"The oval decoration in the floor," Archer said.

"What about it?"

"That's how I'll get inside."

"You will not!" Alessandro bunched his lips. "This church is a holy site. I won't let you violate the crypt."

"I won't violate it. Just jump into it. That's where Rosalina is."

"You don't know that for certain."

"We both heard her screams below here." He stamped his foot on the concrete. "Don't act like you didn't."

Silence beat between them.

"Alessandro! You said they used the oval door to drop bodies into the burial chamber below. How do we open it?"

There was a long pause before Alessandro shrugged. "It's quite simple. Push your finger through a hole and lift."

"You're kidding?"

"They weren't worried about people breaking into the crypt eight hundred years ago."

Archer dashed to the church, launched over the raised entrance and scanned the room to confirm nobody else was there. The eerie silence engulfed him as he strode down the aisle.

At the oval decoration, he found the finger-hole Alessandro described.

The Italian joined his side. "See the hole?"

"Yeah. Will it be heavy?"

Alessandro raised one eyebrow. "I don't know. I haven't lifted one lately."

Archer didn't need the wisecracks. Grumbling under his breath, he pushed his forefinger into the hole and tried to lift.

"What're you doing?"

Archer frowned at him. "I told you."

"Now?"

"Yep."

"Are you crazy? What if someone comes?"

"I don't care. I'm going into this hole. You do whatever you want." He squatted low and pulled. But the damn thing didn't move. He clenched his teeth until his jaw ached. "Come on!" he hissed through clenched teeth.

It didn't move. *Fucking hell.* "Lift you bastard."

The seal broke with a muffled sucking noise.

"It's moving," Alessandro whispered. "*Rapido. Rapido.*"

The oval door lifted from its trap. "Get your fingers under it."

"Me?"

"Yes, you," Archer blurted.

Alessandro straddled the oval and shoved his hands under the sides. The slab was fucking heavy. He would never have lifted it on his own. They wrestled the slab aside and Archer leaned over the hole and peered in.

Nothing but blackness.

He sat on the side and dangled his feet in the hole.

"Jesus, Archer! What're you doing?"

"See ya." Archer slipped into the void.

"Hey," a deep voice boomed from somewhere above.

Archer looked up through the hole. Alessandro froze, and the Italian's eyes were wide. The kind of wide a trapped animal had.

"Run!" Archer yelled. Alessandro looked down at him, his face torn with indecision.

Alessandro's feet appeared above, and Archer stepped back as Alessandro dropped into the burial chamber.

"What the hell're you doing?" Archer dragged Alessandro back from the light.

"Saving Rosalina." The Italian's voice was shrill.

The faint light filtering through the oval was of little assistance in the blackened space and it was impossible to see more than a couple of feet in any direction. Surrounded by shadows, Archer braced for attack from every recess.

As he backed away from the light, a sharp scraping noise raised the hairs on his neck. The light faded, and they were plunged into complete blackness.

"*Dio mio*, we're trapped!" Alessandro's rapid breathing was amplified in the enclosed space.

Archer reached for his phone and illuminated the screen. Alessandro copied.

"Look around for a door." Archer held the glowing screen ahead of him. Despite the low roof, the room felt enormous. It smelled of sweat and grime, but it was the dust that stuck in the back of his throat that dominated.

Archer had the impression this room was once a hive of human activity, but had remained unused for a very long time. A worn path tracked over the uneven cobblestones. It could only have been made from years, hell, more likely centuries of people walking along it.

He followed the path, trying not to picture the piles of bodies that had been thrown down here during the plague.

The path led to a door.

"Over here," Archer whispered. He pushed down on the handle and his breath hitched; it moved. The door opened towards him.

"Turn off your phone." It'd be difficult to navigate without the light, but with it they were glowing targets.

He stepped through the door, and a cool breeze tickled his skin. *A tunnel.* When his eyes adjusted to the blackness, a faint glow filtered from the direction the breeze was heading. "This way." He strode towards the light.

"How do you know?"

"Just a hunch."

"A hunch! Are you crazy?" Alessandro spoke with a forced whisper. "These places are intricate labyrinths. We could be lost for years."

"Okay then." Archer sighed. "Which way?"

Alessandro's silence was irritating as all hell.

By the time Alessandro cleared his throat to speak, Archer's patience was as thin as fishing line. "The oval doorway was centered within the main aisle of the church. Back then, the apse was always built in the east and the stained-glass window was built—"

"Which way?" Archer snapped.

"This way." Alessandro pointed in the same direction Archer had chosen.

With clenched fists, Archer stepped from his hiding spot and strode along the passage. The light intensified with each step and an intersection materialized up ahead.

At the junction, Archer backed against the stone wall and held his breath to peer around the corner. The passage was empty, nothing but sparse hanging lights that barely illuminated the corridor. But that didn't mean it would stay that way.

A door slammed. Heavy footfalls stomped on the cobblestones.

Using his arm, he drove Alessandro against the wall, edging them into the shadows.

Archer stiffened. Someone was coming.

Chapter Sixteen

Rosalina's adrenalin was depleted, replaced with complete exhaustion, and the bruise had swollen over her eye so much she couldn't see.

Her tongue was as dry as her oven-baked croutons, and her back ached with built-up tension that'd stacked higher and higher with each question the madman had fired at her.

Her lack of answers to his barrage had been met with threats and verbal abuse.

Thankfully, he hadn't slapped her again.

Her cheek and eye were throbbing constantly. As was the dread that crawled through her, crushing her sanity bit by bit.

She was alone, but despite telling herself she'd never give up hope of a rescue, she didn't know how much more she could take before she crumpled to the floor.

Fortunately, the rat hadn't featured in her interrogation. Not yet, anyway.

The cage was at her feet and whilst she couldn't see it, the regular thumping of the rodent's tail banging against the wooden bars confirmed the rat was still there.

She shuddered at the horror.

How much longer do I have before he resorted to that hideous torture?

Just having it there, and smelling the rat, was enough to make her nauseous.

The creepy bastard had repeated the same questions over and over and tiny red veins in the whites of his eyes seemed to multiply with each question.

But it didn't matter what he asked, or how he asked; she knew nothing.

She closed her eyes, willing the nightmare to be over.

Jiggling keys had tears springing to her eyes.

She couldn't breathe. She couldn't think.

She wrestled against the ropes binding her wrists to the chair, but it was pointless.

The door bolt thudded open. Unable to move, she clenched her teeth and stared at the entrance. It eased open, and she swallowed hard, bracing for a new round of horror.

But a shrill ring cut through the silence and she jumped. *A phone.*

The door slammed shut. Muffled voices reached her through the dense wood, but she couldn't decipher a single word.

The keys jiggled again. The bolt thumped back into place.

Other than the rat's tail thumping on the cage bars, she was plunged once again into deathly silence.

THE RING OF A PHONE BOUNCED OFF THE STONE WALLS AND ARCHER froze.

The element of surprise was in his favor. But he only had one shot.

He squeezed Alessandro's trembling arm to convey that he'd handle it. A dark-robed figure materialized in the gloom, and despite the hood shrouding half the man's head, Archer knew he was the asshole from the church.

As he strode Archer's way, his gaze was lowered, looking at a phone.

Archer clenched his jaw and waited. Ten steps. *Five. Two.*

He lunged. His first punch landed high in the man's solar plexus and a hideous breath burst out of him. The hooded figure doubled over with a groan.

His second punch connected with a solid jawbone. The force of Archer's blow dislodged his hood as the priest stumbled backwards and hit the floor.

Archer did a double take at the hideous face.

Movement shifted to his left. A second man was in the shadows.

Archer jumped over the ugly creep, and with a lowered shoulder, tackled him.

They were briefly airborne, then landed heavily.

Archer rammed punches into the body beneath him. One. Two.

The man bucked forward and slammed his head into Archer's nose.

A groan burst from Archer's throat. Bright sparks darted across his eyes.

The blow threw him off guard, and the man wrenched Archer over his back onto the stone floor. Archer tried to shake the fog from his brain. Movement shifted above him. But he was too late to avoid a punch to his throat.

Archer clawed for a breath. He tasted blood. He struggled to get onto his hands and knees.

The ugly priest rolled over and crawled away.

I have to finish him.

A scream tore through the silence.

Rosalina!

"Get her, Alex." Archer's voice was a brittle croak.

Alessandro ran into the corridor and vanished into the blackness. Knowing Rosalina was nearby renewed Archer's resolve. He scrambled to his feet; his brain was still foggy.

He shoved from the wall and kicked the ugly asshole in the stomach. His heavy robe swirled in an arc as the priest barreled over.

The other priest lay motionless. With mixed feelings, Archer saw his chest rise and fall.

"Archer! Keys!" Alessandro sounded miles away.

"Okay."

The groaning priest curled into a fetal position.

"You're lucky I didn't kill you." Archer fished a bunch of keys from his robe pocket.

He straightened and nearly smacked into Alessandro. Pushing past him, he rushed towards Rosalina's stricken cries.

"I'm coming, Rosa," Alessandro's cry echoed off the walls.

Archer fumbled with key after key until he found the right one and shoved the door open.

His heart clenched. Rosalina was on the far side of the room.

He was equal parts relieved and fucking furious.

Her hands were tied behind her back. The swollen lump over her eye was black and hideous. Tears pooled in her eyes. Her lips quivered.

"Rosalina!" Alessandro raced to her, fell to his knees, and wrapped his arms around her body.

But she locked eyes with Archer. Her chin dimpled and tears tumbled down her cheeks.

Archer wanted to cast Alessandro aside, to embrace her, to show her his love and tell her how scared he'd been for her.

But all he could do was look into eyes that tore his heart to pieces. He'd do anything to make the pain go away.

"You're bleeding," she said to him.

Typical Rosalina. Putting her own well-being behind that of others.

He huffed. "You should see the other guy."

AS ALESSANDRO GRIPPED ROSALINA, SQUEEZING HER BODY TO HIS, tears spilled down her cheeks. But through her bleary vision, she only had eyes for Archer. Blood trickled from his nose to his lips as his chest heaved with frantic breaths.

She wanted to run to him, to have his powerful arms around her, but the straps biting into her wrists meant she could do nothing but look into his troubled eyes.

Archer strode to the back of her chair and squeezed her hand before he unraveled the ties. The second the straps were free, she stood and wrapped her arms around him, desperately trying to ignore Alessandro's glare.

Their embrace was way too brief.

When he pulled back, Archer placed his palm on her burning cheek. "He hit you."

She leaned into his hand. "I'm okay. You're bleeding."

"He got a lucky head-butt in. That's all. I'm good."

His gaze dropped to the caged rat on the floor and he scowled. "What the fuck is that?"

"A rat dungeon."

Alessandro gasped. "It's a torture device." He bulged his eyes at Rosalina. "Did he use it?"

"No." She shook her head. "Thank God."

"Let's get out of here." Archer gripped her hand and lurched her forward.

Out the door, there were two directions to choose from. She assumed Archer knew which way would lead them out, but he hesitated. He turned left and, hand in hand, they ran along the darkened corridor.

They arrived at an intersection. Archer settled her back against the wall before glancing around a corner.

"Oh no, wait!" Rosalina tugged him back.

"What?" He shook his head.

"I have to show you something back in that room. It's important."

"Nothing is as *importante* as rescuing you." Alessandro's voice was choked with emotion and fear laced his eyes

Her heart squeezed at the twisted situation she'd put him in. Holding Archer's hand while she looked at Alessandro added to her anguish. If she wasn't as scared as Alessandro looked, she would've let Archer's hand go.

Archer tugged her forward. "Alessandro's right. We have to get out of here."

But the sound of stampeding feet made them halt and jump into a shadowy recess. Archer dropped Rosalina's hand and balled his fists; preparing for a fight.

She counted the seconds as the footsteps faded in the distance, going away. *One. Two. Six. Eight.*

"Ready to run?" Archer whispered.

"Yes." She'd run like hell if she had to.

Their footsteps echoing off the walls were so loud she feared someone would attack them at any moment.

A stone wall in the distance looked like a dead end, but as they neared, a doorway that had been discreetly hidden appeared. Archer leaned his ear against the wood. "I can't hear anything."

He let go of her hand. "Stay here."

"No." Rosalina spoke through gritted teeth. "We go together. Three of us will be harder to attack than you by yourself. Alessandro?"

Alessandro's eyes were wide, terrified, yet he nodded. "Absolutely. We stick together." The way he said it, with forced conviction, confirmed he hated the plan.

Archer squeezed her hand one more time before he turned the door handle. The door swung open, and they stepped into a hexagonal-shaped room.

A chunky wooden table was the dominant feature, surrounded by thirteen chairs, each one a work of art on its own. An ancient candelabrum, complete with years of dripping wax, dangled by a chain from the ceiling. The way the room was furnished, she could picture the Knights of the Round Table holding meetings there.

Thumping footsteps echoed off the stone passage, and Archer dragged her across the room to another door. As he put his ear to the wood, all she heard was her own ragged breathing.

He pulled down on the handle, and it opened to a set of steep, narrow stairs. In the gloom they scrambled up them, and at the top was another door. Light streamed beneath this one. She prayed it was the exit.

A long minute passed as Archer again listened for noises beyond the door before he opened it.

They stepped into a normal household kitchen. The room

they'd just left and the room they now entered were centuries apart. This room was modern, bright, and airy. No one would suspect what lay beyond the doorway they'd stepped through.

Squeezing her hand, Archer dragged her a little faster towards yet another door. A window framed the blue cross of a distant church. *We're nearly out.*

"Hey." A voice boomed about the room.

Archer shoved Rosalina behind him and raised his fists.

A young man stood at the back of the kitchen, his eyes wide, his jaw open. He looked harmless, but Archer didn't hesitate. He lunged at the man and, with a swinging fist, knocked him off his feet. As the man hit the floor, dishes shattered onto the tiles with him.

Archer dragged her out the door.

They raced into the fresh night air with Alessandro right behind them, but Rosalina couldn't shake the feeling that they'd escaped the church too easily, as if they'd been set free on purpose.

Street lamps lit every corner of Piazza del Limbo, exposing them as they dashed across the courtyard. Rosalina expected someone to shout at them, but no one did. Her entwined fingers suffered in Archer's forceful grip, but she wouldn't let go.

It was twenty minutes before they reached Alessandro's car. The car lights flashed as Alessandro triggered the key and Archer opened the back door. She climbed into the seat and Archer slipped in beside her.

Alessandro jumped into the driver's seat and sped along the streets of Florence, spiriting them away.

"Are you okay?" Archer caressed her cheek.

Alessandro stared at her in the mirror. The love and care from these two men was a bond she hadn't appreciated. Especially with Alessandro. Her gut twisted over dragging Alessandro into this.

She pulled back from Archer. "Thank you. Both of you. I'm okay. They didn't really hurt me."

"But *mio dolce*, your eye looks−"

"It's okay, Alessandro. Just a bruise." She touched the swelling over her eye and it felt like the size of a plum.

"Did it knock you out?" Alessandro asked.

"Yes." A shiver crawled up her spine as she pictured being unconscious with that hideous bastard nearby. The stench of him was embedded in her sinuses. "That man was—"

"You're safe now with us." Archer ran his hand over her leg.

"He didn't seem human. There were things about him that weren't right."

"Like what?" Alessandro stopped at a red light and looked at her in the mirror.

She pictured remembered the priest towering over her. "His skin was so pale, as if he'd been living in a dungeon his whole life. Not like an albino, more like the pigment had been sucked from his skin. And he stunk like rotten fish."

Archer squeezed her leg. "I saw him. He's a bloody freak."

"What did he do with the rat?" Alessandro asked.

"Nothing. Thank God. Just threatened to use it." She chewed on her bottom lip.

"Do you want me to take you to the hospital?" Alessandro asked.

"No." She sighed. "I just want a hot shower."

"I think we should go to the police." Alessandro blinked at her through the mirror.

"No, Alessandro, we can't. If they find out I was trespassing and you were with me. . . it may ruin your career. I couldn't live with that."

"But what he did to you—"

"I'm okay, Alessandro." Her cheek throbbed. Her eye pounded. But thankfully that was all. "It's nothing really. All he did was ask lots of questions."

Archer intertwined his fingers with hers. "Such as?"

"He wanted to know about the pendant." She studied Archer's dark eyes, wanting to see the truth, but there wasn't enough light in the back of the car. "I told him about you." Her chin dimpled.

"It's okay, Rosa." He squeezed her hand.

She bit back tears. "He got angry because I didn't know anything." Her heart clenched.

Archer's secrets put me in danger.

She tugged her hand free of Archer's grasp.

Has he told me everything?

"I'm sorry, Rosa. If I'd known anything like that would happen, I'd have thrown the stupid pendant overboard years ago."

Did he mean that?

For two decades, the pendant had been a noose around his neck. His world was consumed by it, and yet he'd refused to let it go. Or share its secrets.

"You're the most important person in the world to me." Archer tilted his head towards her. "I'll kill those bastards if they come near you again."

Alessandro tapped on the brakes and Rosalina cringed at the sorrow in his hooded eyes. *It must be gut-wrenching for him to hear this.*

As she looked out the window, rows and rows of patron-filled restaurants whizzed by. Florence's nightlife was thriving. Crowds spilled from bustling cafés onto sidewalks. Scents of garlic and spices and a cacophony of music filled the air. The traffic was peak-hour busy and sounds of carefree laughter were a complete contrast to the torture tearing up her mind.

As the storm of emotions crashed within her, she felt the longing from the two men in her life. Each man wanted her to choose between them. But how could she? They were poles apart in personality.

How can I love them both when they're so different?

One promised safety, stability and a steady future, while the other offered adventure, excitement and passion.

Both risked their lives to save me.

Both loved me.

The last thing she wanted to do was hurt either of them.

Alessandro turned the car onto the main freeway and accelerated away from the city. As the lights of the expressway flashed past, she tried to look into her future, willing divine guidance to show her the way.

Archer's gaze and Alessandro's fleeting glances in the mirror weighed her down.

Closing her eyes, she breathed deeply, trying to arrange her thoughts into something useful, but her mind kept returning to images of the creepy man towering over her.

She laid her head back as the car settled into a rhythm over the asphalt. It wasn't until Alessandro turned into her gravel driveway that she re-opened her eyes. Alessandro parked the car around the back of the villa and jumped out to open her door.

Cupping her elbow, Alessandro guided her along the path to the main villa. Rosalina was thankful Nonna's lights were off. Seeing her like this was a stress her grandmother didn't need.

Alessandro escorted her to the downstairs bathroom, turned on the light, and Rosalina gasped at her reflection. The bruise over her eye was much worse than she'd expected.

It was deep purple, and the swelling had forced her eye closed.

It's just superficial.

Today could've turned out much worse.

Thankfully, nothing was permanent, except for the rotten memories.

But if my bruises were because Archer kept more secrets from me, I will never forgive him.

Never.

Chapter Seventeen

Nox rubbed his jaw. The punch that'd hit him beside his earlobe had hurt like hell. He hadn't been in a physical fight since his childhood, and it surprised him how hard that man's fist was.

Opening his mouth was painful. Talking was agony.

But he needed to block it all out and focus on the men who he'd summoned before him.

His body odor was disgusting in this close space, and the men covered their noses in futile attempts to avoid the stench.

Their discomfort brought him pleasure.

For years, he'd suffered at the hands of those who'd scorned him, but his disease helped to mold him into the man he was today. Rejection came in his early childhood, and he'd dealt with it with varying degrees of success. He'd waited with patience for the day when his tormentors would beg his forgiveness, something he would never give.

The pathetic bunch looked at him with fear in their eyes. If they failed, they'd dread what might come.

Nox slammed his fist onto the table, and the four men jumped. "How the hell did they get away?"

"He knocked me out." The man beside him dabbed a blood-soaked towel to his nose, then checked to see if the bleeding had stopped. "I don't know what happened after that."

Nox knew what happened. He'd seen the footage. They'd taken the keys out of his pocket and helped Rosalina escape, that's what.

Brother Nox glared at the balding man beside him. "And you?"

"He tackled me. I was powerless."

"You fools! Now they have the girl. Our only leverage." A cocktail of anger twisted in his stomach. "Why didn't you stop them?"

"There were three of them and —"

Nox stood, his cloak falling around his knees as he paced the room. The heavy cloth would fail to stop his body odor from seeping into the sinuses of his pathetic group of cohorts. He thrived on watching their vain attempts to block the stink.

At a very early age, Nox learned that if he lingered long enough, the stench would permeate nearly everything. His rare disease would be the undoing of a lesser man, but he'd learned to make the most of Trimethylaminuria. People fled from him. They dropped their eyes and scurried away, as if his odor were poison.

He never found out what happened to his actual parents. Nor did he care. The church-run orphanage he'd grown up in had been a haven for children for hundreds of years, but to him it'd been hell.

Every day had resulted in varying degrees of torment until he'd learned to fight back or to wait in the shadows, listening and learning, until the perfect chance for revenge arose.

Ironically, having the disease saved him from growing up in that horrid dormitory. He remembered the day he was chosen by Father Benedici, like it was yesterday.

When Nox was twelve, he'd been caught putting rats' tails into a large pot of spaghetti. He'd expected to be punished, but instead, Father Benedici had taken him from the overcrowded dormitories and given him his very own room, deep within the church.

Over the years, Father Benedici had treated him like the son he never had. And Nox grew to love him like the father he never knew.

Nox had tried to talk to Father Benedici about the secret treasure once. It was just after he'd overheard a conversation that he shouldn't have. Father had known he'd heard it and had initially tried to convince him it was just tomfoolery.

But when Nox had questioned him over what would happen should the elusive treasure ever be found, the answer the old fool had given him was worlds away from the answer Nox had expected.

Never would Nox have kept the treasure hidden, as his father had planned.

When I find it, I have every intention of using it.

From the moment that conversation had ended, Nox's father had proved he could never be part of his glory.

Nox had no qualms about eliminating the old man. . . when the time was right.

His heart thundered with anticipation at the concept of watching his father writhe in agony after ingesting the poison Nox had already prepared.

He contemplated the enormity of today's events and sucked in deep breaths, oblivious to the air's tainted tang.

When that man with the pendant around his neck showed up in his church, it proved Nox was the chosen one. He would be the victor among centuries of fools who had failed to find the missing treasure.

With the valuables in his hands, he would finally have the money he needed to treat his disease properly and he would return to Florence a new man.

But he had to get that necklace.

Before that man figured out that the pendant around his neck was a key to a vast fortune.

Chapter Eighteen

Alessandro placed his hands on Rosalina's shoulders. "Let me help you out of those clothes, *mio dolce*."

She wrapped her arms around him instead, and unable to hold back her tears, she sobbed. Alessandro squeezed her to his chest. As his heart beat against her ear, he smoothed her hair and whispered reassurances she couldn't decipher. Her tears were a good release, and his embrace was wonderful. The tension drifted away as she calmed down.

When she could cry no more, she kissed his cheek and stepped back. "I'll be okay. Let me shower. Then we'll have hot chocolate and talk."

He rested his hand on her shoulder. "Okay. I'll get your robe."

Rosalina turned the shower faucet on and held her hand under the water until it was hot. Alessandro returned quickly and draped her bathrobe over the hook. Rosalina was grateful he didn't say anything else before he walked out and shut the door behind him.

Alessandro was a true gentleman. Kind, caring, dependable, and today he'd shown a side of him she'd never seen before — courage. But despite all that, she wasn't sure if she could ever truly love him. At least not in the way she'd loved Archer. Archer set her heart racing. And when they weren't together, it was like a piece of her was missing.

She never felt that connection with Alessandro.

Lathering with her favorite orange-scented soap, she allowed the hot water to massage her aching skin. Washing her hair was the therapy she needed and she let the conditioner rest while she scrubbed her skin again. When she could no longer smell the devil, she emerged from the shower, dried off and moisturized her face, carefully avoiding the bruise.

She pulled on her robe and went to her room to dress. Running a comb through her hair, she walked from her bedroom and over-heard the men talking in the kitchen. The sweet scent of chocolate brought a smile to her face.

"Are you feeling a little better?" Alessandro pulled out a chair, and she sat. He placed his hand on her shoulder before he went to the stove and stirred a heavy-based pot with a wooden spoon.

"I'm okay. Don't burn the chocolate."

"Of course not." Alessandro adjusted the flame down a notch anyway.

Archer winced. "Your eye looks terrible. I'll get some ice."

Alessandro placed a steaming mug in front of her with one of her pistachio biscotti balanced on the saucer. Rosalina was impressed. "This is lovely. Thank you."

"You haven't tasted it yet, *il mio dolce*."

She blew on the top and then took a sip of the sweet velvety chocolate. It was the perfect temperature, not so hot that it burned her tongue, but heated enough to enhance the rich flavor and warm her insides. "It's perfect."

Archer returned with ice in a plastic bag and instructed her to hold it onto her bruise. Then he sat with his own cup of hot choco-late nestled within his palms.

Alessandro placed his hand over Rosalina's. "I think it's time you two told me what's going on."

Rosalina turned to Archer. His eyes were downcast, staring at his fingers as they tapped his mug.

Alessandro tenderly cupped her cheek. "Whatever is going on

with that pendant put Rosalina in danger, and that means I need to know. All of it."

Archer cocked an eyebrow at Alessandro.

Rosalina eased back from Alessandro's warm palm. "He's right, Archer. You need all the help you can get."

Archer tilted back in his chair and squeezed his temples with the tips of his fingers. For several beats, Rosalina thought he was going to clam up. But finally, he released a massive huff, and once he began telling his childhood story, it was like he couldn't stop.

Archer did hold back, though; it seemed he couldn't bring himself to mention the shark attack again. He simply labeled his father's death as a diving accident.

Alessandro was a superb listener; barely making a sound during the entire telling. He'd be taking every little detail into that amazing brain of his.

Oh, my God. Alessandro and Archer were meant to meet.

And she was the master of this destiny who'd put them together. But she'd also be the one to decide who she wanted to be with.

That thought horrified her, and she wanted to crush the idea like pine nuts in a mortar and pestle. Rosalina thrived on conflict resolution, rather than conflict instigation.

The only time Archer paused during his childhood story was to change from hot chocolate to wine and to replenish Rosalina's ice.

"So. . ." Alessandro's frown deepened and his lips pouted. . . it was his professor's face. "You have known about this treasure for how long?"

"Twenty-two years."

Alessandro's facial expression switched from a concerned frown to incredulous. "And you've found *nothing*."

Archer stiffened and Rosalina cut in. "To be fair, Archer didn't have the entire word on his pendant."

Rosalina could almost see the cogs working in Alessandro's brain.

"True, but still. . ." Alessandro let the sentence hang and Rosalina was thankful Archer didn't bite.

The image of the lion carved on the crypt lobbed into her mind.

"Oh Archer, I forgot to tell you. That room I was trapped in had the crypt of Robert. . . umm." She scoured her brain for the precise name, but it eluded her. "I can't remember his real name, but they called him Robert The Wise."

Alessandro clicked his fingers. "Oh, that's Robert D'Angiò, King of Naples. He has a fascinating history—"

"You can tell us later, Alessandro." She cut off Alessandro's impending lecture. "Anyway, a lion was carved into the stone beneath the effigy. Around the lion's neck was a necklace, but half of it was missing. I honestly think your pendant will fit into the other half. You have to see it."

Archer reached for his pendant, wrapping his hand right around the finger of gold. "You think this fits into the crypt somehow?"

"It's possible. It was very similar."

Alessandro chuckled. "Maybe it opens a trapdoor."

Archer rubbed his chin. "Don't laugh, Alessandro. I've seen it before. What do you know about this church?"

"I can tell you everything about how it was built and restored over the years, but not a lot about other aspects of its history. We could try the library." Alessandro cocked his head at Archer.

"Great idea." Rosalina agreed.

"What time does the library close?" Archer asked.

"Ten o'clock. Why?" Alessandro glanced at the clock over the fireplace and she followed his gaze, it was just after seven thirty.

"You and I can go now. Rosalina might want some—"

"Hang on a minute." Rosalina cut in. "If you think you're going anywhere without me, think again."

"It's not that I don't want you along." Archer shook his head. "But I have a feeling these bastards are watching us now. It's not safe."

"Exactly! That's why I should be with you two." She folded her arms across her chest.

Alessandro checked the clock. "If we go now, we'll have about two hours. Lucky for you, I know the library like the back of my hand."

Archer looked at her, no doubt debating whether this was a good idea.

"Let's go then." Rosalina made the decision for him and pushed back her chair.

Both Archer and Alessandro stood together. Hiding her smile, she claimed her bag from a side table and Alessandro was a pace ahead of her before she reached the door. He opened it, and with his hand under her elbow, he guided her towards the car.

"Lock the door behind you," Alessandro called to Archer over his shoulder.

As she walked to the car, she tried to work out the logistics of who should sit where. She didn't need to show any favoritism to either man. There was only one solution. "I'm going to lie down in the back seat. Alessandro, you drive." There, decision made.

But lying down increased the throbbing in her bruised eye, so it wasn't long before she sat up again. She wriggled to the middle, and from this angle she could see Alessandro's eyes through the rear-vision mirror.

"Do you have any idea where to start, Alessandro?" she asked.

He glanced at her in the mirror. "Actually, I do. I just hope the books we want weren't lost in the flood."

Archer eyeballed Alessandro. "What?"

"In 1966, about a third of the library was flooded by the Arno River. Most of the Magliabechi collections were damaged. And it's his collection we want to get our hands on."

"Who?" Archer's exasperated voice indicated his frustration over Alessandro's cryptic responses.

"In 1714, Antonio Magliabechi donated more than thirty thousand volumes to the city of Florence. Some of them were letters from the cardinals of the thirteenth and fourteenth centuries to very influential people of that time."

"And why is this important?" Archer threw his hands out.

Alessandro furrowed his brow. "Why are you so cantankerous?"

"Why can't you just get to the point?" Archer cracked his neck from side to side. "I just don't understand what a collection of ancient letters has to do with the church."

Alessandro winked at Rosalina. "You'll see. In fact, I predict in an hour or so you'll be apologizing to me."

The library was a grand building with high arches of carved stone adorning the entrance. Alessandro led the way and Rosalina and Archer followed up the large marble steps into the building. Archer's shoes squeaked on the marbled floor and people turned towards him as he rushed ahead.

Alessandro darted across the foyer and stepped into an elevator. She and Archer followed. With highly elaborate wrought-iron decorations and a manual handle, the elevator looked as old as the man who operated it.

Twice Alessandro had to tell the man which floor they needed, the second time several decibels louder. Archer fidgeted with the pendant beneath his shirt as the elevator moved at a snail's pace. They could've walked up the stairs faster.

At the second floor, Alessandro handed his satchel over to a guard who checked its contents before handing it back. Rosalina did the same with her handbag.

They walked through enormous double doors and Rosalina blinked at the thousands of books lining the walls of the three-story room. As she followed Alessandro up a set of spiral stairs, she had a dreadful feeling they were wasting their time. But they had no other ideas.

Archer leaned into her ear. "I feel like I'm putting my faith in the hands of a tarot card reader." He rolled his eyes at Alessandro.

She squinted at him and whispered, "Maybe it's a chance worth taking."

They scooted along the second landing to yet another set of stairs. Alessandro was panting when they reached the top, but he didn't stop there. He went to the second last column of shelves and scoured the bookends as if he knew exactly what he needed.

"What're you looking for?" she asked.

"I've seen a book here on the construction of churches during medieval times."

"What's it called?" Archer asked.

"If I knew that, I'd look it up."

"Well, how are we goin' —"

"Here it is!" Alessandro turned to Archer with a triumphant grin. The book was blood-red leather, bound with gold trimmings and, from the way Alessandro was carrying it, it looked like it weighed at least ten pounds. He lugged it to a nearby table, and it released a soft *crack* when he opened it.

Rosalina nestled in beside him as he skimmed over the first couple of pages. Archer leaned over her shoulder, but as the book was written in Italian, he grumbled and eased back, shaking his head.

Archer started pacing behind them.

"Hey, listen to this," Alessandro said. "The crypt was built by Baccio Pontelli in the thirteenth century to house the tomb of Robert the Wise. He incorporated a large passageway to accommodate the thousands of pilgrims that were expected to visit the church to view his tomb." Alessandro looked up with satisfaction.

"So?"

"So, I was correct about the long passageway."

"That's great. Well done." The mockery in Archer's voice was unmistakable. "But it doesn't help."

Unperturbed, Alessandro kept reading. "The tomb was later moved to Santa Chiara Convent in Naples in an unprecedented move by Pope Clement VI. Apparently, our little church could no longer accommodate the swelling crowds."

He turned to the next page, and Rosalina frowned at the jagged edges along the spine. A page had been torn out. Sitting up straight, she tried to read the Italian inscription on the opposite page. A name stood out. "Hey Alessandro, look."

"Oh no, someone's torn out a page."

"Yes, and it's referring to that Pontelli fellow you just mentioned."

Alessandro twisted the book sideways. "This can't be a coincidence." He pulled his wallet from his pocket, tugged out a ten euro note and used it to mark the page. Then he snapped the book shut, clamped it under his arm, clutched Rosalina's hand and strode towards the stairs.

"Bring my satchel." He called over his shoulder to Archer.

Rosalina was swept up in Alessandro's excitement and tried not to look in Archer's direction.

By the time Archer caught them, his clenched teeth showed his frustration. "Where are you going?"

"The microfiche room. Hopefully, this will be one of the books they've filmed, and the missing page was there when they did it."

They dashed beneath an enormous clock over the arched doorway. It was already past nine o'clock.

Rosalina's thoughts clanged over the significance of the missing page.

Could Archer finally get some answers?

They passed through several rooms so fast people glanced in their direction. At the end of one enormous book-lined room, they climbed a set of marble stairs and entered a narrow hallway through an arched doorway.

A burly woman with breasts that threatened to escape from her tight uniform greeted them.

Alessandro advised the woman where they were going and she pressed a button to open a two-inch-thick glass gate. Stopping at the first computer, Alessandro dropped the heavy book onto the table and clicked the mouse to bring the monitor to life.

Rosalina felt rather than saw Archer fidgeting behind her. He wasn't usually one to keep quiet and Rosalina was impressed with his restraint.

It was wonderful to watch Alessandro work. His fingers glided over the keyboard as if he were a musician at a grand piano. He was elegant, treating the letters with delicate respect.

It was a full two minutes before Alessandro uttered any words. "Here we go." His voice brimmed with excitement. "What page are we looking for?"

Archer opened the book and flicked to the page with the euro marker. "Page 762."

After a couple of mouse clicks, the screen filled with a copy of the missing page. Along with several paragraphs of typed print, there was a drawing of a tomb with a knight's body atop it. "Perfect. We can see what it looks like inside the crypt."

Alessandro tapped the screen. "That's not the tomb."

Archer frowned. "I'm no Italian scholar, but I'm sure this says Robert the Wise."

"But it's impossible." Alessandro leaned closer to the screen.

"What? Why?"

"I've been to the tomb of Robert the Wise at Santa Chiara Church in Naples and it doesn't have the —" Alessandro turned to face him. "Have you got a credit card?"

"What? What doesn't it have?"

"*Per favore*, Archer, put your credit card in here. We need a copy."

Rosalina bit on her bottom lip, stifling a giggle.

Archer clenched his jaw. Alessandro's reluctance to reveal what he was thinking was infuriating him. Archer swiped his credit card and Alessandro pressed a series of buttons, then winked at Rosalina and ran to the printer to remove the copy.

Alessandro studied printout. "The room is different too, so it must be the original crypt. However. . ."

The muscles in Archer's jaw bulged as he clamped his teeth.

Rosalina blinked at Alessandro, waiting for his revelation.

"What?" Archer threw his hands out.

"Back to the shelves." Alessandro grabbed her hand and raced off. "Bring my satchel."

Archer grumbled behind them as they fled away. *He's going to kill Alessandro.*

She smiled at the buxom woman as she and Alessandro dashed past her. They returned to the upper floor bookshelves and Alessandro resumed scanning the bookends with his finger.

Archer returned and tossed the pack onto the floor. "However, what?" he demanded.

Rosalina spied the guard below looking up at them. She waved over the balcony at him. "Archer, keep it down or they'll throw us out."

"Well, he's deliberately keeping me in suspense."

"*Un momento.*" Alessandro continued scanning rows and rows of bookends. "Let me show you a picture of Robert the Wise's tomb and you will understand."

Rosalina stood back, watching the two men. Alessandro was the picture of concentration: fierce gaze, pursed lips, eyes scanning with dedicated focus. Archer was high on the prospect of revelation, fidgeting from foot to foot and watching Alessandro's moves like a hungry lion.

Anticipation hung in the air, and Rosalina felt like she was about to watch an act of magic unfold.

Alessandro clicked his fingers at Archer. "Bring me that ladder."

Archer rolled the ladder along the rails, and Alessandro jumped on before it stopped. He climbed to the next level of shelving and plucked a book from the shelf. With it hooked under his arm, he climbed back down.

"Where's the photocopy?"

Archer handed it to him.

Alessandro slid the new book onto the table and as Rosalina sidled in beside him, he flicked through the pages until he found what he was looking for. "See. . . what's different about the two tombs?" Alessandro's eyes shimmered with excitement as he laid the photocopy next to the picture in the book.

Archer leaned in to compare the book picture with the printout. "Okay. . . he's wearing the full regalia of his knighthood. The spurs on his ankles are usually only reserved for knights, so that fits," Archer mumbled, talking himself through the picture. "His sword, belt and the sheath are fitting for that era."

Finally, Archer shook his head. "I don't see anything unusual. They're both the same."

Alessandro's expression confirmed his surprise. Rosalina was also impressed.

"What?" Archer shrugged.

"I had no idea you were an expert." Alessandro nodded in approval.

"Far from expert. I spent a lot of my childhood in museums. I guess I learned a bit."

"You impressed me. But take a closer look at the lion in the copy."

Archer lifted the photocopy, then he jumped like he'd been stung by a bee. "Holy shit!" This time Rosalina didn't offer an apology to the guard below. Beneath the feet of the knight in the photocopy lay a roaring lion. Around the lion's neck was Archer's pendant.

"Alex, do you realize what this means?"

A sly grin tugged at the sides of Alessandro's lips. "You owe me an apology."

"You're right and I'm sorry." Archer reached for his pendant, drawing it out from beneath his shirt. He ran his thumb over the finger of gold, as Rosalina had seen him do thousands of times before. But this time he looked as if he were drawing some kind of energy from it, as if the gold was finally speaking to him.

Archer tapped the photocopy with his finger. "Someone went to a lot of trouble to create a replica of the first sarcophagi, but deliberately removed the necklace from the lion. This is the first clue in over twenty years."

Archer clutched Alessandro's cheeks and kissed his forehead. "Thank you, man."

Rosalina giggled as Alessandro squirmed away.

"All right, that's enough." Alessandro pushed back but beamed with satisfaction. "We have work to do."

Archer punched his fist into his hand. He smiled at Rosalina and for the first time in a long time, he looked genuinely happy. "What do we do now?"

Alessandro ran his hand through his thick hair and it fell right back into place. "I wouldn't mind a drink."

"Be serious."

Alessandro clicked his fingers and strode away, disappearing into the bookshelves again.

Archer turned to her, still smiling. "He's a strange one."

"Be nice."

Archer palmed his chest. "I'm always nice. You know that."

Alessandro looked as happy as a puppy at the seaside when he returned a couple of minutes later with another book. He sat beside Rosalina and began scouring the pages.

"Listen to this," Alessandro said. "The Arte della Calimala guild were major textile merchants during the thirteenth century. They grew very wealthy and owned several buildings in the neighborhood of our church, including the buildings immediately attached to it."

"And?"

"Well, they were direct rivals with the Arte del Cambio guild, who were also wealthy, but through banking. These guilds acted as *consorzi*, ummm, how do you say it in English…cartels. You know?"

Archer nodded, but his eyes grew dark as he frowned. He was obviously tiring of Alessandro's long-winded history lessons. *Why couldn't Alessandro just get to the point?* They were running out of time.

"So, although the local archbishop was the leader of the government, he depended on armed local nobles to execute the law." Alessandro clicked his fingers. "But, of course, they only cooperated when it suited them. The city was ultimately overrun by graft and corruption. As a consequence, many Florentines took governing into their own hands."

Archer folded his arms. "Thanks for the history lesson. . . but it's not helping."

Alessandro groaned and rolled his eyes. "Throughout the eleventh and twelfth century, Florence was basically a small town, but by the end of the thirteenth century, it was one of the biggest and most influential cities in Europe."

"Come on, Einstein, we don't have much time here. What's the point?" Archer put his hands on his hips.

"That is the point. The Arte della Calimala guild would have amassed an extensive fortune, and with the bankers as their rivals, they had to hide their wealth somewhere."

"Are you suggesting the church?"

"Well, it is interesting that they purchased much of the property around the church, and then in 1348, they sent a fake tomb to a church in Naples to stop people from visiting their church."

Archer slapped Alessandro on the shoulder. "You're a genius. That fits perfectly."

"You know what else is significant about that year?"

"What?" Rosalina asked.

"That's the year the black plague decimated the city. Nearly half the Florentine population perished."

Rosalina shrugged. "And what's the significance."

Alessandro leaned back. "During that time, the executors of the law would have either fled the city, lived in seclusion, were dying, or, in high probability, already dead. That meant, with no one to enforce the law, people could do as they pleased."

Rosalina scrunched her nose. "But why would they duplicate the tomb of Robert the Wise and claim to have moved it, when, in fact, they kept it hidden in the Church of St Apostoli?"

Archer clicked his fingers. "Because there's something hidden within it."

Alessandro nodded. "Right. That makes sense."

"I need to see if my pendant opens that hidden vault. I'm breaking into the church again."

Alessandro's eyes bulged. "Jesus! You can't be serious!"

Archer pulled the pendant from beneath his shirt. "Do I look like I'm joking?"

Alessandro glared at him. "No. But you must have a death wish."

Chapter Nineteen

It would be a miracle if they entered the church unnoticed for a second time, but Archer had no choice. The element of surprise was in his hands. No one would think they'd break in for a second time.

At least, that's what he was banking on.

As Archer descended the library's front steps, he pictured the church's layout. It was symmetrical, with the main aisle dividing the church in half. The oval trap door was halfway along the aisle and in full view of anyone.

The three of them stepped into the cool night air and Archer held back from the bustling crowd as Alessandro hailed a cab. Rosalina hovered between the two men as if unsure which man to go to.

He didn't blame her.

One minute she was cruising along with the Italian gigolo and then Archer waltzed back into her life after eight months apart. Add in all the church craziness, and it was no wonder she was confused.

But he'd do anything to win her heart again. He'd take it slowly. Whatever it took. And if, in the end, she went with Alessandro, then he'd accept that.

Even if it crushed him to let her go for a second time.

Archer's galloping heart elevated when a man in the shadows of the library quickly looked away from his gaze. But either he was becoming paranoid, or the stranger wasn't interested in him, because the man strolled off without haste.

"Archer," Alessandro yelled from an open taxi door.

Archer jumped into the rear seat and stifled a laugh. Rosalina was now squashed between the two men vying for her heart. She seemed to take it all in her stride, though. Rosalina was like that, strong, confident. . . goddamned sexy.

There were so many things he loved about her.

Peering through the back window of the taxi, the stranger Archer had noticed lifted a phone to his ear. The knots of tension in his stomach wound a little tighter.

Is that bastard reporting our moves to someone?

The taxi took forever, winding its way through the bustling Florence streets. Finally, it pulled into the curb alongside the deserted Piazza del Limbo and both Archer and Alessandro offered to pay the bill. Archer triumphed and instructed the driver to keep the change.

They strode across the piazza, and Archer directed both Rosalina and Alessandro to the side of the church. He gripped Rosalina's arm, drawing her attention. "Rosa, I know what you're going to say, but−"

"No!" she said it, anyway.

"You don't know what I'm−"

"You want me to stay here while you go back into the church. The answer is no. And nothing will change my mind." She folded her arms over her chest. It was hard to argue with a woman with a black eye; she looked mean.

And angry.

Damn, she was stubborn. Time for damage control. "Okay, so here's the plan. This is going to be fast. Real fast. The three of us stick together. That's not negotiable. Alessandro, you look after Rosalina and don't let her out of your sight. I'll handle anyone we come across. Okay?"

Alessandro grinned. Pleased with his role in the plan.

Rosalina was a brave woman; even after all she'd been through today, she simply nodded.

Archer released a forceful breath, readying himself. "With a bit of luck, we'll be in and out before anyone even sees us."

Rosalina cupped his ears and kissed both his cheeks. "Be careful."

She did the same to Alessandro. "You too."

There was nothing left to do but pray. Not that he was a praying man. "Let's go."

Taking the lead, Archer ran around the corner of the church to the front door. He jumped over the raised entrance, ran down the mosaic-checkered aisle, dropped to his hands and knees and tugged on the oval door.

Rosalina was right there with him and, unlike Alessandro had been earlier today, she was ready to slide her hands under the slab as soon as it released. It shifted quickly this time and, with the slab out of the way, he dropped into the room below.

Rosalina was next and, as she lowered into the room, he caught her. If it weren't so damn risky it could've been a romantic moment. As he carried her aside, Alessandro joined them.

Archer eyeballed Alessandro. "Look after her."

"There's no need to say it again." In the dim light, Alessandro's clenched jaw accentuated his determination.

Maybe I underestimated the professor.

Maybe Alessandro was a lot more of a man than I'd given him credit for.

I damn well hope so, because with what we're about to do, I may need his help.

Archer strode to the door and cracked it open. Confirming it was all clear, the threesome ran along the same passage they'd traveled hours earlier.

Every tunnel looked identical to the last, and Archer hoped he could remember the way. Moving fast, they arrived at the room with the crypt much quicker than he'd expected and they rushed to the stone effigy.

Rosalina lowered to her knees and ran her finger over the carved necklace on the lion. She pointed out the groove where half of the pendant was missing. "See what I mean?"

Archer's heart skipped a beat. "You're right." Reaching behind his neck, he unclipped his necklace and slid his pendant into the slot and pushed. A whoosh of air sounded as a secret door popped beneath the lion's feet.

"Wow," Rosalina whispered.

"Oh, *dio mio*," Alessandro murmured.

Crowding together, they squatted to look beneath the tomb. Despite its vast size, the only item in the sarcophagus was a book. Rosalina lifted it from the secret vault with a delicate touch.

"A book?" Alessandro frowned.

"A book people will kidnap for." Archer used his phone to photograph the vault and the tomb.

Rosalina turned over the leather front cover. Centered in the middle of the first page was the date: 1st January 1325. She gasped. "It's nearly seven hundred years old. I wonder how long it's been here?"

"From its appearance, I'd guess most of that time," Alessandro said.

She flipped over another couple of pages. "It's a diary."

"Time to get out of here. Alex, you hang onto that book and whatever you do, don't let go."

Alessandro nodded, clutching the leather-bound cover to his chest.

Archer popped out his gold pendant and clipped it around his neck again

"Let's go." Archer made for the door and turned left. He raced along the same passages they'd sprinted earlier, and pausing outside the closed door of the hexagonal room, he waited for Alessandro to catch his breath.

Archer turned the handle and burst in. A group of men were inside.

They jerked back.

Archer did too.

A heartbeat later, all hell broke loose.

Chapter Twenty

Brother Nox jumped to his feet as the Australian with the necklace, Rosalina, and another man charged into the room. Under the stranger's arm was a book.

Fire rage inside him. He knew what that book was.

He'd been searching for it for decades.

Releasing a guttural growl, Nox lunged for the book.

But the book thief ducked away from Nox's charge.

Nox lunged again, but a fist connected under his chin.

Searing pain ripped up his neck. His legs crumbled.

He fell hard. Hit the ground and struck the stones face-first. Pain ripped across his knees and up his spine as he blinked at a white pebble on the stone floor.

It was a tooth. His tooth.

A scream burst from his throat. Warm liquid dribbled down his chin.

It all happened so fast.

And not one of his men had moved.

Nox rolled to his hands and knees.

The Australian shoved Rosalina up the stairs. The man with the book followed behind her.

"Chase them!" Nox screamed through the pain in his jaw as he pushed up from the floor.

But his men were pathetic. None of them moved. Not one.

"Get them." Nox gathered his coat from around his ankles and climbed the stairs two at a time. With every step he took towards the front door, he knew it was pointless.

He ran across the kitchen and stood at the exit. Clutching the doorframe, he scanned left and right.

They were gone.

Nox balled his fists, ready to hit anything or anyone that got in his way. His mind scrambled to work out why they came back.

They'd found the vault. That book under the man's arm was the sacred journal.

Ever since he'd discovered that scroll in the statue, he'd searched for three things.

A key. A vault. And an ancient journal.

The pendant around that man's neck was the key.

But despite spending decades searching every crack, every hiding space and every hidden passage in this church, he'd never found what the key opened.

They'd been here one day and they found the other two.

He was going to kill someone. It didn't matter who.

Grabbing a dish towel as he strode through the kitchen, he wiped his mouth and chin. There was so much blood.

Someone was going to pay.

He stormed back to the Esagonale room and the men fled like scared mice.

Nox strode the halls, searching for what the threesome had found.

He returned to Robert The Wise. The crypt had a very special place in his history, but what he saw now tipped his already racing heart into overdrive. A door at the end of the crypt was ajar. The bastards had left it open to mock him.

Crouching down, he peered into the space beneath Robert The Wise's tomb. It was empty.

"No!" Clenching his fists until his nails dug in, his eyes snagged on something that nearly drove him to hysteria.

The necklace around the neck of the stone lion statue.

He'd been around this very crypt for decades and not once had he noticed that necklace.

Now, though, the necklace, and the section of the pendant that was missing, stood out as if it had been slathered in fluorescent paint.

I am a fool. A stupid, stupid fool.

They'd found the secret vault that had been within his reach all this time.

Not knowing what was in the book gnawed at his sanity. But if it was the journal detailed on the scroll, it was of huge significance.

Nox fell to his knees and screamed until fresh blood poured down his chin.

The words written in that book could expose the secret the church had contained for nearly seven hundred years.

Then everyone would be after my treasure.

I need to kill that Australian bastard and get my book back.

Chapter Twenty-One

As much as Rosalina wanted to crawl into bed and sleep, she did not want to miss looking through the diary they'd stolen from the crypt.

She fought the throbbing headache behind her eyes with a couple of painkillers and at the kitchen table, she sat between Archer and Alessandro. "I hope breaking the law was worth it."

"It will be." Archer's eyes shimmered as he slid a mug of hot chocolate toward her.

Alessandro wore a pair of white cloth gloves that he'd removed from his car, and with a very delicate touch, he turned the pages. "It dates from 1325 to 1348."

"Seven hundred years ago. Wow," Rosalina said.

"Does it say anything about the pendant?" Archer was an impatient man.

Alessandro shot Archer a glare. "I've only just started reading it. Give me time."

Alessandro's gaze was intense; his eyes darkened even further. His brows were drawn, but not quite together. He turned the yellowed pages, covered in decorative cursive, slowly, as if he feared they'd crumble under his touch. Rosalina studied the pages. Great care had been taken with the delicate calligraphy. Intricate designs colored in pinks, greens and blues adorned the page borders.

Alessandro skipped forward to the last page. The left-hand side had writing on it, but the right-hand side was blank. "This is the last entry."

He cleared his throat before he read.

Rosalina wouldn't be surprised if he did that before every one of his lectures at the university.

"JUNE 13, 1348,

Each day I wait for the hideous disease to take me like it has taken those around me. As I am forced to watch my brothers die, I am forced to wonder why.

Are the sinners being sacrificed?

But now I have fallen to even greater depths as I refuse to give my dying family and friends' last rites. My fear of the evil is so grim that I abandon the ill. I have ceased my God-given duties to ensure my own safety.

Does this make me a sinner too?"

ALESSANDRO LOOKED UP FROM THE PAGE.

"What were they dying of?" Rosalina asked.

"The plague," Archer said.

Rosalina cocked her head at Archer.

Archer wiggled his eyebrows. "Alex gave me some history lessons while you were in the shower."

Rosalina tried to picture how those history lessons were received. Archer was impatient and Alessandro had the patience of a saint.

Alessandro shrugged. "In 1348, the plague ripped through Europe like a tornado. More than twenty million people died. At that time, they had no idea what caused the disease."

Rosalina cupped her mouth. "My God. That's huge."

Archer tapped the book. "Go back and see if we can work out why he hid the book."

As Alessandro turned over the pages, reading in silence, Rosalina hugged her mug to her chest and evaded Archer's gaze.

"Listen to this," Alessandro said.

"JUNE 1, 1348,

A papal edict has been released stating that God's poison is punishing all Christians. For three days, thousands of people, both believers and heathen, have attended processions led by the Pope. The people implore the mercy of the Virgin Mary by praying, weeping and pulling their hair out."

"NASTY, BUT NOT HELPFUL. KEEP GOING." ARCHER SHOOK HIS HEAD and rolled his eyes at Rosalina.

She ignored his impatience. It helped that she couldn't stop picturing a world where an unknown disease was killing her loved ones. It was a horrifying thought. "It would've been terrifying."

Alessandro jabbed his finger at the table, seeking their attention. "Actually, it wasn't until the early 1900s that the cause of the plague was discovered."

"Focus!" Archer pointed to the book.

Alessandro glared at him and turned another page. "Okay, this is interesting."

"MAY 21, 1348,

God came to me in a vision and told me to leave this place of suffering. He said, "The bridal chamber is decorated, the banquet is overflowing and the treasure house is open."

ALESSANDRO'S EYEBROWS SHOT UP.

"OUR DIVINE LEADER SAID HE WILL LEAD ME FROM THIS UNGODLY PLACE and show me paradise. He said I must use the treasure to build a church in honor

of those who have succumbed to this silent evil. Then, and only then, will I be blessed in Heaven."

"WHAT TREASURE?" ARCHER SAT FORWARD IN HIS SEAT.

"Do you remember me telling you about the great wealth in the Arte della Calimala guild?" Alessandro met Archer's gaze.

"Of course."

Alessandro brushed his gloved hand over the ancient pages. "During the thirteenth century, three powerful guilds dominated Florence. One guild, the Arte della Calimala, bought many properties around the church. They were so paranoid about one of their rival guilds, who were bankers, that they hid their valuables rather than giving them to the bankers."

"Right," Archer interrupted. "We have three guilds, all dripping with money, and then the plague rolls in and spoils everyone's day."

"And," Alessandro swept his attention to Rosalina, "that meant all the governors and lawmen were either dead or trying not to die. Florence became a lawless city."

"So." Archer nodded at Alessandro. "The people entrusted the church to watch over their valuables during that time of uncertainty."

"But our priest here." Alessandro tapped the book. "May have taken the treasure instead."

Rosalina felt like the prize in a jousting match as each man sought her attention.

"And somehow, *this*," Archer reached for his necklace, "ended up in the middle of the ocean."

As she sipped her hot chocolate, Rosalina mulled over the information. Archer's eyes were distant, as if he was reliving the moments when he'd found the pendant.

Alessandro scrolled through the diary, his finger skipping down pages as he read in silence. After several pages, he sat up. "Listen to this."

· · ·

"MAY 2, 1348,

The earthquake was so powerful it has fouled the air with vile odors and provoked God's wrath. Black Death, so colossal and ruthless, has possessed the land, punishing mankind for its sins.

I am overwhelmed with the burden of guarding great treasures. The people believe a man of God will not be struck down. But I have heard of a great monastery where the infection of one led to the death of all.

I wait for guidance, before my death lays the treasures bare for all to plunder."

"YOU WERE RIGHT," ROSALINA SAID.

Archer put his mug down and shoved it aside. "What earthquake?"

"The same year the plague roared through Florence; a powerful earthquake hit the region."

"That's a little unfortunate," said Archer.

"The earthquake hit in January and coincided with the beginnings of the plague. These two events fueled apocalyptical fears. They believed they were acts of God. People abandoned everything and literally ran for their lives," said Alessandro. "They left their valuables with men they trusted the most."

"Men who should've guarded the treasure with their lives." Rosalina tried to stifle a yawn. Her eyes were heavy. Her body ached. As much as she didn't want to admit it, it was time for sleep. "I'm sorry, but I'm too tired. Can we take this up tomorrow?"

She stood, and both Archer and Alessandro rose at the same time. The look of hope on both of their faces made for an awkward moment.

Thankfully, Archer nodded and discreetly winked at her before sitting back down.

Alessandro gave her a gentle hug and kissed her forehead. "See you tomorrow, *mio dolce.*"

"Goodnight." Rosalina tightened her robe around her waist and left the kitchen. She trod lightly as she climbed the grand staircase to her bedroom, hoping to hear any conversation from the men.

But the only sound was the town clock chiming out at two o'clock in the morning. With each step the weight of exhaustion sunk deeper into her bones.

After a brief refresh in her restroom, she wriggled under the soft bed covers and listened to the never-ending sounds of the ancient building.

It was just like the never-ending guilt that blazed through her over the attention from both Archer and Alessandro.

How can I want both of them?

What am I going to do?

ARCHER STUDIED ALESSANDRO'S EXPRESSION AS HE WATCHED Rosalina leave the room. The man was in love with her. There was no doubt of that. But does she love him?

She clearly had feelings for him, but was it love?

Today could have ended in disaster, but with the help of Rosalina's lover, it had finished well. It was an awkward situation, sitting with a man who was also in love with his woman.

But was Rosalina *his* woman? He'd driven her away. And now he regretted it. Alessandro seemed like a good man, someone who was safe, reliable, and someone who Rosalina could trust. Maybe he was worthy of Rosalina. *Maybe.*

Alessandro dragged his fingers through his hair as he turned to Archer. "So, will I have to fight you for her?" He raised his chin in what looked like bravado.

Archer chuckled. It seemed Alessandro was also a mind reader. "You mean an actual fight with fists and grunting?"

"If necessary." Alessandro fired a glare that could carve ice.

"She's worth fighting for."

"You had your opportunity. You failed." Alessandro sneered.

"I know." Archer reached for his pendant. "But things have changed."

"For you, maybe. But not Rosalina."

"Then, may the best man win." Archer held his hand across the table and Alessandro pumped out his chest like he was preparing for an arm wrestle before he returned the shake.

It was very late. But Archer had no intention of strolling off to his room, knowing Alessandro was here in the kitchen and Rosalina was just two floors above.

If there was one thing he'd learned during his years in the orphanage, it was to study your enemy before you challenged them. Now might be the perfect time to get to know Alessandro. "Fancy a glass of wine? Celebrate our successful rescue."

Alessandro's lips parted, like he was lost for words. Then he nodded. "Sure. I shall choose the wine."

Alessandro disappeared down a set of steps, and Archer rummaged through the fridge. He removed a selection of cheeses and olives and had them presented on a plate by the time Alessandro returned carrying both white and red wine bottles.

"I wasn't sure of your preference, so I brought both."

"Red. Thanks." Alessandro seemed like a decent guy.

I may have my work cut out for me after all.

But Rosalina was worth it. I should never have let her go. I'll do anything to have her come back to me.

Anything.

Alessandro twisted a corkscrew into the cork. "So, what do you do for a living?"

"I'm a treasure hunter."

"*Mi scusi?*" Alessandro chuckled.

"I take rich tourists on fake treasure hunts."

Alessandro gawked at Archer. "And you make money doing that?"

"Sure. It's fun, too. I set up a fake treasure hunt and when my customers find it, they think they discovered it on their own."

"A stable income, then?"

Archer shrugged. "I'm usually booked up solid through the summer, and during winter I do a little hunting of my own."

Alessandro cocked his head. "You only work half the year."

"I'm comfortable."

Alessandro's dark eyes drilled into him, as if digging for dollar signs. Archer didn't want Alessandro to learn of his wealth. Winning Rosalina had to be about him as a person, not what he could offer her financially. He already had that aspect of life covered. Money would never be a problem for him or Rosalina.

Winning back her love, however, was not as certain. "What do *you* do for a living?"

"I'm a Professor of Ancient History and Architecture at the Università degli Studi di Firenze."

Archer clicked his fingers. "The University of Florence, right?"

"*Sì.*"

"That sounds interesting."

"It's fascinating in a city like Florence. My faculty is in the Accademia di Belle Arti, where Michelangelo's statue of David is. Have you seen it yet?"

"No. Maybe you can show me?"

"Of course."

Alessandro swirled wine around the glass before he swigged it, and Archer wondered if the academic could actually handle his liquor. Maybe plying him full of grog would be a good way to get to know him. *But would that really be fair?* Archer reached for the ancient book that sat between them instead.

Alessandro crossed his arms. "So, discovering this book was a typical day for you."

"No, I wouldn't say that. It's the most exciting thing I've found in decades." Archer opened the book to a page covered in elaborate writing. It was inscribed with a heavy pen, as if they wrote it in anger. *Shit! It's in Italian.*

He twisted the book to Alessandro. "What does it say?"

Alessandro ran his finger down the page as he read.

"*January 25, 1348,*

Something strange has happened. First, the earth was shaken to its core and now we are surrounded by an unnatural silence. Like everyone on earth is waiting for the King to awaken.

But when he rises, I dread what he has planned for us.

I fear something unearthly is about to happen."

"His premonition came true, huh," Archer said.

"*Corretto.* He predicted the plague four months before it hit Florence. You can almost feel his fear."

Archer couldn't help but like Alessandro. He was a good man. Stable. Reliable.

Maybe I should let Rosalina go.

Hell no!

May the best man win!

Alessandro turned each page like they were made of gold. When he paused at a page filled with a detailed table, Archer sat forward. Although it was written in Italian, it was obvious the far-right column with a series of numbers was a value. "What's that?" It annoyed him that he had to prompt Alessandro to share the information.

"It looks like a list of items the church was holding on behalf of its constituents. They've written the date, the name of the donor, a list of the goods and the value."

Archer's heart almost burst with excitement. This was every treasure hunter's dream. The list went on and on for several pages.

Archer reached for the pendant around his neck. This finger of gold was only one small piece in what appeared to be an extensive collection. He tried to visualize the size of the haul and frowned. "Do you think this priest escaped with all those items?"

Alessandro rubbed his chin as he scanned down the page. Finally, he looked up. "It must have been an enormous haul."

Archer tried to picture how a treasure-trove this large could have been moved around, especially as transport would've been very limited in those times. "It must've taken some planning."

Alessandro rested his elbow on the table and pointed a finger at Archer. "You know, the reason Florence flourished while other cities in Europe floundered was because of its slow-moving Arno River. It allowed goods to be shipped in and out with ease."

"By boats." That makes sense. Archer's mind catapulted to the location of the pendant's final resting place. This new information proved that his pendant was once part of a shipment being transported by an ocean-going vessel.

Archer's heartbeat stepped up another notch.

We are one step closer to finding the treasure.

"Now, we need to establish where the treasure went after it left Florence." Alessandro reached for his wine.

"Not really." Archer bunched his lips, and the Italian cocked his head. "I kind of know where it ended up. We don't need to know how it got there."

"You know where the treasure is?"

Archer sucked air through his teeth. "Not exactly."

"What does that mean?"

"I told you about scuba diving with my dad. But I'm not entirely sure where we were." Archer scraped his hand over his chin and the weight of exhaustion hit him like an unclipped anchor. "Let's meet for lunch tomorrow and take it up from there?"

Alessandro clenched his jaw; clearly unhappy with that answer, but a heartbeat later, the Italian professor relaxed. Defeat came pretty damn quick. "I'm working tomorrow," he said. "We will meet here at six?"

He made it sound like he was calling the shots. And that had the hairs on Archer's neck bristling. But playing it cool, Archer pushed back in his chair. "Six o'clock it is then."

He offered his hand and let Alessandro dominate the handshake.

After Alessandro left in his car, Archer returned to his room.

He lay in bed, wide awake.

Sharing the information on the treasure with Rosalina had been one thing. But sharing it with Alessandro? That seemed like a very bad idea.

He could trust Rosalina to keep it a secret.

But he didn't know enough about the Italian professor to make that judgment.

It would only take one wrong person to find out that Archer was going after an ancient treasure and every ghost from his past would be on his ass.

And thanks to both him and his father, Archer had a few of them.

Chapter Twenty-Two

R osalina woke to a throbbing headache and groaned when she tried to open her eyes. As the town clock in the distance chimed seven, she slipped from her bed and headed for the nearest mirror. A gasp tumbled from her throat.

The bruise over her left eye was the size of a plum and as black as a storm cloud.

Just the slightest touch had her wincing.

Gripping the basin, she stared at her reflection. Her throat constricted as she relived the fear that had nearly driven her over the edge of sanity yesterday.

She couldn't handle it if she ever saw that priest again.

His eyes were horrifying. Soulless.

He'd have no hesitation in killing her.

Or everyone she loved.

She'd never been so scared in her life.

A tear squeezed out of her swollen eye and, as she wiped it away, she vowed that no man would ever scare her like that again.

The bruising and swelling were much worse than she'd hoped for. *I can't go to work looking like this.*

That decision created two problems — one, being her boss

wasn't very forgiving. The other, and the more important one of the two, was that she was likely to spend the day with Archer.

The prospect delighted and perplexed her at the same time. She showered, dressed in jeans and a cotton shirt, applied her favorite perfume and cruised downstairs, hoping Nonna wouldn't rise for another couple of hours.

If there was one thing that was guaranteed to make her feel better, it was cooking, so Rosalina set about making pastries for breakfast. It wasn't long before she was humming to herself and cinnamon and coffee aromas wafted about the kitchen.

Soon she forgot about her injuries, but she constantly glanced out the window for Archer. Each time, she chastised herself and turned the music up a little more.

The timer sounded, and she opened the oven door.

"They smell divine."

She nearly dropped the hot tray at the sound of Archer's deep voice. "Don't you believe in knocking?" She nibbled her lower lip at the sight of him in jeans and a white T-shirt that hugged his toned biceps.

"I've been knocking for a while." He glanced at the radio.

Rosalina turned the music down, gathered her coffee cup and backed up against the counter, determined to remain aloof, despite her thundering heartbeat portraying otherwise.

He pointed at the coffeepot. "May I?"

"Sure. The mugs are over there."

He bent over to choose a mug, and his muscular rump begged to be checked out in those jeans. But she forced her gaze away, angry that she couldn't control herself.

Archer sipped his coffee, and the silence between them was as awkward as two strangers in an elevator. "Your eye looks better."

"Liar."

"You're right. It looks worse. Does it hurt?"

"It throbs like crazy."

"I hope you're not going to work." His eyes twinkled, showing off that golden halo she'd missed more than she cared to admit.

She sighed. "I can't. Not looking like this."

His face lit up with a sassy grin. "Great. Maybe you can show me around your home."

Rosalina's heart skipped. Villa Pandolfini had been in her family for four generations, and she'd love to show him how special it was.

But being alone with Archer would create opportunities she didn't want to contemplate.

"I promise to behave myself." He grinned like he'd been able to read her mind.

Rosalina softened. "Okay then." She held the tray of steaming cinnamon scrolls towards him. "Well, for starters, this is where I learned to cook. I practically lived at Nonna's side, begging to learn everything."

Archer held a pastry up as a toast. "Here's to Nonna."

"You'll get to meet her later. But I'm warning you, she'll say what's on her mind." Nonna was just as likely to beat him over the head with a rolling pin as to give him a smothering embrace. Her grandmother knew all about Rosalina's broken heart.

"I deserve whatever she dishes out."

"That's true."

Archer released one of his rare, hearty laughs.

"Grab another pastry and I'll show you the cellar." Rosalina topped up her coffee and, cradling her mug, she moved around the rustic kitchen table. "All the rooms in the villa have fourteen-foot ceilings, except this one. It was originally the maids' kitchen, so it's only ten feet. It's probably the least decadent room in the villa, but it's my favorite. I spent most of my childhood in here." She shrugged. "It feels like home."

Rosalina walked past a fireplace that was no longer in use. The ancient stone-lined oven was much smaller than the other seven fireplaces in the villa, but it was also the hardest to clean. It hadn't seen a flame in two or so decades.

She paused at a side door. "Watch your head on this." Rosalina touched the top of the frame.

The doorway down to the cellar was just over five feet high, and Nonna was the only family member who hadn't hit her head on it. As she opened the door, the old hinges screeched as if protesting the movement. Rosalina switched on a light and held the balustrade as she stepped onto stairs that'd seen centuries of wear.

The cellar had a distinct, musty smell, with strong, earthy overtones. She loved it. Many fond childhood memories began or ended down here. "It hasn't always been a cellar. Over the years, it served as living quarters for the hired help, a hospital during the war, and a bunker." She turned on another light to reveal rows and rows of shelving, all heavily laden with dusty bottles of wine.

"Oh, wow. It's huge down here." Archer ducked his head as he stepped off the last step. The darkened ceiling was much lower than regulation. At six-foot-two, Archer could stand, but only just.

"It runs nearly the full length of the villa." She backed up against a row of bottles and took another sip of coffee. As Archer slipped past her and reached for a bottle, she inhaled his musk cologne. It was her favorite, and he knew it.

Having him there, so close and so damn sexy, was dangerous.
Stay strong, Rosalina.

"This is the wine tasting area." She indicated to a row of ancient oak barrels that'd been converted to tables.

He cocked his head. "People come down here?"

"Sure. People come from all over the world to stay at Villa Pandolfini. We offer cooking classes, too. Even royalty has stayed here."

"You're joking?"

She hugged her coffee to her chest. "About the cooking classes or the royalty?"

"Both. Either."

"We're fully booked for the next two years and many famous people have stayed. Including Napoleon."

Archer whistled. "I can't believe you never told me about this."

Resisting a nasty comment, she sipped her coffee instead.

He held up a bottle. The black rooster symbol on the label was steeped in history that she'd love to mention. Some other time, maybe.

"What's the rooster about?"

Wow, his new-found intuition was spooky. "It's a long story."

Their eyes met and she could tell a question was burning on his lips, but he held it and her gaze. Her heart beat faster. He did that to her, and he knew it.

He slid the bottle back into its slot in the row. "Maybe you can tell me over lunch."

She shrugged. "Maybe."

He walked further along the row of bottles. "Do you make this wine here?"

"Yes. We have several acres of vines and we make it in the cottage near your room."

He selected another bottle and read the label. "Red Chianti."

She walked towards him. "It's good. Most restaurants in Florence stock it."

Archer placed the bottle back onto the shelf and before she knew it, he'd reached for her and slipped his fingers into place between hers. "Why didn't you tell me about all this before?" He cupped her chin and gently tilted her head until she had no choice but to look into his eyes.

Rosalina fought the urge to pull back. She shrugged. "You never asked."

"But how would I know to ask? Your home is an ancient palace; your family makes wine. These are things you should've mentioned."

"You never seemed interested."

His eyes glazed, and his shoulders sagged. He squeezed her hand and let go. The room seemed to darken with their mood.

"Rosa, the things I didn't talk about were horrifying. I tried to erase them from my memory. But these aspects of your life are fun, interesting. I want to know everything about you."

"It's too late, Archer. For three years I tried to get to know you; you not only made it impossible, but you also showed no interest in discovering the true me. I can see that now. Before I was blind, but now I can see our relationship was incomplete."

"No, Rosa. Don't say that. We had the most beautiful, amazing thing. I blew it. It was me, and my stupid idea that I could handle everything. I was wrong. I want you. I need you."

Her heart crumbled into tiny little pieces. "It's not that easy now. I was young and naïve when we met. I've done a lot of growing up since I left you, and I won't settle for anything less than perfect anymore."

"I know. . . I know and I'm sorry. I was holding back, but now I'm ready. I'm an idiot for wasting years by not seeing that everything I wanted was right in front of me."

Rosalina shook her head, resisting the urge to crumble into his arms. "I'm not ready, Arch." She drained her coffee and took a step towards the stairs.

He rubbed his face and sighed. "Okay. But don't cut me out altogether. I've changed, Rosa, and I want to show you."

Rosalina wanted to believe him. But he needed to prove himself first. "I'm not going to commit to anything right now. I need time. Okay?"

He nodded. His eyes reflected his disappointment.

"Do you still want to see the rest of the house?"

"Of course." He reached for her hand and his fingers again interlocked with hers. "Where to next?"

"How about the ballroom?"

"You have a ballroom?"

"Well, it was a ballroom once. Last time I saw it, it was being used for storage. But it's still beautiful."

"You really have been keeping things from me."

"Ha, very funny."

A gallery of paintings led the way up the two flights of stairs. Rosalina had no idea why her stomach twisted tighter with each step upward but suspected Archer, who still clutched her hand behind her, and his declaration that he'd changed, was the reason.

She wanted to believe him.

But he had to do more than just say it. . . he needed to prove it.

If he doesn't, she'd walk away.

Forever.

Chapter Twenty-Three

I t had been several years since Rosalina stepped into the ballroom, and she hoped someone had taken the time to restore it to its original glory, but she didn't really expect that miracle. Much like the Archer's promise that he'd changed. That would be a miracle too.

Grasping onto that little ray of hope, she pushed on the double doors. The sun filtered through three full-length casement windows, welcoming them into the grand room.

Archer strolled to the middle of the room and paused beneath the elegant glass chandelier. He turned, his hand reaching for her. "May I have this dance?"

Rosalina palmed her chest, just above her heart. "You dance?"

"Allow me to show you." His dimples punctuated his cheeks.

"Archer Mahoney, you really are a mystery."

Archer held a pose, right foot forward, right arm high, silently willing her to step into his embrace. She strolled to him and clasped his hand. Her heart skipped when he placed his other hand on the small of her back and drew her to him.

Their eyes met. What she saw in those dark eyes, the raw sexual tension dazzling across the surface, was enough to make her knees weaken. But he clutched her to his body, and when they moved, it was like two pieces of a puzzle finding their perfect places.

She'd seen him at work many times, manhandling heavy objects with brute efficiency, but right now, despite his rugged athletic build and their hips anchored together, he glided her across the floor with surprising elegance.

Rosalina didn't know the tune he hummed, but she recognized the four-step beat to his smooth footwork. She felt as if she were floating on air.

Archer drew her closer and lowered her in a gentle dip. She dropped her head back and his hot breath teased her throat. A delicious shiver tantalized her skin as he touched his lips to her cheek. The golden halos around his dark irises were pure electricity in this light. They appeared almost magical. He stared at her mouth. He glided his tongue over his bottom lip.

Oh God, I want him to kiss me.

It was the slow motion that had her mesmerized, as he pulled her towards him. His tongue flicked out over his lips. Every ounce of her wanted him.

To kiss him. To hold him. To make wild, passionate love to him.

But her sanity finally kicked into gear, and she took control by placing her hand on his chest. She pushed to her feet and cleared her throat as she stepped back. "You really can dance."

The dazzle in his eyes vanished in a flash and his shoulders, so strong and proud during the dance, sagged.

Nervous, she dragged her gaze away from Archer and the confusion drilled onto his expression.

A fine layer of dust covered the once highly polished floor and in the far corner, next to the ornate fireplace, several pieces of furniture were covered in white sheets. At least their numbers hadn't multiplied since she was last there.

Paintings of exotic birds and flowers adorned the vaulted ceiling. It was a shame that such an amazing room had become nothing more than storage space.

Archer cleared his throat. "My mom would've loved this room."

Rosalina froze. Rarely did he speak of his mother, and never with any fondness.

"She loved Trompe l'oeil paintings." He glanced at the decorated ceiling. "These are magnificent."

"You know this style of art."

"Mom would point them out all the time."

Rosalina wanted to know more. So much more. Archer never spoke of his parents. "Did your mom dance?"

"As a matter of fact, she taught ballroom dancing. But my father dragged us all over the world hunting for treasure, so she had to give it up. We often spent months at sea. Sometimes, when I was bored out of my brain, I'd let Mom teach me a few moves."

"Careful, Archer. You're showing me a side to you I didn't know existed."

"I've learned my lesson. You can ask me anything."

"Anything?"

"Anything." He led Rosalina to the window, and she tugged off a white sheet that covered the bay seat and allowed it to crumple to the floor. She sat on the overstuffed cushion and admired the view down the tree-lined driveway.

Archer sat beside her and placed his hand on her knee, drawing her attention back to him. "Anything, Rosa. I promise." His Adam's apple bobbed up and down.

"Okay." A vision of yesterday's madness flashed into her mind. "I saw you knock a man off his feet with one punch yesterday. Where'd you learn to fight like that?"

Archer eased back ever so slightly, but then he caught himself. She could almost hear his mind working his mouth into action. It was a long pause before his Adam's apple moved again, as if he were swallowing a huge lump of regret.

Finally, he said, "After Mom and Dad died, they bounced me from orphanages to foster homes like a football." He inhaled and reached for her hand. "There were some dark times when I had to fight for my life."

"Oh Archer, I never knew."

"Well, how could you? I'm not proud of some things I did."

"You were a kid, all alone. You did what you had to."

"I created some of those problems. I was angry at everything and everyone."

She was falling for him again and wasn't sure she wanted to stop. "It's understandable, after what happened."

His eyes lowered. "The authorities were just trying to help. I made their lives hell."

Rosalina was beginning to believe that maybe he was a changed man after all. She waited until their eyes met. His eyes had darkened, shadowing his memories like a cloak. "You were a child, Arch. All alone."

His lips drew into a thin line, accentuating his dimples, but he refrained from speaking. His childhood had festered into an angry memory, and she could see him chewing over his bottled-up secrets.

He squeezed her hand. "I'm going after the treasure, Rosa. Will you come with me?" His eyebrows drilled into a frown, and his eyes pierced hers with their intensity.

Rosalina cupped her mouth, mulling over the idea. This challenge could make or break their relationship. Exactly what they needed.

She dropped his hand. "I'll think about it, okay?"

He nodded. "Jimmy's bringing *Evangeline* to the Greek Islands—"

"The Greek Islands? I thought you didn't know where to look?" She'd suffered because he hadn't told her details.

"I don't, exactly."

"Stop being cryptic," she snapped, and touched her bruised eye.

"Sorry." He released a deep sigh. "After Dad's. . . *accident*, I spent months recovering in an Athens hospital. So, although I'm not sure which island we were diving off, it must've been the Greek Islands." He reached for the pendant. "There are over six thousand islands to choose from, but I assume one of them has their graves."

"Oh, Arch." Rosalina reached for his hand again. "You don't know where they're buried?"

He shrugged. "I guess I was told at some point, but I don't remember."

"Don't you have any paperwork?"

"They gave me some." He lowered his eyes. "I burned it all a long time ago."

She blinked at him.

"Don't look at me like that. I was angry. I hated my mother." He drove his fingers through his hair. "She abandoned me."

"She didn't abandon you."

"Hell yes, she did. She blamed me for Dad's death and never forgave me. Then she left."

"Archer, she. . ." Rosalina didn't know what to say. No words could express the horror Archer and his family had suffered all those years ago.

"I was still in the hospital when Dad was buried. I didn't see Mom before she died and I wasn't allowed to go to her funeral either."

His knuckles on his clenched fist bulged large and white through his tanned skin. She placed her hand on top of his and it was a long moment before he unfurled the tension and rolled his hand over. Their palms met and Rosalina welcomed the touch.

"I was in a strange country, unable to speak the language. I knew nobody, and they shuffled me from one authority to another as they decided what to do with me."

"You can't blame your mother." Rosalina cupped his cheek, drawing his eyes to hers. "She was hurting and fell into a downward spiral she couldn't get out of."

"Mom couldn't live without Dad." His eyes flared. "It was love that killed her."

Rosalina's heart crumbled and, as she stewed over how to respond, she caught a movement near the door.

"Ahhh, here you are."

"Nonna." Rosalina jumped to her feet.

Her grandmother shuffled across the room toward them and as Rosalina's mind raced over how this was going to go, she strode to greet her half way.

Nonna reached her hands up to grasp Rosalina's cheeks in what had become her signature kiss, but she gasped instead. "*Oh mio Dio, cos'è successo?*"

Rosalina grasped her grandmother's hand in hers. "It's okay Nonna."

"It not okay. Look very bad."

"Nonna, I want you to meet someone. Do you remember me telling you about Archer?"

The wrinkles on Nonna's forehead deepened as she peered around Rosalina. The wrinkles became a scowl when Archer stood. "Archer? The man who break your heart."

Apprehension riddled Archer's expression as he walked toward them. "Hello, it's a pleasure to finally meet you."

Nonna's eyes narrowed. "Pleasure? It no pleasure for me."

Rosalina cringed as she touched her grandmother's arm. "He's come all the way from Australia to see me, Nonna."

"I no care if he came from the moon." She shook her head and the second Archer was within reach, Nonna jabbed her finger at his chest. "You hurt my Rosalina."

"I know. I was stupid."

"Stupido." Nonna flicked her hand to her forehead.

"Yes, I know." Archer nodded.

"Knowing you are stupid no make it better." Nonna was not one to mix her words. "You no deserve my beautiful granddaughter."

Archer eased closer to Rosalina. "I assure you. I will never hurt her again."

"Hmmm." Nonna shifted her dark eyes to Rosalina.

"Nonna, please." Rosalina placed her hands on Nonna's frail shoulders. "Can you give us a moment? I've made a batch of cinnamon scrolls. How about you make a fresh coffee and we'll come down in a moment?"

Her frown gradually faded. "Okay." She nodded. "Okay."

"Thank you Nonna." Rosalina leaned over to kiss her grandmother on both cheeks. "Love you."

Nonna glared at Archer, then turned on her heel and shuffled from the ballroom.

Once she was gone, Archer let out an enormous sigh. "Jeez, she's a fiery one."

Rosalina turned to him. Nonna's timing had been inconvenient.

Now that Archer had told her why he couldn't commit to a relationship, she felt like she was finally understanding the hurt that affected his emotions.

Not only did he see his father die in the most horrific way, he also blamed himself for both his parents' deaths. She tried to imagine the childhood Archer had suffered after their passing.

Archer touched her shoulder, luring her from her tumbling thoughts. "Jimmy should have *Evangeline* in Athens in a week or so. Will you at least think about coming with us?"

Rosalina gathered her thoughts, trying to compose the right words to say. The tightened muscles along Archer's jawline added to the stubborn look in his eyes, confirming it was pointless continuing with the previous conversation. For now, anyway.

Rosalina was determined to prove to him that love was worth fighting for and a couple of weeks on *Evangeline* would be the perfect place to start. "Okay. I'll come with you."

The tangle of emotions that had shattered his handsome face melted away. His features softened and reassembled into the man she knew and still loved. A smile changed his whole look and the old Archer was back. "Excellent. You won't regret it." He held out his hand.

She reached for it and he twirled her around the dance floor. After a series of dips and twirls, he pulled her to his chest. Her skin tingled as he ran his hand up the inside of her shirt to touch her bare back. "What about your job?

She shrugged. "I hated it anyway."

"What about Alessandro?"

Rosalina recalled Alessandro's excitement over the ancient diary. "He's involved now." She raised her chin in defiance. "He has to come, too."

"Well." Archer directed her into an elegant spin. "I hope he doesn't get seasick."

And I hope it doesn't end in a brawl between Archer and Alessandro.

Chapter Twenty-Four

B rother Nox stepped into his bedroom, shut the door, and slid the bolt into place.

A sliver of sun penetrated the split in the drapes, creating a line that ran across the stone floor and up the wall. The beam crossed over a large glass tank, dividing it in half. The vision wasn't lost on him. He already kept the mushroom-filled tank divided.

Half of the mushrooms were known for their hallucinogenic properties. The other half were as deadly as poison.

Closing his eyes, Nox reached into the tank to pluck two mushrooms at random, one from each end. Then he tossed them around in his hands before placing them on his desk. It was a little game he performed almost daily. A test.

Mushroom Russian roulette.

To an untrained eye, the mushrooms looked identical: small, brown, and sticky. The wood-rotting funguses preferred decaying conifers, and over the years he had perfected their germination by maintaining his room as a dark, humid space.

The rotten smell almost masked his body odor. Almost. It also ensured nobody ventured into his room. Exactly how he liked it.

Shadow appeared out of nowhere and wove in and around

Nox's ankles. The silver-gray Chartreux had an uncanny way of knowing exactly when Nox would walk through his bedroom door. "I'll get to you in a moment, Shadow." He resisted the urge to pick the cat up.

If he chose the correct mushroom, he would experience mild hallucinations for an hour or so.

But if he chose poorly, he would most likely spend the afternoon in the restroom with diarrhea and vomiting.

One mushroom would only cause mild symptoms, good or bad, but he resisted the urge to have more today. He needed to maintain control.

After years of experience though, he could usually tell the almost identical mushrooms apart, but he was still caught out on the odd occasion. With the decision made, he flicked one mushroom across the table and tossed the other into his mouth.

He chewed on the meaty fungus with tingling anticipation, then followed it with half a glass of red wine. A few drops trickled down the glass stem as he placed it back on the table. The drip stain would add to all the others dotted over the dark wood.

He turned towards his bed and gently shoved the cat aside to tug on his mattress. When it was half off the frame, he removed a few planks of wood and reached into the void. He fingered a dozen or so metal boxes until he located the one he wanted, removed it and carried it to the table.

The brass latches were no longer the shiny metal that had caught his eye several decades ago. After unclipping them, he lifted the lid and smirked at his creative foresight. Finally, his years of meticulous planning were going to pay off.

The box contained a small notebook, much like the ones sold in all the tourist shops at the Vatican City. The pope smiled at him from the cover. Nox flicked through the pages, allowing a scramble of details to flash past.

He stopped at the page with a list of names and numbers. To anyone else, this list meant nothing, but to Nox it highlighted his detailed planning. His eyes fell on his father's name; beside it was the number 17.

Placing the book aside, he reached into the box for the videotapes. He sorted through them, readjusting the order until he found tape number 17. There was no need to watch it; he had long ago memorized every second of his video footage. His time would not have been wasted.

Nox twisted his bulky ring over and unclipped the jeweled lid. He licked the tip of his little finger and dipped it into the vial concealed within the ring. His fingertip caked in black powder as fine as the ashes they removed from the crematorium. He resisted the urge to lick it off, knowing just how potent it was.

Damn it! I might need every trace of this poison.

And it takes months to make.

Now he couldn't put it back, nor could he use it.

Stupido! Focus!

With clenched teeth, he wiped the powder onto his robe. He shoved the book and all the other videos back into the tin and returned the box to its hidden chamber in his bed. After tugging the mattress back in place, Shadow jumped onto the bed. Nox again ignored the cat as he placed tape 17 on his bookshelf, amongst his collection of bibles.

The time for using it would come around soon enough.

He turned to Shadow. The feline sat up tall, his yellow eyes alert, his tail a controlled movement from side to side, as if performing a hypnotic induction.

"You looking for dinner?"

Nox gathered him into his arms and smoothed Shadow's thick fur. "Soon, I won't be around much. So, you'll have to get your own dinner."

Shadow had been his roommate for years. The feline had turned up one day and although he could leave through a small air tunnel at the back of the room, he always came back. Nox liked to think Shadow enjoyed his company, but it was probably because of what he fed him.

Nox lowered the cat to the stone floor and, as he walked towards a second tank hidden behind his bookshelf, the cat meowed. "You know what's coming, don't you?"

Nox glanced at the wall behind yet another tank. He stared at one brick, ensuring there was nothing distinguishing about it. It was important that it remained an identical replica of every other block in the wall. Because behind that brick was the one piece of evidence that had been driving him for decades. The scroll would stay there for now. Nox didn't need it where he was going, and he'd already memorized every word, anyway.

He reached into the glass tank, and with expert swiftness, latched onto the tail of a scampering mouse. Shadow went crazy at the sight of his dangling dinner and voiced his excitement with a deep growl.

Nox tossed the rodent onto the floor, and Shadow dashed after it. Although Shadow was at least ten years old, he still had the agility of a kitten.

It was over in a matter of seconds. Shadow would survive well without him; rodents were all over this damn church.

He'd miss his feline friend, though.

"Good boy." Nox ran his hand down the cat's back. When Nox returned to this room later, there would be no evidence of the bloody meal.

Nox handpicked a dozen mushrooms, tucked them into his robe pockets, and walked out the door. He turned and locked it behind him and then went in search of his father.

Although the old man had been helping at the orphanage all day, he would most likely know about what had happened yesterday. The cunning old bugger still had his spies all over the place.

As Nox traveled along the dark corridors, he embraced the familiar sensations flowing into his mind from the hallucinogenic mushroom.

In the small kitchenette, Nox stirred his steaming pot of mushroom risotto. Nox had been practicing his mushroom risotto for years, waiting for this exact moment. His stomach fluttered with excitement. Adding his dried mushroom powder to the risotto, already filled with an abundance of mushrooms, he hoped it wouldn't affect the taste too much. The added poison would ensure the deadly result would happen swiftly.

Treasured Secrets

It was nearing perfection when his father entered the kitchen and took a seat at the end of the table.

"Good evening, my son."

"Hello, Father. I'm making your favorite meal." He turned off the gas but continued to stir the risotto until it was ready. Then, with his back to his father, he scooped the potent meal into a fine china bowl and spooned his own meal from another pot.

He turned with the two dishes, and his father looked at him with interested eyes. The old man's mouth opened, readying to speak, but then he closed it without uttering a word. It was like his father knew what was coming and was preparing for his ultimate sacrifice.

As Nox placed the plate before his father, he smelled his own body odor, a rare occurrence; he had become almost immune to it. It was usually only present in times of stress or excitement. He believed today was the latter.

Nox slipped onto a chair at the opposite end of the table and the old man scooped a spoonful of risotto into his mouth. The taste between the two almost identical mushrooms was similar, but he could barely breathe as he waited to see if his father detected a difference.

"Mmm, delicious as usual."

"Thank you." Nox's voice trembled and his mouth was so dry he wasn't sure he could even eat. He reached for the glass of wine and sipped at the full-bodied nectar without losing sight of his father.

With breathless anticipation, he waited for the moment when Father Benedici would be gripped with pain.

"Did you get over to the orphanage today?" His father paused with a fully laden spoon at his lips.

"No, I didn't. I'll go tomorrow," Nox said.

Father Benedici spent many hours at the orphanage, but he only used the orphanage to wield his authority like it was some kind of divine power. With the flick of his bony hand, he could change the life of any child.

Nox ran his tongue over the new gap in his teeth, waiting for the deadly toxins to attack his father. The poison would penetrate his father's liver first, causing vomiting and diarrhea.

163

Next, he would be struck down with excruciating stomach cramps, his body heat would rocket into extreme temperatures, causing hyperthermia and, within a very short amount of time, he would be dead.

Death would be a welcome relief from the crippling pain his father would suffer.

Father stopped again with his spoon to his lips.

Nox stared. *Is this the moment I've waited years for?*

"I heard you had a bit of excitement here yesterday. Want to tell me what happened?" His father pressed his lips together in a look that was meant to reflect his authority. Nox was a regular recipient of this look and knowing this would be the last time he saw it; he studied every line and wrinkle of the old man's face.

"I wondered if you'd heard."

One of his own men would have told him. Their twisted loyalty couldn't be trusted. But then again, not much went on in this church that Father didn't ultimately learn about. It was another reason tonight's meal was justified.

"I hear everything. I've told you that."

Over the years, Nox had found his own way to keep secrets. And he'd heard his share of them. One benefit of crawling all over the church looking for the treasure meant that he'd also discovered all the key places in the building where sound traveled. He often hid in the shadows and listened to a conversation that was being held one or two corridors away.

Bribery, he'd also learned, was the most successful way to contain secrets.

"Yesterday was one of the most exciting days in the history of our church."

Father Benedici lurched, clutching his stomach. His spoon flew from his hand, spewing rice across the table.

Brother Nox reached for a grain that landed near him and lifted it onto his finger. "You are about to be a part of that history."

"What have you done?" Benedici pitched sideways, scuttling the bowl. It shattered into a sticky mess on the stone floor. The old man dropped from his seat and landed on it.

Nox placed the rice on his tongue and bit into the softened grain, but was disappointed when he couldn't taste the poison.

"What have you done?" Father repeated his question.

Nox moved to stand over him.

Benedici writhed in pain, contorting his body in violent moves that threatened to snap his neck at any moment.

"Father, don't pretend you didn't know this day would come. This is why you chose me. I am destined to find that treasure and you know it. Yesterday's events prove you chose well."

"I saved you!" As Benedici spat the words, chunks of rice sprayed from his bluing lips.

"No, Father, it is I who is saving you." Nox held a pen forward. "You should have let me into your secret little group a long time ago. I told you not to mess with me. You have given me no choice but to do it this way. But I am a forgiving man. If you sign this document, declaring me as your successor, I will save you."

Nox showed him a syringe. "I have the antidote here." Even in the dimmed light, the blue liquid inside the plastic cylinder had an unusual glow, as if it were somehow alive.

Benedici reached out with shaky fingers, his eyes riddled with red spider veins. "Save me. I did nothing but the best for you."

Nox handed the pen to the trembling fingers. "Sign the power over to me and I will save you." Nox reached for a clipboard and cried out. Pain shot up his leg.

Benedici had stabbed the pen into his ankle, right into the soft skin between his Achilles tendon and his ankle bone.

Nox dropped to his knees and resisted the urge to strangle his father with his bare hands. When he pulled the pen out, blood oozed from his wound. But he savored the pain when he saw the look of pure anger in his father's eyes.

"Sign the document and I will save you." An unearthly calm washed over Nox as he cleaned his blood off the pen and placed it in his father's hand.

Father Benedici gripped his knees to his chest, squeezing into a tight ball.

Nox placed his hand on his father's shoulder. "Sign the document and I will stop the pain." Father rolled onto his side, the pen trembling in his fingers.

Nox guided him to the paperwork.

The signature was an erratic scrawl, but satisfied it was sufficient, Nox whipped it away before his father threw up on it. He placed the clipboard on the table, folded the paper and tucked it into his robe pocket, along with the syringe.

The blue fluid inside was nothing but liquid soap, anyway.

His father's moaning became pathetic sobs, and Nox ignored the pain in his ankle to kneel beside him.

"I will do great things. This I promise you." He bent over and kissed his father's blazing-hot forehead. Not a drop of perspiration confirmed hyperthermia had already kicked in.

Death would not be long now.

"You would have been proud of me."

Nox wiped up his own blood and washed out his bowl. Now it looked like Father Benedici had eaten alone. And died alone. Nox had detailed footage of his father gathering mushrooms in the fields around the villages.

On this occasion, it would seem he hadn't chosen wisely.

His death would look like an awful accident. Videotape number 17 was going to come in handy, as Nox had always known it would. As he hobbled from the kitchen, his father vomited.

Brother Nox smiled.

In a couple of minutes, the old man would no longer be in pain.

And Nox would have got away with murder again.

Yet he still had so many more people to kill to get his revenge.

Chapter Twenty-Five

Before Rosalina had analyzed the repercussions of what she was doing, she boarded a flight to Athens with Alessandro and Archer. Once she'd decided to do this treasure hunt with Archer, her life became a chaotic whirlwind of packing, planning, excitement and severe trepidation. They had no idea what they were heading into. Archer had told her many times that treasure hunters were ruthless. And they'd already seen one crazy creep. She had a terrible feeling he wasn't going to be their last.

Nonna had taken some convincing before she'd given Rosalina her blessing to go with Archer, and Nonna had also given Archer a stern talking to that he'll never forget.

Alessandro had been like a giddy schoolkid when he agreed to join them. He didn't even hesitate to take time off work, which was very surprising to both Rosalina and his employer.

It was only a two-hour flight from Rome to Athens, yet Alessandro was driving her crazy. Fidgeted with all the buttons and knobs on the seat. Adjusting his position. Looking out the window non-stop. He was like a child who'd consumed an abundance of red candy.

Despite being seated between two men who were vying for her

attention, Rosalina was trying to remain calm. After all, both men would do anything for her.

Not too many women could boast of that luxury.

Yet it didn't stop it from being awkward.

Red wine warmed her insides, and the sound of Archer's calm breathing comforted her heart.

He seemed at peace. As his chest rose and fell, his pendant moved beneath his T-shirt. The golden enigma was about to change the course of her life.

Rosalina was a firm believer in destiny.

This trip was her destiny, and that of Archer and Alessandro.

In contrast to Archer, Alessandro was a bundle of nervous energy and incapable of hiding his feelings for her. She dreaded when he'd have to accept she'd never be his. Deep down, she'd always known that. And she hated that he had fallen so deeply. But that was the type of man he was.

Passionate. Loyal. Decent.

Archer however, was the stronger of the two. In both body and determination.

She hoped this trip didn't turn into an all-out brawl between them.

She couldn't handle that.

During the flight, to keep up with Archer, Alessandro had drunk several glasses of whiskey. And the silly bugger was giggly with intoxicated excitement by the time they landed in Athens.

Rosalina tried to conceal her amusement as Archer manhandled Alessandro through the airport. But Archer masked his annoyance with a smile and gave the impression he was helping an old friend.

When a taxi pulled into the curb, Rosalina bundled Alessandro into the back seat while Archer attended to their luggage.

With Alessandro snoring the entire way, the taxi pulled to a halt alongside the marina and Rosalina breathed in the crisp night air. The smell of the ocean was like a welcome-home present.

Alessandro was impossible to wake, and it took all her might to drag him from the back seat. She was about to help him out of the car when she heard a familiar whistle.

Smiling, she turned. Jimmy's distinct swagger was unmissable as he strode up the pontoon towards them.

"Hey, Jimmy," she called.

"Hey, Princess."

Rosalina had initially hated being called Princess, but right now it was simply perfect.

He embraced her in his signature bear hug and spun her around. "What the hell happened to you?"

Rosalina reached up to touch her bruised eye. She'd completely forgotten about it. Even after all this time, faint bruising was still visible. "Oh, it's nothing."

"Right," Jimmy said suspiciously. He transferred the suspicious look to the body in the back of the car. Alessandro was still passed out, with his legs on the curb, but the rest of him sprawled over the seat.

"I'll tell you about it later."

Archer dropped the last suitcase from the cab onto the sidewalk and he and Jimmy shared a hug and slap on the back. "It's good to see you, man."

"You too, buddy."

"How's my baby?" Archer was referring to his precious yacht.

"She's perfect. I treated her just like my own."

"Shit! Now I'm worried."

"Okay, I treated her better than my own."

Jimmy helped Rosalina tug Alessandro from the cab and she draped the Italian's heavy arm over her shoulder to help him stand. Alessandro was at least holding his own weight, otherwise there was no way she could carry him.

Archer and Jimmy gathered two suitcases each, and indicated to Rosalina to lead the way. Despite all Rosalina's efforts to keep Alessandro walking straight, his drunken wobble risked plunging them both into the water.

"Who's the drunk?" Jimmy asked.

"Rosalina's boyfriend," Archer said before Rosalina could answer.

Over her shoulder, she cast a sideways glance at Archer. In the dim marina lights, his cocky grin was unmissable. And that was a worry. She didn't want, nor need, Archer thinking that mending their relationship was going to be easy.

He had a lot of work ahead of him before she was going to fall for him again.

If ever.

"Alessandro is a good friend of mine," she said. "He was attempting to keep up with Archer. And he would have, too, if Archer hadn't switched from wine to whiskey on purpose." She glared at Archer.

He poked his tongue. "Alessandro's not much of a spirit drinker."

"No shit. You could've fooled me." Jimmy loved his sarcasm.

Evangeline dominated a double-sized berth at the end of the marina. Her precision lighting accentuated her stylish curves and her sleek style showed off her power. She was the envy of the motor yachting elite, no matter where she was moored in the world.

Rosalina was pleased to see Jimmy had taken the time to wash off the sea salt that would've peppered the deck during their weeks at sea, because the moment Archer stepped on board, he'd be scanning every inch of the deck like an overprotective parent.

Two crewmen raced forward to help Rosalina with Alessandro.

"Take him to the Fraser suite," Archer said.

Alessandro began to sing and the combination of his Italian accent and liquor-affected brain made him impossible to understand his muffled tune.

Jimmy's laughter was genuine and boisterous.

She'd missed having Jimmy around.

It'd been Rosalina's idea to name each of the yacht's six bedrooms after islands off Australia's Eastern coastline. The Fraser suite was a VIP cabin with a double spa bath, fully stocked minibar and king-sized bed, and as Alessandro was carried towards it, Rosalina suspected he wouldn't appreciate its luxury until well into tomorrow.

Rosalina tried to blink back her exhaustion, but it was impossible. The demands from the last couple of days had finally caught up with her, and she needed to crawl into bed. She stifled a yawn and turned to Jimmy. "So, Captain, what room shall I take?"

Jimmy did a double take, glanced at Archer, then shrugged. "You should have the Hamilton Suite."

Hamilton was the superior master suite and the star bedroom of the yacht. She gripped the handle of her suitcase and tugged it towards the central stairs. "I can't have that room. I'll let you two fight over it. I'll take the Moreton suite."

Heavy footfalls sounded behind her, and she turned to see Jimmy reaching for her case.

"I'll be okay, Jimmy." His eyes were troubled, and she touched his arm for reassurance. "See you in the morning."

Jimmy nodded and pivoted away.

She opened the door to her room and dragged her case to the corner. In the restroom, she stripped down to her underpants, splashed water on her face, brushed her teeth and examined her bruise.

The swelling was long gone, but the bruise had mellowed to an interesting potpourri of plum and yellow. The memory of how she got it though, would never fade.

It was well past midnight when she finally crawled into the king-sized bed.

Pulling the crisp sheet up under her chin, she sighed and hoped the sounds of the marina would put her overactive mind to sleep.

Rosalina was more than happy with the Moreton suite, and she couldn't stand being alone in the Hamilton suite, anyway. It would bring back too many impassioned memories of her time with Archer.

The next time she returned to that suite would be when everything was perfect.

Either that, or she'd never return to that suite again.

And if that happened, she wasn't sure she'd ever be whole again.

Chapter Twenty-Six

Archer lay in his enormous bed alone and the emptiness smothered him like the air itself. He rolled onto his side and his heart clenched as he spread his palm over the unwrinkled sheet on the other side of the mattress. Knowing Rosalina was asleep in the room just two doors down was disappointing, yet comforting at the same time.

He didn't expect her love to be offered to him on a platter, but he had hoped the lure of *Evangeline* would have softened her resolve somewhat.

After what seemed like only twenty minutes, it surprised him to feel the sun streaming in through the window onto his face. He was even more surprised that he'd actually slept through the night and cursed himself for not closing the electric blinds the night before.

He reached for the remote, ready to go back to sleep, but the familiar smell of Rosalina's morning pastries baking had him up and into the shower.

As if riding first-date jitters, he struggled to decide on what to wear. Eventually choosing a pair of khaki cargo pants and a white button-up shirt. He splashed on cologne and then headed towards the galley.

His breath hitched at his first glimpse of Rosalina. The oversized T-shirt she wore had slipped to the side to expose one very sexy shoulder. Her olive skin was flawless, and with her dark hair pulled back into a ponytail, she looked like a goddess.

He would've stayed right where he was and watched her weave her magic in the kitchen, but she saw him. Her smile lit up her face, and as she twirled a lock of hair behind her ear, her cheeks flushed.

It was a delightful greeting.

"You're up earlier than I thought." Looking unassumingly sexy, her fingers curled around her coffee mug, caressing it. Her standard morning pose took his breath away, and boy, had he missed it.

He strolled to her and, resisting the urge to pull her into his embrace, kissed her cheek. "I forgot to lower the blinds."

"Ahhh. Coffee?"

"Yes, please."

Rosalina filled a mug from the coffee machine and their fingers touched briefly as she handed it to him. It was too brief. He wanted more. So much more.

But he had to give her time. He'd wait as long as it took to receive her forgiveness.

His first goal was to ensure the treasure hunt was fun. And while they were hunting, she could fall in love with him all over again.

At least, that was his plan.

Alessandro staggered into the saloon, squinting against the morning sun. "Where am I?"

Archer's heart sank. He'd forgotten all about the Italian thorn in his plans. "You're on my yacht."

"This?" Alessandro's eyes bulged. "You told me you owned a boat, not a multi-million-dollar yacht."

Rosalina shrugged. "He can be modest sometimes."

Alessandro crumpled in what looked like a wave of defeat. He rubbed his hands down his cheeks, as if trying to clear the fog from his mind.

"Coffee?" Rosalina asked.

Alessandro flopped onto a leather sofa and covered his eyes with his forearm. "*Si, grazie.*"

Archer suppressed a grin as Rosalina filled a mug with a fresh brew and sat beside Alessandro to hand the coffee to him.

Watching the two of them together, Archer understood Alessandro's pain. Rosalina was a woman any man would want to hang onto, and Alessandro must've thought he'd won her over.

Before I'd returned, that is.

A woman dressed in a bikini top and a tiny pair of white shorts entered the room. Archer did a double take. He'd given Jimmy strict instructions to steer clear of the bikini babes.

Jesus. What expertise did this young woman come with?

And do I want anyone else knowing what we're up to?

Hell no!

But Archer had to trust Jimmy's judgment. Although, Jimmy was always a sucker for a pretty lady.

"Hello." The blonde held her hand towards him. "You must be Archer. I'm Ginger."

"Are you one of the crew?" He took her hand. Based on her soft skin, he doubted she did any manual labor.

"I'm the chef. Not that I have any qualifications, but Jimmy is so nice. He likes my cooking."

"I'm sure he does." Archer bit back laughter.

Rosalina stiffened. Cooking, and *Evangeline's* galley, were her domain.

Well, it had been. But that was nine months ago. As a fiery Italian, Rosalina wouldn't give up her domain lightly. He just hoped the inevitable takeover wasn't a nasty one. Ginger might be reluctant to give up such prestigious surroundings.

Alessandro stood and held out his hand as Ginger walked towards him. "I'm Alessandro, or Alex, if you prefer."

Rosalina stood, too. "I'm Rosalina."

"Oh, yes. I've heard all about you. Jimmy tells me you're an amazing chef. Maybe you can teach me some of your home secrets."

"Sure. I could do that." Rosalina offered a tight-lipped smile.

Alessandro groaned and flopped back into the seat.

"Are you okay?" Ginger sat beside him.

"He's got a hangover," Archer said.

"Oh, I've got the perfect cure for that. Come with me." She dragged Alessandro to his feet and led him towards the galley. "Have you ever heard of Vegemite?"

Archer and Rosalina laughed, and Alessandro's brows bunched together as he glanced their way.

"Looks like he's in excellent hands," Rosalina said.

"She's a real gem. But Jimmy's got some explaining to do."

"Be nice." Rosalina scowled at him.

"Always." He gasped in mock hurt.

"Ha ha. So, did you sleep well?"

"Not too bad." *I would've slept better with you beside me.*

She squinted at him like she was reading his mind.

The fact that she was asking showed how much she cares. Her concern elevated him like a thoughtful promise. "I slept right through until morning. It's the truth."

She draped her delicate fingers over his forearm. Her touch was electric, but way too brief. "Good."

Rosalina strolled back to the coffee pot. "What do we do now?"

"We might as well get going. Jimmy will probably sleep until midday. He's had a huge couple of weeks."

"He's done a marvelous job."

"So, he should, the amount I'm paying him."

She shifted her gaze from the dripping coffee to Archer. "That's not the point."

She was right. Paying good money didn't always equate to work done well. The person needed to have a genuine passion to do a great job. And Jimmy had done damn fine in cruising *Evangeline* halfway around the world. Regardless of who he'd hired for the crew. "You're right. I'll thank him properly later. Want to help me with the ropes?"

"Sure, let me clean up first."

"Ask Ginger to do it. After all, she's paid to be the chef."

They found Ginger with Alessandro. The Italian was slumped in a chair with a cloth over his eyes while Ginger massaged his shoulders.

Archer thought it was a match made in heaven.

At least, he hoped so. Any attention Ginger sent Alessandro's way, especially if it took the Italian's focus off Rosalina, had to be a good thing.

Greece's Fliszos marina was one of the biggest in the world, and it was more than half an hour before Archer had navigated *Evangeline* out of the marina and into open waters.

It wasn't until the marina was a blurry white splash on the horizon that Jimmy finally emerged from his bedroom. "Aye, who's taken over my boat?"

"Hey, Jimmy." Archer shook Jimmy's hand, and they clapped each other's backs. "Thought you'd sleep for a week."

"And let you run amuck on my ship? I don't think so."

"Well, you're just in time to help me decide on our heading."

As they motored past an enormous cruise liner, bikini-clad Ginger stepped onto the front of the yacht and waved to the abundance of passengers high on the ship's balconies. "I see your lady friend is enjoying herself." Archer nudged Jimmy.

Jimmy flushed red. "Oh, so you met Ginger. She's a great cook."

"Yes. She told us that," said Rosalina.

Jimmy groaned.

Archer pushed the throttle forward, increasing the speed, and they sliced through the beautiful azure waters, leaving silvery bubbles in their wake.

While nearly everything was perfect now that he had both Rosalina and Jimmy onboard *Evangeline*, Archer couldn't shake the feeling they were heading into trouble.

Just like the turbulent waters they carving through, Archer feared he'd have zero control over the danger.

Except now everyone he loved was also in the firing line.

Chapter Twenty-Seven

Rosalina rode a wave of guilt as she typed Archer's name into the Google prompt. She was spying on him, and he'd be furious if he found out. But she was trying to help him.

She had researched Archer's name before. Except her previous search was focused on his business, as she'd wanted to know all about it before she'd started working for him.

But now that she knew about his shocking childhood, she focused her search on his earlier years.

She'd had to wait until Jimmy and Archer were busy plotting an appropriate course to the surrounding Greek islands before she slipped into the computer room.

Several sites populated the screen, mostly advertising *Evangeline* and the unique charter service Archer provided. With one eye on the door, and hoping nobody came in, it took half an hour to find a reference to Archer's father's death, but the newspaper article was surprisingly brief.

"Famous treasure hunter killed by shark."

The small heading, several pages into a copy of the *Makedonia Newspaper*, was in Greek. However, like many Europeans, she understood most languages of her surrounding countries. Her résumé listed five languages, but she'd fail if she ever had to prove she was fluent.

She fought alternating waves of guilt over what she was doing and horror at what she was reading. The paper detailed how Wade Mahoney's body was only partially recovered and, as if it were unimportant, it only briefly mentioned that Wade had an eleven-year-old son.

Rosalina couldn't understand why the paper didn't highlight that they were diving together when the shark attacked. Reporters usually sensationalized a story. Not the opposite. Wade's horrific death warranted more detail than the tiny article in the paper.

Was the reporter forced to withhold information?

The following day's paper was a rehash of the same story, however it also included the details of Archer's hospitalization and his likelihood of recovering from serious decompression sickness.

Neither article mentioned which Greek island they were diving near when the shark attacked.

Rosalina continued scanning for a further ten minutes, but she only found one more article. This one, also brief, was about Archer's mother. It, too, was merely a sidebar to the shark attack story. Although it did mention that Archer, now an orphan, remained in a stable condition in the hospital.

With each website she shut down, she clenched her fist harder. By the time the desktop background photo of tropical Australian waters returned to the screen, her nails had left deep grooves in her palm.

She closed her eyes, picturing a frail, young boy being told of his mother's death, barely weeks after he'd seen his father killed by a shark. Comprehending Archer's tragic childhood was impossible. Especially when her own childhood had been complete bliss in comparison.

But this only made her more determined to make sure this treasure hunt gave Archer the strength to forgive himself.

Maybe then he could heal, and hopefully, he could learn the splendor of love.

Six islands were within an hour's cruise from Athens and as they motored towards the closest island, Rosalina settled at the dining table with a fresh coffee. The others joined her. But a heavy mood fell upon the group. She believed it stemmed from Archer, who was mostly quiet, as if internalizing their prospects.

He crossed his arms over his chest and fixed his face in a nasty scowl.

"It's going to be impossible to do any secret diving with all these bloody people around." Archer jabbed a finger toward the windows that ran the length of the saloon. The number of nearby boats was ridiculous. Dangerous too.

He was right. Trying to keep their treasure hunting a secret would be a miracle.

Every once in a while, Archer went to the bridge and gazed out at the passing waters.

Was he looking for signs that would help him remember that dreadful day all those years ago?

After about thirty minutes of Archer disappearing, and returning looking even more dejected each time, Alessandro left the room. He returned, dragging the whiteboard from the computer room.

Finally, someone had a plan.

Alessandro reached for a marker and looked every bit the professor he was. "What do we know about the treasure?" He pointed at Rosalina and Archer with the pen.

Archer threw his arms out in frustration. "It's lost in the ocean somewhere near a friggin' Greek Island."

Deflecting Archer's negativity, Rosalina responded to Alessandro's question instead. "An Italian priest stole from the Church of St Apostoli in 1348."

"*Correcto.* And people entrusted the church with their valuables before trying to escape the plague." Alessandro jotted his own comment on the whiteboard.

Rosalina pushed her coffee mug aside. "We have a diary that lists pages and pages of the treasure."

The seven-hundred-year-old journal was sealed in a plastic ziplock bag in Archer's safe. It would be very useful. If they ever found the treasure, that is.

Jimmy cocked his head. "Sounds like a lot."

"You should see, Jimmy. I've never seen anything like it." Archer's eyes brightened. "Loads of details. . . descriptions of the pieces, who they belonged to, how much they were worth back in the thirteenth century. It's gotta be priceless now."

Jimmy's eyes sparkled as he tapped his finger on the table. "So, the treasure must've been huge and bloody heavy."

Ginger raised her hand and Archer shot her a you've-got-to-be-kidding look.

"Yes, Ginger?" Alessandro tipped his pen towards her, taking his professor role way too far.

"Could we narrow down the type of boat he used?" Ginger blinked at him like a star pupil. "Couldn't have been too many choices back then."

"We can look at known shipping routes from that century, too," Rosalina said.

Alessandro listed their comments as bullet points on the whiteboard.

"I suggest we begin with inhabited islands. That narrows the field down from about six thousand islands to two hundred or so." Frowning, Alessandro shook his head. "But some islands that were inhabited back then are no longer lived upon."

Jimmy leaned back in his chair. "It'll take months to scour that many islands."

"I can narrow our search again by researching the oldest churches on these islands. I'll be back in a minute." Alessandro rubbed his hands together, winked at Rosalina, and then marched away.

"I'll see if I can help." Ginger chased after Alessandro.

"Where'd you dig him up?" Jimmy thumbed in Alessandro's direction.

"We went to college together," Rosalina said.

"Right." Jimmy didn't sound convinced. He stood. "I'm going topside for some fresh air."

Suddenly Rosalina was alone with Archer. Archer had an aura she couldn't ignore and even when she closed her eyes, she could feel his presence.

But he downplayed his charisma, even shied away from attention, preferring instead to remain aloof.

Knowing his childhood, she could blame that trait on his orphanage upbringing.

Never trusting, always defending.

She placed her hand over his and he raised his intense, smoldering eyes to her and blinked as if he hadn't noticed they were alone. "Thank you for coming." Archer turned his hand over and she relished the warmth of his palm.

"I'm glad I'm here." They remained in comfortable silence for a long time, happy to watch smaller boats cruise past.

Alessandro strode into the room and Rosalina snatched her hand from Archer's.

Shit! Alessandro saw that.

Alessandro's eyes clouded, and he heaved a mournful sigh. "I may have established the ideal island to start with."

"Already? Excellent. Which one?" Archer said.

"Andros Island. It's approximately two hours away."

"Why Andros?"

"A couple of reasons, actually. The island has been occupied since at least the second century. It's home to a very impressive monastery and has a well-documented maritime history."

Ginger returned to the table, and Alessandro pulled a chair out for her before he sat beside her.

He placed a sheet of paper with lines of his neat handwriting down the page. "It has an award-winning Maritime Museum. And for the *pièce de résistance*, I found an article about a thirteenth-century ruler who sought a dedicated priest to build a church to help bring security and financial and demographic strength to the island."

"Oh Alessandro, you're brilliant!" Rosalina said.

"He is, isn't he?" Ginger grinned like a schoolgirl with a new love interest, then giggled like one too.

"Okay, well, I guess I'll get some lunch on the go for everyone." Ginger flicked her braid over her shoulder.

"That would be nice," said Rosalina.

"Good." Ginger strode away, swinging her hips like she was on a dance floor.

Alessandro seemed unable to drag his gaze from her butt. When Ginger slinked behind the kitchen counter, he turned his gaze back to Rosalina.

Rosalina grinned at him.

"What?" His cheeks flushed.

"Nothing." Rosalina tried to pretend it was nothing. But it wasn't. Alessandro had barely looked at any other women since their one crazy mistake together all those years ago. Just seeing him ogle Ginger was a step in the right direction.

The trouble was, though, he'd feel like he was cheating on Rosalina.

He wasn't.

Alessandro swallowed loudly and cleared his throat. "We could start at the Maritime Museum. It's next to the large statue called the Unknown Sailor."

"Sounds like a plan." Archer stood and strode towards the door. "I'll let Jimmy and the crew know where we're heading."

Once Archer left, Rosalina dreaded facing Alessandro. But she had to before guilt and embarrassment shared the same space in her mind. With Archer back in her life, she'd put Alessandro in a rotten situation. Alessandro was a good man, and he'd always been open and honest about his love for her. But it was time to voice what she hoped he already knew.

He pushed back from his chair, "I'd better go—"

"Alessandro, we need to talk." Rosalina reached for his arm. "Will you come sit with me?"

Lowering his gaze, he nodded.

She led him to the sofa. When they sat, he kept at arm's length from her and his shoulders sagged, as if heavy with sorrow.

She tugged on her gold hoop earring as she stewed over how to say the obvious. "I'm sorry to drag you along on this trip."

His eyes met hers. "Are you kidding? I'm having the most fun since. . . well, ever."

Rosalina's stomach settled, and she let out a sigh. "I'm glad it's not all a waste of your time. Alessandro, you're an amazing man but —"

"You don't need to say it." He draped his hand over her leg. "You've never looked at me the same way you look at Archer. We never had those sparks. I know when I'm defeated, or not even a contender. Rosalina, I want you to be with Archer. He's obviously the man of your dreams."

"Oh, Alessandro, you're wonderful. I know you'll find the perfect woman. But I would never be that for you. You and I, we —"

He squeezed her knee. "I know. But it was *magnifica* while it lasted."

She half sighed; half giggled. "Yes, it was *magnifica*. And I hope we always have time for each other."

"My love will always be there for you. But I'm telling you now. Archer had better not break your heart again or I'll find nasty ways to hurt him. I'm thinking along the lines of a big, black rat."

Gasping, the memory of that rat crawled through her. "Alessandro, that's not like you."

"I mean it." He pinned her with his dark eyes.

She slid towards him and wrapped her arms around his shoulders. "Thank you."

He curled her hair over her shoulder and snuggled in. "I'm going to miss you."

"I know. But we have —"

A huff at the door made Rosalina jolt away from Alessandro and her breath caught.

Archer glared at her from the doorway with his arms folded and fists bunched.

Without a word, he stormed away.

Chapter Twenty-Eight

S *hit. Shit.* Rosalina jumped to her feet. "I'm sorry Alessandro, but I have to go after Archer."

"Of course. Go."

She kissed Alessandro's forehead and sprinted after Archer.

Archer marched along the passageway with his hands swinging at his sides. "Archer, wait! It's not what you think."

"It's exactly what I think."

"Don't be a jerk."

"I'm a jerk? You're the one who's jerking Alex and I around." His voice boomed off the walls.

"Will you just stop and listen for a minute?"

"I just saw you together." He increased his pace.

She lunged forward and grabbed his arm.

He spun towards her with a mutinous glare.

"Archer, listen! I just told Alessandro he wasn't the man for me."

"What?" His fury hung in the air like smoke.

"Alessandro already knew. He said I never look at him like I look at you."

"Oh. He's —"

She folded her arms and jutted her chin at him. "He's a good man. He also said if you ever break my heart again, he'd find that torture rat."

Archer's shoulders relaxed. "Ha. He's got a weird sense of humor."

She stared at him, taking in the crinkles by his eyes that deepened with his frown, and vanished completely as his expression morphed from anger to relief.

He reached for her hand, pressing his palm to hers. "I'm sorry. But seeing you in his arms made me crazy."

Rosalina liked the sound of that. She wanted passion and desire and love that he would fight for. The tapestry of his heart was finally being stitched together. "That's good."

Archer hugged her to his chest, and she inhaled his scent. This wasn't the aroma of a cologne that pretended to be a man. This scent was Archer. Her hot-blooded man.

God, I've missed his embrace.

His beating heart was a beautiful melody. It felt good to be in his arms. No, it was better than that. It felt right.

All too soon, he let her go and stepped back. "Thank you."

"For what?"

"For letting Alessandro go."

She nodded. "It was the right thing to do."

He cocked his brow.

"And I meant it."

He tilted his head, treating her to his incredible gaze. "I'm so pleased to hear that."

His intense eyes captured her so fiercely that she wanted to jump into his arms and make him march to his room. But she fought that desire. Fought it hard. Her body was oh so ready for that glorious adventure, but her head was still working through some things.

Archer squeezed Her hand. "Ginger has made us lunch. They'll all be waiting for us."

"Excellent." She made a show of rolling her eyes. "I can't wait to see what we're having."

He cupped her cheek. "Be nice. Or else you'll have to do all the cooking."

"Exactly!"

Hand in hand, they strolled to the galley together. Jimmy and Alessandro were already seated and Ginger was at the head of the table, ready to dish whatever was in the steaming pot before her.

Jimmy grinned like a proud parent and Rosalina couldn't decide if he was nervous or excited about their first meal together.

Archer led Rosalina to a seat, and as she sat, he reached over the table to shake hands with Alessandro.

Ever the gentleman, Alessandro accepted his handshake.

Rosalina's heart swelled as months of burning tension melted away.

Archer filled their crystal glasses with wine and then raised his. "Here's to good hunting."

"To treasure hunting." Jimmy swigged his wine down in one gulp.

Alessandro cleared his throat. "With these solid leads —"

"Whoa. Hold your horses there, Alex." Archer jabbed his finger at the table. "What we have is a couple of interesting facts and ideas that may lead to nothing at all. Believe me, most treasure hunting is days, even months, of endless disappointment."

"Maybe. But it's going to be one hell of a ride," Jimmy said. "And I can think of much worse ways to spend the summer."

"It sounds like fun." Ginger flipped her thick blonde braid over her shoulder and then scooped a spoonful of rice onto Jimmy's plate.

"What're we having?" Jimmy asked.

"Chili con carne." Ginger glanced nervously at Rosalina.

Rosalina cringed at the thought of eating such a heavy dish for lunch and hoped Ginger hadn't overdone the chili.

"I hope you like it." Ginger spoke over Rosalina's shoulder as she dished a spoonful of the dark stew onto her rice.

"It smells good." Rosalina inhaled the lovely aromatics. With a delicate hint of garlic, it smelled delicious. As she waited for everyone to be plated, Jimmy grinned at her. He was waiting for her approval as much as Ginger was. *Hopefully, the chili won't blow my mind.* She was more of a sweet tooth girl.

Ginger sat between Alessandro and Jimmy and gathered her fork. "Dig in."

Rosalina spooned a couple of kidney beans and a chunk of meat into her mouth and braced for the spicy impact. But the dish was deliciously spiced and mild in heat. The beef was tender and sweet and a hint of smoky flavor added an interesting twist. Ginger watched her eat.

Rosalina nodded. "This is fabulous. How did you produce the smoky flavor?"

Ginger winked. "My secret ingredient. Smoky barbecue sauce."

A tiny laugh slipped from Rosalina's throat, and the others laughed with her.

She and Ginger were in for some interesting times ahead in the kitchen.

"I told you she's a good cook." Jimmy refilled their glasses with a generous swish of wine.

Lunch was the reverse of their earlier gathering. The level of excitement had risen several notches and for the benefit of Jimmy and Ginger, between Rosalina, Alessandro and Archer, they told the story of what had happened in Florence as if it were all just a bit of fun.

She was happy with that. There was no point in rehashing it completely.

And this was the first time she'd heard all the details about what Archer and Alessandro had done before finding her in the church dungeon.

The way the men told it, disagreeing on every detail and no doubt exaggerating everything else, made it much more enjoyable.

Lunch reminded Rosalina of mealtimes with her family. In some ways, the surrounding people were her family. A lovely warmth washed through her and she hoped this was just one of many great times together.

"When we get to Andros, we should split into two teams." A deep frown crossed Archer's forehead. "Rosalina and Alex, you go to the museum and see what you can find out. And Jimmy and I'll go to the graveyard."

"No way." Jimmy abandoned his knife and fork and folded his arms across his chest. "I'm not goin' to no graveyard. What the hell would we wanna go there for, anyway?"

"We believe Archer's parents are buried on one of these islands." Rosalina answered on behalf of Archer. 'If we find their graves, at least we'll know we're in the right area."

"Hey Archer, no offense, man, and you know I'll do anythin' for ya, but I can't do that." Jimmy shook his head but maintained eye contact with Archer. "I don't do graveyards."

"It's okay, I understand." Archer raked his hand through his wavy hair.

Jimmy's reluctance wasn't unexpected. In the last twelve months, he'd buried his mother, father and only sister. After each of their funerals, Jimmy had gone on a huge drinking binge, and it'd taken Archer several nights of serious poker playing to drag Jimmy out of those downers.

"I'll go." Ginger put up her hand as if she was volunteering to taste dessert.

Rosalina's mind raced at Ginger's enthusiasm. "It's okay, Ginger. I'll go with Archer, and Jimmy can go with Alessandro."

"Rosa. No." Archer's gruff tone unsettled her.

She cocked her head. "Why not?"

"You need to go with Alex. With your language skills, you two will interpret better than any of us."

Damn it. He's right. "Okay," she mumbled.

Archer reached for his drink. "Jimmy, you can run us over to the island and back. And Ginger, you're with me."

"Sounds like fun." Ginger giggled.

Rosalina's stomach clenched. "I doubt that searching for Archer's parents' graves will be fun."

Ginger slapped her hand over her mouth. "Sorry. I'm such a ditz."

"It's okay." Archer turned to Rosalina, drawing her eyes to him. "I'll be okay. The likelihood of this being the right island is minuscule."

"I know, but —"

A knock on the door interrupted her. "Excuse me, Mr. Mahoney." It was one of the crew.

"Yes, Tim?"

"Sir, we'll be throwing anchor in approximately ten minutes. Do you want to check our positioning?"

"No. I'm sure you know what you're doing."

"Yes, sir. Thank you, sir." Tim nodded and backed out of the room.

"Does the crew know about the treasure?" Ginger whispered.

"No," Jimmy blurted. "Nobody else must know. I've been thinking we should let them off for a bit, anyway. They've worked for five weeks solid."

"I agree. Patmos Island isn't too far away, and it looks like an ideal place for them to stay for a while."

"Unless we succeed at Andros Island," Alessandro said.

Jimmy snorted. "If we get lucky at Andros Island, I'll get 'Alex is a God' tattooed on my ass."

Alessandro reddened and Archer chuckled, and the laughter that followed from everyone else, including Alessandro, was loud and genuine.

But finding Archer's parents' graves was a double-edged sword.

On one hand, it may provide a clue.

On the other, there's no telling how Archer would react.

And if he does shatter, I won't be there to pick up the pieces.

Chapter Twenty-Nine

Rosalina tried to pretend she was a tourist enjoying the scenery, but her growing worry about Archer made it impossible.

Few Greek islands had a marina to suit a motor yacht the size of *Evangeline*, and Andros was no exception. With the anchor in position, Jimmy helped Archer with the crane to lower the tender over the back of the yacht. The small boat was only just big enough to carry the five of them.

Within forty minutes Rosalina, Ginger, Alessandro and Archer were walking along the wooden jetty and Jimmy was returning the tender back to *Evangeline*.

The island was quite mountainous, and it was one of the bigger Cycladic Islands. Port Gavrio was the principal port where the ferries arrived into, and it catered well to tourists with souvenir shops and little outdoor bars dotted along the beach. But, on this Tuesday afternoon there were barely any tourists. In fact, there were hardly any people at all, and many of the shops were already closed.

It didn't matter how much Rosalina wanted to explore the vast selection of local produce at the few remaining market stalls, her mind wouldn't shake the sense of dread enveloping her.

Even the smell of vine-ripened tomatoes, sitting plump and bright red at the corner of the stall, couldn't drag her mind from what Archer was about to do.

She wanted to be with him in case he found the graves. He seemed okay at the moment, strolling along as if he was enjoying the scenery, but who knew what reaction he'd have if the graves were here?

Archer hired a taxi and Alessandro, Rosalina and Ginger climbed into the back seat. From the front seat, Archer instructed the driver to take them to the Maritime Museum. As they drove along, the driver rambled a monologue of tourist information, but he soon quietened down when none of them responded to him.

The taxi pulled up alongside the statue of the Unknown Sailor and Archer jumped out to help Rosalina from the car.

He pulled her close. "I'll be okay, babe. Get as much info as you can. Ginger and I'll come back to you once we're done."

Rosalina's throat tightened, but she was determined not to lose control.

Archer kissed her briefly and then climbed back into the front seat of the taxi.

Her feet were glued to the pavement as she watched it drive away.

"There it is." Alessandro pointed at the museum sign. "This is going to be fascinating."

Rosalina didn't share his enthusiasm.

The Maritime Museum wasn't very enticing for a tourist attraction. It was set back from the street. A large, rusty anchor adorned the narrow doorway. The entrance smelled of dust, ropes, and cold cement.

Light filtering in from a series of windows fell upon a man who was slumped in an overstuffed chair. Rosalina paused. The man, in faded denim overalls and an off-kilter sailor's cap, was unnaturally still. He was either a mannequin or he was dead. She was too scared to find out which.

"Hello." Alessandro's voice echoed about the sparse room.

The overall-clad man jumped from his seat and stumbled

towards them. "Hello, folks." With eyes as bloodshot as a drunken sailor and cheeks that contorted like plasticine as he rubbed them, Rosalina guessed he was at least eighty-years old.

She'd already seen enough weird men to last her a lifetime and was tempted to run the opposite way.

"Welcome to Andros Island Maritime Museum." Even his voice sounded weathered, but when he smiled at Rosalina, her perception changed. He may look old and bedraggled, but his sassy grin indicated he still had a good deal of life in him.

"Thank you." Rosalina relaxed.

The man motioned for them to come further into the room. "Let me know if I can help you with anything."

"As a matter of fact, we're interested in seeing any maps you might have that detail shipping lanes of the thirteenth century." Alessandro got straight to the point.

"Ah, treasure hunters."

Rosalina's mouth fell open.

"Um, no." Alessandro tucked his arm around Rosalina's waist. "I'm doing a research paper for Florence University and I've convinced my poor fiancée here to help me."

The man nodded, but his raised eyebrows indicated he didn't believe a word Alessandro said.

"Why do you think we are treasure hunters?" she said.

"I've been working here for over forty years. Seen my share of them. Though they're not usually as pretty as you." He tilted his hat at Rosalina.

"Have you had many treasure hunters recently? Where were they looking? Did they find treasure?" Alessandro fired rapid questions, without pausing for an answer.

"Jeez, hold up on those questions, my boy. My mind isn't as quick as it used to be." He walked towards a bank of glass-topped tables. "Our oldest maps are over here. Let me show you what we have, and while he's looking, you and I can grab a pot of tea." The old man winked at Rosalina.

Rosalina couldn't decide whether his wink was him flirting with her, or if the tea he'd mentioned wasn't the herbal kind.

Either way, it was a great chance to pick the old man's brain about the maritime history of the area. Alessandro's nose was pushed up against the glass cabinet, so she had no idea if he noticed the old man shuffling her towards the back of the room.

"My name is Yanis." He opened a door, and a creaking hinge welcomed her into the kitchen area.

"Rosalina."

Yanis filled the kettle with fresh water. "So, what really brings you to Andros?"

His fingers trembled as he filled the kettle, and a fleeting image of her grandmother flashed into her mind. It was as if Nonna was telling her it was okay to trust this man.

She let out a long sigh and hoped she was doing the right thing. "You've got me. We *are* looking for treasure."

"I knew it." He exaggerated a wink.

She chuckled. "But how?"

"No camera. Tourists carry a camera. You're not. And if you're going to pretend to be engaged, you should've made him buy you a decent ring."

Rosalina glanced at her naked fingers and chuckled. The old man's ancient appearance contradicted his sharp observations.

He laughed with her. "Green or black tea?"

"Whatever you're having,"

He poured boiling water into a white china cup. "Green it is, then."

He carried the cups towards the table and when he sat beside her, she met his gaze with new respect.

"So, what do you want to know?"

"We're interested in ships that passed through the Greek Islands in the thirteenth century."

"It's funny, you know? I don't get too many requests for wrecks that old. But I did have a fella in here a while back looking for thirteenth-century wrecks. We tracked down some information about an Italian ship called the *Flying Seahorse* that disappeared around that time."

"Did he find it?"

"No idea. The poor bugger was killed by a shark."

A gasp released from her throat, and she dropped her cup into the saucer.

"It's okay, love. He wasn't anywhere near here." He whipped a handkerchief from his pocket to wipe up her spilled tea. "We rarely see sharks in the Mediterranean, anyway. He sure was unlucky."

Rosalina leapt to her feet. "Sorry, but I have to go." She dashed out the door.

"Are you okay?" Yanis yelled after her.

She raced for the front door. "Alessandro, we have to get to Archer."

"What? Why? What's wrong? Rosalina. . . wait!"

She didn't wait. The chances of him finding his parents' graves just went from negligible to possible and she had to be there when and if he did. She ran across the square, squinting against the sun's glare off the whitewashed walls of the surrounding buildings.

"What happened?" Alessandro reached for her arm.

"That man knew Archer's father." She waved at a taxi parked farther up the street.

"You're kidding. I told you this island—"

"He knew about the shark attack—" Gasping, she covered her mouth.

"What shark attack?" Alessandro gripped her arm, but she yanked it free and dashed up the hill towards the taxi.

Archer asked me to keep the shark attack a secret.

And now I've broken my promise.

Will he trust me with his secrets again?

Chapter Thirty

Archer couldn't believe there were two graveyards on this tiny island. But he shouldn't have been surprised. Nothing about treasure hunting was easy.

He instructed the driver to take them to the nearest one. As they drove along the winding road up the bluff, the vista revealed dozens of islands in the distance.

How many would they need to visit before they found anything?

It could be months of disappointment. Years.

Rosalina was adamant that this treasure hunt was his salvation. He didn't share the same confidence.

At the top of the hill, the driver pulled to the side of the road. Behind a stone wall with a wrought-iron gate, the graveyard seemed to stretch forever.

He asked the driver to wait, then stepped out.

With Ginger at his side, he crossed through the entrance and heaved a sigh of annoyance. The gravestones were scattered everywhere, with no semblance of order.

He'd expected them to be in neat rows, but this was far from it.

As he strolled towards the nearest headstones, his brain was all over the place. For years, he'd fought to forget his mother. And he'd tried damn hard to forget his father's horrific death.

Would finding their graves make my nightmares worse?

Would finding their graves even be a clue?

It might take them in a direction that's all wrong.

Wiping his sweating palms on his shorts, he forced the impossible questions from his mind.

Ginger walked towards a large headstone that was tilted at a nasty angle. "We're looking for Wade or Helen Mahoney. Right?" Ginger's chirpy voice was out of place with their surroundings.

"Yes." Hearing their names turned a heavy knot in his stomach. At thirty-one, Archer was nearly the same age as his mother had been when she'd died.

It hit home. She'd barely lived.

Coincidently, the first headstone he reached was for a man who was also thirty-one years of age when he died in 1893. The next one was decorated with a cherub. Its dates on the inscription confirmed it was for a nine-month-old baby.

He fought sadness as he moved from one headstone to the next. Ginger called out a few names and dates as she continued to move further away.

Another taxi drove towards the cemetery gate and before it had even pulled over, the door swung open.

Rosalina jumped out and her hair danced in long ribbons behind her as she dashed towards him.

His heart lurched at the distress on her face. Her urgent stride scared the hell out of him.

"What's wrong?" He reached for her outstretched arms.

"The man at the museum knew your father. He mentioned the shark attack."

"Tell me what he said." Gripping her elbow, he directed her back towards the taxi.

Alessandro climbed from the back of the taxi. His wide eyes suggested he had no idea what the hell was going on.

"Alex, you stay here with Ginger." Archer yanked the taxi door open again.

"Where are you going?" Ginger yelled across the gravestones.

"Just keep looking. We'll be back later."

They climbed into the taxi's back seat and Archer directed the driver back to the Maritime Museum.

He squeezed Rosalina's hand. "Tell me exactly what he said."

As the car followed the winding road around the cliff, Rosalina relayed what the old man had said.

Archer's mind was a scramble as he tried to fit the pieces together.

Rosalina was on edge, but the second she re-entered the museum, she froze.

Archer halted too.

The museum was still and quiet. Even the howling wind outside failed to penetrate these concrete walls.

A smell, as distinct as it was offensive, invaded his senses. The smell was like no other.

It can't be a coincidence.

Could the priest from Florence be here?

He shuffled Rosalina behind him and stepped further into the room. "Hello?"

Rosalina pointed at the glass-topped tables. "Alessandro was looking at these maps when Yanis took me into the kitchen for tea."

Acid churned in Archer's stomach as he stepped towards the kitchen. "Hello?"

Voices echoed down the hall, and a man in overalls stepped from a doorway.

Rosalina released a sigh of relief. "That's Yanis. The man I told you about."

That was good, but Archer didn't settle his guard. Something wasn't right. And he'd learned to trust his gut a long time ago.

"Oh, it's you," Yanis said. "The way you raced out of here, I thought I'd never see you again."

"Do you have someone with you?" Archer's voice bounced off the concrete floor.

"Yes, Nathan is out the back. I'll let him know you're here."

"Who?" A rush of breath escaped Archer's throat.

"Your brother. He said you'd be back."

Archer grabbed the old man's arm. "That man's not my brother. He's very dangerous. Where is he?"

Janis jolted back. "He's in the back room. What's going on?"

Archer pointed at Rosalina. "Stay here."

Striding toward the doorway, he clenching his fists and forged his anger from visions of Rosalina's black eye and her emotional scars that ran even deeper.

He squinted into the dimly lit hallway. His heart thundered in his chest.

"I'm calling the police," Yanis yelled after him.

With each step, Archer's mind slammed from one unanswerable question to the next.

Was he following us?

What did he know about the treasure?

Did he have a weapon?

That last question had Archer halting.

Maybe I should wait for the police.

The sound of shattering glass broke the silence, and Archer raced towards it.

With a clenched jaw and anger clawing through him, Archer stormed into the room. He glanced left and right. But the room was empty.

A small glass panel within the door was broken, and shards were scattered over the floor. But the door was closed. His neck hairs bristled. Archer spun around.

He saw the chair too late.

The blow stuck him square in the forehead and knocked him flying. His head hit the concrete floor.

Pain speared behind his eyes. The room spun.

The creep loomed into his vision. The chair slammed into him again.

Everything went black.

Chapter Thirty-One

The ugly priest came out of nowhere and ran straight at Rosalina. His hooded cape was gone, replaced instead with a flannel shirt and a tattered beanie over his bald head, but there was no mistaking his evil eyes.

She scoured for a weapon. Terror clawed at her throat. Adrenalin shot through her veins.

Oh God, is Archer hurt?

Riding a wave of fear and fury, she gritted her teeth, snatched a picture off the wall and, with the determination of a snared animal, she smashed it over his head. The glass shattered, trapping his neck within the jagged shards left in the frame.

The priest tumbled over.

His agonized screams tore at her sanity.

But he wasn't done. He scrambled to his hands and knees.

She jumped onto his back, clutched the picture frame and pulled with all her might, determined to strangle him.

Despite her full weight on top of him, he continued to rise. His stench made her gag.

She yanked even harder, pulling on the frame like she was riding a bucking bronco.

He changed direction and slammed her back into the wall. The wind exploded from her lungs. The wood fell from her hands.

She tumbled to the floor, her hip taking the full brunt of the fall.

Gasping for air, she watched him run from the building. A trail of blood marked his escape.

"Archer!" Pushing through the pain in her hip, she scrambled to her feet and ran to the rear of the museum. The silence was deafening and her heart was in her throat as she prepared for what she was about to see.

Archer lay sprawled on the floor, his mouth slightly ajar, a swollen lump was on his forehead. She fell at his side, scooping him into her arms.

His eyes flickered. His breaths were short and sounded painful.

"Archer, wake up."

"I'm okay." He tried to push up, but crumbled to the floor with a groan.

Relief flooded through her as she adjusted her legs so his head fell into her lap. "Don't move. I'm getting a doctor."

"I don't need a doctor."

"Yes, you do. You were unconscious and there's an enormous bump on your head."

He reached up as if to touch his forehead, but his hand touched her breast instead. "I'm good now." A sexy grin formed on his lips as he fondled her.

"Stop that." She guided his hand to her lips and kissed his fingers. The redness of his eyes failed to mask his desire for her. "You're obviously not feeling too bad."

"Told you. Help me up. We need to find out as much as we can before the police get here."

Rosalina hooked her arm around his waist, and they hobbled along the hallway. "What's all this glass?"

"I smashed a picture over his head."

His eyes filled with curious amusement. "Hope it wasn't a priceless artifact?"

She shrugged and scrunched up her nose. "Me too."

He pointed at the trail along the hallway. "Blood?"

"It's his." This was the first time she'd inflicted harm on anyone. She felt no remorse.

"I wonder if the police can use it to find out who this asshole is."

They rounded the corner. Yanis was still on the phone in the front office. He cupped the mouthpiece. "They have me on hold."

Archer indicated to the leather lounge that Rosalina had originally found Yanis asleep on and they limped to it. Rosalina flopped into the chair and yelped in pain.

"What's wrong?"

"I bruised my hip."

"Did he do it?" A look of hatred darkened Archer's eyes and hardened his features. It was a side of him she'd never seen before. Driven by hatred, Archer might be capable of dangerous things.

"I tried to strangle him with the picture frame, but he threw me against the wall. I'm okay. I think he's worse."

"I hope he bleeds to death. Save me the job of killing him."

Archer was serious.

Yet as much as it horrified her to admit it, she'd do the same if Archer were being threatened.

Yanis finished the phone call and walked towards them. "The police are on their way. Are you two all right?"

"We're fine, Yanis, but we need to know what he wanted?"

He flopped into a chair beside them. "He wanted to know what you were asking about."

"What did you tell him?" Archer was forceful, and Rosalina squeezed his hand.

"We didn't get very far. I was telling him about Petro Zeno, the leader of Andros in 1349, and about The *Flying Seahorse*, and how—"

"The *Flying Seahorse*?" Archer touched the lump on his forehead and winced.

"Yes, it's one of the oldest maritime mysteries we have. It was a ship that was carrying a priest who Zeno had commissioned to build a church, but it disappeared out there, somewhere between Malta and Rhodes."

Rosalina's breath caught, and her pulse hit overdrive.

Archer shifted forward. "Rosalina tells me you knew of another man who was searching for that boat."

Yanis cocked his head at Rosalina and she assumed he was nervous about mentioning the shark attack again. She nodded at him.

"Yes, I remember him well. He was such a lovely guy, so full of excitement, a real charmer, and his wife, she was beautiful. Wade and Helen, if I remember correctly. I'll never forget—" Yanis froze. His hand snapped to his mouth.

He blinked, then he lowered his hand. "He was your father, wasn't he?"

Archer's eyes widened.

Yanis nodded. "You look just like him."

Rosalina gasped. Is this the clue they've been looking for to find where Archer's father was killed?

Archer seemed to crumble with the weight of the world.

Oh God. I hope these answers don't pitch Archer even deeper into his nightmares.

Chapter Thirty-Two

By the time they returned to *Evangeline*, the sun was gliding into the horizon and Rosalina's hip was seizing up. With the amount of pain she was already suffering, she'd have a bruise the size of a dinner plate by the time she went to bed.

Pink hues colored the low-lying clouds and blue sky morphed into violet, but the pretty sunset couldn't distract her from the turmoil racing through her brain.

Determined to hide her pain, she went straight to her room and, for the second time in a month, examined an enormous bruise on her body. The blue stain covered her hip, buttocks and most of her thigh, and looked as bad as it hurt. She cringed as she touched it and gasped at how dark the bruise already was.

After a brief shower, she dressed and chose a pair of silver drop earrings she'd bought from the feeble man at a Bali market. She didn't think they were genuine silver, as the man had touted, but she couldn't resist the smile from the little girl sitting on the man's knee.

Rosalina turned off the light and went to find Archer. She stepped into the bar area, and Archer swiveled on his stool towards her. "I thought you'd be in the shower for hours."

"Are you kidding? And miss all the excitement?"

"Do you want champagne?" Ginger offered from behind the bar.

"That would be lovely." Rosalina accepted the fluted glass Ginger held towards her. Alessandro and Jimmy sat in the white leather lounge and, judging by Alessandro's pink cheeks, he was already a drink or two ahead of her.

Archer guided her to one of the bar stools and she was careful to put her weight onto her good side as she slid onto the chair. "What did I miss?"

Jimmy grunted. "Nothing much. Just Alessandro gloating about being right about Andros Island."

"I *was* right." Alessandro waggled his head.

"I better get another rum. It's going to be a long night." Chuckling, Jimmy strode to the bar.

Before leaving Andros, Yanis had helped them make copies of maps, captains' logs, transcripts from ancient diaries and any other document that might've contained information to help them with their search. Now the entire assortment was spread out across the bar top.

When Archer shook Yanis' hand before they'd left, he'd asked the old man to keep the details of their research a secret; and, with a grin and a wad of cash he'd quickly shoved into his pocket, Yanis had assured Archer their secret would go with him to the grave.

Rosalina sipped her champagne, listening to the friendly banter.

As the conversation moved to the attack, Rosalina watched the people she considered her family. But as usual, Archer brushed off the danger. He always pretended that it was nothing. But it wasn't.

He could have died today.

And I could have killed someone.

Oh, God! What if he *is* dead?

I could be arrested for murder.

Anxiety gnawed at her stomach. But everyone else seemed oblivious to the danger they'd been in. Danger they could still be in.

Nox may never let them be.

Was any treasure worth that?

Rosalina helped Ginger prepare a meal of fresh fish and a selection of local vegetables, and not long after she finished eating, Rosalina struggled to keep her eyes open. She blew them all a kiss and retired to her bedroom.

A knock on her door had her smiling. She pulled on her silk nightgown and tightened the belt around her waist before opening the door. Archer greeted her with a bag of crushed ice. "Thought you might like some help with your bruises."

"Really?" Despite her intended rejection, she grinned as she welcomed him in.

"I noticed you favoring one side of your delicious derriere. Let me see it."

"I don't think so."

"I won't take no for an answer. On the bed. Lift your skirt."

She huffed. "That's romantic."

"Rosa, I know you're hurt, so stop faking it and lift your skirt."

He eased her onto the bed and she stared into his smoldering eyes as he lifted her skirt over her hip.

"Oh shit! Babe, why didn't you tell me it was so bad?" He sat beside her and his eyes filled with concern as he rolled the ice bag in his palm and then cradled it to her thigh. "I think I need more ice."

"My butt's that big, huh?"

"Your butt's perfect. The bruise isn't."

The coldness of the ice stung, and she winced against it. But he wouldn't let her withdraw. She laid her head back on the pillow and tried to relax. "Archer, I'm terrified. That was too close."

He tilted his head. "I know, but he won't get near us again."

"What do you think he wants?"

"I know what he wants. The treasure."

"So, what do we do?"

"We just keep an eye out all the time. And be very careful with any more enquiries we make. I don't think we'll see the priest again, anyway."

"I hope not."

The ice was melting, and a droplet tickled as it rolled down her inner thigh. She moved to wipe it but Archer caught the drip with his thumb. Their eyes met.

"If something happened to you, I couldn't live with myself." His voice was barely a whisper, but his words spoke volumes. He leaned in to kiss her forehead, and she moved to catch his lips with hers.

A soft moan tumbled from his throat and she tasted sweet Frangelico on his probing tongue.

They parted, and she cupped his neck. "Nothing's going to happen to me, not now that we're back together."

"From now on, we stick together. Joined at the hip."

"I'm okay with that." She patted the bed and Archer lay down beside her. He draped his arm over her waist and whispered something unintelligible in her ear.

Did he say he loved me?

She didn't want to ruin the moment by asking him to repeat it.

Closing her eyes, as she listened to the therapeutic sound of water lapping at the side of the yacht, she willed her exhaustion to lull her to sleep.

But unanswered questions racing through her mind kept her awake.

And the biggest question of all. . . *was Nox really gone?*

Because she could not handle another encounter with the ugly priest.

Chapter Thirty-Three

Nox checked his neck wounds and, wincing, he wiped away dried blood. He couldn't believe that bitch had attacked him. The cut on his neck was deep. One inch over, and he would have bled to death.

Bitch! She is going to die! They all are!

As he redressed his bloody wounds, the disgusting groaning sounds that had been emanating from Brother Bonito's bedroom next door finally subsided.

Without knocking, Nox opened Bonito's bedroom door. A naked woman stood at the side of the bed.

Her body and breasts and white flesh repulsed him.

Brother Bonito sat rigid on the end of the mattress. His slow reaction to cover his nakedness indicated the hallucinogenic powder Nox had secretly given him was still in effect.

The guilty pleasures the prostitute provided to Brother Bonito could never be satisfied any other way. It hadn't been too hard to find her, and he didn't mind paying handsomely for her discretion.

Her duties, as necessary as they were disgusting, would ensure Brother Bonito gave Nox his undivided attention. Nox instructed her to cover up and paid her well before she scurried out the back door of their tiny rented cottage.

Bonito had not followed Nox to the Greek Islands willingly. Nox had only convinced him after a very brief discussion over a series of photographs he still had in his possession. None of the photos were as salacious as the ones he had now. But they had depicted Bonito in compromising positions and were perfect for blackmailing the younger priest.

Yet, nearly a month after that initial discussion, the pathetic Bonito had begun to question Nox's authority.

It had been time to show Bonito the type of control Nox wielded and reaffirm his domination.

As Nox strode into the room, Brother Bonito's weakened form shrunk further into itself. His beaded brow and shifty eyes said more than his ragged breathing. He was a lost soul sinking into the trappings of a guilty man.

But Nox held ultimate control over him, and this was only the beginning. When Nox removed a camera he'd hidden in the overcrowded bookcase at the end of the bed, he made no effort to conceal the device.

Bonito's eyes bulged when he saw the camera and his body shriveled further as he slumped his head into his hands.

Nox was looking at a shattered man. No longer a man of faith. His choice of intimacy had destined him for a life at the mercy of Nox, forever trapped by guilt.

As a tear slipped down Brother Bonito's red cheek, Nox smiled wide enough to reveal the gap in his yellow teeth to the weaker man. "Now you will do anything and everything I tell you to."

Dabbing at the bandage bloody around his neck, Nox left the sobbing priest.

Nox hated that he needed Bonito's help.

For now.

But once Nox killed Archer and that bitch Rosalina, he would kill the pathetic priest too.

Chapter Thirty-Four

Archer's scare at Andros Island had been a wake-up call, and since that bullshit he'd kept constant watch on the surrounding boats to monitor if they were being followed. So far, everything appeared normal and yet he couldn't shake the persistent worry.

Since they left Andros, they had settled into a pattern of cruising to an island to investigate the gravesites. When that turned out to be fruitless, Rosalina insisted they sample the local cuisine at a café or taverna and then they would settle back on *Evangeline* before the sun set each evening.

Each morning, Jimmy, Alessandro and Ginger slept in while Archer and Rosalina woke early and, with coffee and fresh pastries in hand, pored over the charts provided by Yanis to decide on the next island to visit.

Archer loved watching Rosalina's decision-making process. She was methodical, decisive, and always adamant she was right. But Archer didn't mind. Letting her win each debate was part of the fun.

After nearly a week of island hopping, Archer set a course for Patmos Island.

Patmos was like every other island they'd visited, in that Archer's luxurious yacht didn't fit in the marina. So, he had to anchor offshore and they used the tender to transport everyone onto the island.

They had the disembarking process down to a fine art, and within a couple of minutes of anchoring, they cruised towards the island famous for the Cave of the Apocalypse. According to Alessandro, this was where John the Apostle was said to have written the Book of Revelation.

Unlike the first couple of islands they'd visited, Patmos was not known as a party island. Its deeply religious past dictated its low-key nightlife, and a quiet night was exactly the type of evening Archer needed.

Jimmy guided the tender to a crumbling jetty and Archer jumped out to tie the boat to wooden pillars that appeared centuries old. He helped Rosalina climb out of the boat first and turned back to the tender.

Alessandro seemed mighty comfortable placing his hands on Ginger's hips to help her out and as Alessandro climbed out, Archer whispered in his ear, "You old devil, you."

Alessandro looked at him as if he had no idea what he was talking about, but his act wasn't lost on Archer. Archer winked, and Alessandro dismissed him with a nervous laugh before following the ladies along the pier.

The town of Skala was not only the major town on Patmos, it was also the island's chief port. And despite being the most populated town on the island, it still retained its relaxed atmosphere.

As they strolled along the jetty towards the shore, Archer couldn't shake the feeling he'd been there before. A knot tightened in the pit of his stomach and he had no idea why.

Rosalina reached for his hand, and as he welcomed the clutch of her fingers, he tried to shake his unjustified nervousness.

"For thousands of years, people from all walks of life have passed through this little town to visit Patmos." Alessandro was in professor mode. "Did you know Skala means 'stairway'?"

Jimmy clapped Alessandro on the back. "You're a regular *Funk and Wagnall.*"

"What does that mean?" Alessandro shrugged off Jimmy's muscle-clad arm.

"Relax, Alex," Archer said. "It's a compliment. *Funk and Wagnall's* are a brand of dictionary."

"I know that." Alessandro blushed as he glanced at Ginger, and she smiled, seemingly oblivious to the joke at his expense.

"Tell me about Patmos." Ginger sidled up beside Alessandro and blinked at him like an overzealous student.

Alessandro puffed his chest. "Patmos was once the perfect place to house criminals, as it was so inaccessible."

Ginger tucked her arm into Alessandro's elbow.

He seemed lost for words, and it was a few beats before he cleared his throat. "It's believed Saint John the Divine was exiled here. During that time, he lived in a cave where he apparently heard the voice of God, and that's why he wrote the Book of Revelation. It's hard to believe this beautiful island was the setting for such a dark book."

"How do you know all this stuff?" Ginger said.

"I'm a historian. It's my job."

"I thought you were an architect." Jimmy scratched his chest through his shirt.

"As a matter of fact, I'm a professor of history and architecture. I majored in Ancient History."

"Wow, you're so smart." Ginger fluttered her lashes.

Archer rolled his eyes at Rosalina, and she wriggled her brows.

The beach was dotted with an assortment of boats, from abandoned wrecks to little fishing vessels fitted with all manner of modern equipment. Pelicans cruised across the smooth water in an elegant aquatic dance while seagulls squawked noisily above, performing nimble acrobatics.

Many couples sat at the small tables decorated in the blue-and-white checkered tablecloths and shared bottles of wine as they gazed out over the ocean. The fiery backdrop of the setting sun transformed the couples into romantic silhouettes.

Ginger and Alessandro looked very comfortable, strolling arm in arm along the beach as if they were lovers. Rosalina tugged on Archer's arm and a look of satisfaction brimmed in her eyes as she nodded towards Alessandro and Ginger. Archer couldn't decide if their meeting was by design or accident, but he sure was grateful Alessandro's focus had shifted from Rosalina to the blonde Australian.

Alessandro pointed high up the hill. "See that building?"

Ginger squinted into the distance and Archer followed Alessandro's outstretched finger.

"It looks like a Byzantine fortress, but it's actually the Monastery of St John the Theologian. It was built in 1088."

"Holy cow, that's nearly a thousand years old," Ginger said.

Alessandro continued to detail the features of the monastery. But Archer's gaze snagged on a much smaller building high on the bluff. His heart skipped a beat. *I've been here before.* The knot in his stomach twisted tighter and his nerves set to crack.

Ginger jiggled with girlish excitement. "Oh, Archer, it's so beautiful here. Can we sit at one of these tables and watch the sunset? Please?"

Archer sought Rosalina's approval, and she nodded.

As Jimmy tugged two tables together, Archer went to the bar to order a round of drinks. He sat on a stool and stared into the mirror behind the bar. It was not his usual relaxed reflection that looked back. Something was about to happen. He felt it as sure as he smelled the salty sea air. The waitress returned with his order.

"Say," he said, "you don't happen to know the name of that little church up on the hill?"

In response, she pointed at a coaster on the bar. He gathered the coaster and flicked it between his fingers. The sense of déjà vu was overwhelming. The coaster had a picture of a building with white-washed walls and bold pink flowers. The words "Zoodochos Pigi" written upon it made his gut drop.

Memories burst from his mind like buckshot.

Uncontrollable tears rolling down his cheeks.

Cold stone walls that sucked every ounce of his energy.

Flowers that smelled sickly sweet.

Robed women with no answers.

He spun away from the bar. The band in the corner blurred into insignificance as his brain tangled with the long-forgotten memories. The path beneath his feet crunched in time to his urgent stride.

He dropped four hundred euro on the table for Jimmy and told him to enjoy the night.

Archer grabbed Rosalina's hand, lurching her upright, and tugged her along the path with him. Jimmy called after them, but Archer was a machine; focused, driven, determined. No longer in control of his thoughts.

He flagged a taxi and directed the driver to the convent.

"What's wrong, Arch? Where're we going?"

Incapable of answering Rosalina's questions, he squeezed her hand and stared out the window, searching for signs of recognition. The church was drawing him with an urgency he'd never felt before. With each turn around the cliff, the whitewashed walls of Zoodochos Pigi flashed in the setting sun like a warning signal.

The taxi turned into a road full of bumps and sharp turns. Archer remembered some of the curves as if he'd only traveled the road yesterday. The drive was a random concoction of familiarity and mystery.

The car stopped at the end of the road, and Archer paid the driver. Gripping Rosalina's hand like a safety harness, he stepped beneath an enormous stone arch leading into a large courtyard. Decorated with an abundance of flowering vines and flowerbeds overloaded with blooms, the pretty setting failed to settle the turbulence in his stomach. The sickly-sweet scents provoked waves of nausea.

Archer let his intuition take over. He diverted from the main doorway and down a narrow alley that circumvented the grand, white building centered in the perfectly manicured yard. At the back of the convent was a series of shelters, and he strode towards the one furthest from the monastery.

"Can I help you?" A voice interrupted the silence.

Archer turned and froze. Snippets of memory raced across his mind as he stared at the nun. Her silver-framed glasses were new, but he'd met this woman in the white robe before.

"Archer?" Her voice was a loaded question.

Archer's knees wavered, and he gripped Rosalina's hand harder.

"Oh, Archer, it *is* you. I never stopped praying you would return to us." The nun reached her fingers towards him and clasped his hand between her soft palms. "You have your mother's eyes," she said.

Rosalina gasped.

Archer's trembling knees set to crumple him to the ground. "You knew my mother?" His voice was barely audible.

"Yes. Don't you remember me? I guess it has been over twenty years, and you were so young."

Archer's world tumbled out of control and he didn't know how to stop it.

"You lived here for a brief time after your father passed away." The nun shook sadness from her eyes. "My name is Mother Maria."

She released Archer's hand and reached for Rosalina's.

"Hi, I'm Rosalina."

"You must come inside. We've waited a long time for your return."

The nun moved ahead of them; her heavy skirt cloaked around her as if she floated on air. She glided up a small set of steps into a room Archer knew would be the kitchen. "Please take a seat. I'll make some tea." She turned her back on them and made herself busy with the kettle and teacups.

The chairs were heavy and noisy on the stone floor as Archer dragged them out from under the table. The cold, hard wood of the seat was built for resilience rather than comfort.

Archer sat beside Rosalina and she placed her hand on his forearm and mouthed, *are you okay?* Although he nodded, he was a million miles from okay. His mind was a raging torrent of questions, begging for answers.

The building was eerily silent, but a distant bird singing a melodious tune didn't seem out of place. A slight breeze came in through the open door and blew a wisp of hair across Rosalina's nose. Archer reached for it and tucked the wayward lock behind her ear. He attempted an easy smile, but knew it offered no reassurance to Rosalina.

The nun presented two china cups of steaming tea. "It's such a lovely surprise to see you. What brought you back?"

Archer cleared his throat. "I. . . I. . . we, um——" Words failed to form.

Rosalina patted his leg. "We were sailing in the area and to be quite honest, Archer doesn't have much memory of that time in his childhood. But when he saw your beautiful building, it was like he was drawn to it."

The nun nodded. "I know exactly what you mean." She sat opposite and reached for her teacup. It tinkled with her trembling fingers. "It was a long time ago and a dreadful time for all of us. Your mother tried so hard after what happened to her, but it was not to be."

What happened to her? What about what she did to me?

She might've been perfect to everyone else, but to Archer, his mother was a quitter. Archer placed his palms on the cold, hard table and glared at the old woman opposite. It was all he could do to stop himself from ranting.

"She thought she was going to lose you, too."

Archer cocked his head, confused.

"For nearly six months, you were in the hospital. She wrote a letter to you every day, telling you what was happening, your father's funeral, your tests, what she was feeling, other things. . ." her voice trailed off. "But then it got too much."

Archer sat up and curled his hands into fists. "I never saw any letters."

Mother Maria lowered her eyes. "Your mother was in a very dark place. Some letters were. . . difficult. I guess she knew that. Despite her fractured mind, she recognized that what she was writing was not suitable for the eyes of her young son."

"Do you still have the letters?" Rosalina asked.

She nodded. "We knew you would return someday, so the other

Sisters and I held onto them for you." Mother Maria's eyes brightened. "And here you are."

She pushed back in her chair and stood. "Follow me."

Little light crept into the corridor, and the cold from the walls leached into his skin. He tried to shrug off the feeling as they stepped down a series of curved steps into a large open room.

The setting sun streamed in from five small square windows set high in the stone wall, casting shadows around cloth-covered furniture. The room had a damp, musty smell and reminded Archer of the halls of the church in Florence. That memory already seemed like years ago.

Archer followed Mother Maria as she inched around shabby furniture with faded pillows and fraying fabric. She navigated a stack of sagging boxes and finally reached a row of dust-covered bookcases. The overloaded shelves were piled high with trinkets, books, candles, crockery, cloth, and a heap of other discarded knickknacks.

"I know they're around somewhere. Please excuse me. It's been a long time since I've been down here. Ahhh, this looks like it." She reached in to move a large floral bag from a shelf and a flurry of dust floated about the room. Archer leaned over to help her and the old nun looked at Archer with a mixture of sadness and honor.

Archer accepted the two handles and was surprised by the bag's size and weight. "Why didn't you send these to me?"

"We couldn't find you. You were whisked away so fast and all our searches ended in disappointment. We had no idea where you went or how to find you. But we prayed you would return, and thankfully, our prayers have been answered."

Archer shook his head. He was a fraud. He wasn't there in search of his mother's history; he was there for treasure. He tugged the heavy bag to his chest and retraced his steps around boxes and furniture back to where Rosalina stood in the doorway.

"Would you like to see her?"

Archer frowned. "Who?"

"Your mother."

His heart leapt to his throat. "My mother died twenty years ago."

The nun's eyes widened. Her hand shot to her mouth. "Is that what they told you?"

"What're you talking about?" Anger drilled into his voice.

"Your mother. . . she didn't die. She slipped into a very dark place and never came back."

"No. No. You must be wrong." Archer reached for the wall, needing the support.

"She was no longer capable of looking after you, and the authorities took control. It all happened so quickly."

"Where is she?"

"She's here. But Archer, she's not the woman you remember."

"You don't want to know how I remember her."

"Archer." Rosalina reached for his arm, but he yanked it back.

"Don't. You don't know what I've been through. She's dead. I was *told* she was dead. I thought I was an orphan and now. . . I find out she's alive. Don't tell me how to react!" He squeezed his thumbs to his temples.

Mother Maria clasped her hands in front of her chest. "Oh Archer, no. She's not dead. She's here. Alive." Although her eyes were filled with dread, she looked and sounded completely calm. "But I need to prepare you, Archer. She hasn't spoken in nearly twenty years. You have to understand, she suffered greatly after what happened."

"*She* suffered? So did I!" He swallowed hard, biting back fury.

Mother Maria nodded with heavy eyes. "I will take you."

As he followed the nun through a series of corridors deep into the ancient convent, he tried to organize his thoughts. But all he had were questions. None of this made sense.

Mom can't be alive. She must be wrong.

They arrived at a large wooden door and Mother Maria placed her hand on his shoulder. "Be gentle with her."

The nun opened the door, and Archer followed her into the room. A frail woman sat upon a small bed nestled against a wall. Archer didn't recognize her until she looked at him. Her eyes had lost their sparkle, shrouded in eternal sorrow, but there was no mistaking this woman was his mother.

"Helen, you have a visitor."

Helen rose from the bed, and when her dress fell into place, Archer cringed at her pale skin shriveled around shrunken muscles. He reached for her, afraid she was too frail to walk, and his fingers wrapped right around her bicep. Archer slid his arm around her waist and led her back to the bed. He sat beside her with his words frozen in his throat.

What do I say?

She looked at him and deep within her eyes, he saw recognition. Her pale lips parted. Her sad eyes widened. "Archer?"

Mother Maria gasped and Rosalina reached for the nun's hand.

Rosalina and Mother Maria backed out of the room and closed the door.

Archer wrapped his arms around his mother's frail shoulders and held her to his chest. "I'm here, Mom. I'm here."

Archer could no longer be angry with his mother. She'd suffered, too.

He fought threatening tears but was unable to contain them when a single tear trickled down his mother's sunken cheek.

Once again, his life was thrown into turmoil.

But this time, he wasn't walking away without all the answers.

Chapter Thirty-Five

A cocktail of anger and shock raced through Rosalina as she tried to understand how someone could lie to Archer about his mother being dead. Especially when he had already been through so much horror after his father's shocking death.

She frowned at the nun seated opposite her. "How did they get away with such terrible lies?"

Mother Maria lowered her eyes. "We may have made it easier for them, I'm afraid. By taking Helen in, they only had to look after Archer. As far as they were concerned, Helen was already gone."

Rosalina recalled Archer's confession in the glow-worm cave weeks ago. "He doesn't have much memory from that time, but he remembers the authorities were unsure what to do with him. For years, they shipped him from one home to the next."

"Oh, poor Archer." Mother Maria clutched her chest. "We assumed he was with family."

"No. There was no one else."

The silence between them thickened the air.

The elderly nun took a deep breath and let it out slowly. "Helen was already sick by the time Archer came out of hospital, but after he was taken away, we almost lost her several times. Some of those times were by her own hand." She twisted her fingers into knots and stared at them as if they weren't her own. "She would spend hours and hours simply sitting at his grave."

Rosalina took a moment to register what she'd said. "Whose grave?"

"Oh, my." Mother Maria covered her mouth, and as Rosalina stared into the older woman's eyes, she feared they were going to succumb to tears. But the nun blinked them back before she spoke. Her shoulders sagged even deeper. "Archer's father is buried here."

Rosalina sighed. "We've been looking for his grave."

"The grave is in a beautiful spot. Helen often sits there looking out to sea. Lost in her own world."

How will Archer cope with this new information?

His entire childhood was a concoction of lies. But then, what sort of life would he have had living with a mother who was no longer sane? Wade had died in a truly horrific way and after what Helen had seen, it wasn't surprising she'd dealt with it the way she did. "How does she communicate?"

"She doesn't, really. She stopped writing in her journals about a year after Archer was taken away and she stopped talking soon after that. Her world is consumed with her inner torment."

"What does she do all day?"

"We make her join us for breakfast and dinner. And sometimes she sits with us and does needlework, but mostly she stares out at sea as if searching for something."

"Maybe she's found what she's looking for?"

The nun blinked. "Archer?"

Rosalina nodded.

ARCHER HELD ONTO HIS MOTHER FOR A LONG TIME. BARELY A WORD was spoken. All his questions could wait, and now he wasn't sure she'd have the answers, anyway. If the authorities had lied to him, then there was every chance they'd lied to her, too.

He helped her lay back on the bed, and she drifted to sleep. He tucked the sheet under her arm and kissed her forehead.

Leaving her to rest, he shut the door and by the time he returned to the kitchen, he was mentally and physically drained. Rosalina wrapped her arms around him. He squeezed her to his chest and his thumping heartbeat pounded in his ears. "Mom's sleeping now."

"Did she say any more?" Mother Maria asked.

"No."

"Archer, there's something else." Rosalina stepped back and looked up at him. Her chin dimpled and the worry in her eyes deepened. "Your father's grave is here."

Archer huffed out a breath and closed his eyes. He never believed they'd actually find his grave, so he'd never prepared for it. He should be overwhelmed with sorrow; strangely though, he felt at ease.

Maybe it was time…

"Do you want me to come with you?" Rosalina pleaded with her eyes.

Archer was crippled with turmoil, unable to move. Rosalina clutched his hand and led him behind Mother Maria. They arrived at the end of a gravel path, stepped onto a large grassy field, and Mother Maria pointed to the top of the hill. "I'll leave you two alone."

Archer squeezed Rosalina's hand, seeking reassurance. Finding his father's grave had always seemed an impossible dream. Now, with each step he took towards the headstone, drops of sorrow pooled in his heart.

The father he remembered was vibrant, full of life, capturing every experience with gusto and driving his wife crazy with his boyish enthusiasm.

Would seeing his grave change all that?

Twenty-two tombstones occupied the gravesite, and they quickly found the headstone they were looking for. A white marble cross marked its place, and the inscription read:

Wade Thomas Mahoney
Feb 16th 1961 - June 14th 1992
Husband and father.
A man who knew how to live.
May Heaven be as exciting!

ARCHER BRUSHED AWAY STRAY BLADES OF GRASS AT THE BASE OF THE marble and sat beside the headstone. Rosalina settled next to him and drew her knees to her chest. He draped his arm over her shoulder and stared into the sunset.

The view was truly magnificent. Beyond the luscious green field, the scene took in the entire town of Skala and almost three quarters of Patmos Island. The surrounding waters were still a vibrant blue, despite the fiery setting sun. Many islands dotted the ocean. Some showed signs of occupation. Others were a jumble of green vegetation and white cliffs.

He could picture his mother sitting in this very spot, staring out over the ocean, day after day. "I've wasted years hating her."

"You didn't know the truth."

"She was hurting so bad. I never stopped my hate long enough to consider what she went through. What she saw would've sent anyone crazy."

"It would have been horrible."

Just before the sun completely absorbed into the horizon, Archer and Rosalina used its final rays to help them find their way back to the kitchen. Mother Maria was waiting for them, with the floral bag propped on the table like a grand trophy.

Archer didn't want to open the bag at the convent, so they said their goodbyes with promises to return soon. They began their walk down the steep, winding road, both quietly contemplating the last couple of hours. The full moon popped up and provided ample light to guide them.

"So, what do we do now?" They were nearly halfway down the road before Rosalina spoke.

He was surprised she'd waited that long.

There was only one thing to do. "We finish what we started. What Dad started. We find the treasure. He would've wanted that."

She smiled, and the glow from the moonlight made her look even more beautiful. He was grateful Rosalina had been there to share today with him, and the overwhelming current of desire he had for her was now even greater.

But he had to wait. Rosalina would tell him when she was ready.

A car pulled over, and the matronly woman behind the wheel offered them a lift. They accepted and arrived at the beach a short while later.

As Archer stepped from the vehicle, Jimmy's laugh drifted to him. The raspy, deep-throated cackle was unmistakable, and by the sound of it, Jimmy had a few drinks under his belt. But the laughter made everything seem normal again.

Jimmy, Alessandro, and Ginger were still seated at the same table. A dozen bottles cluttered the checkered cloth, and by their boisterous chatter and garbled speech, they'd all had more than their fair share of liquor.

Alessandro could barely sit up. Jimmy and Ginger were debating something, and it was near impossible to follow Ginger's slurred words. Jimmy, however, seemed to manage, and was still topping up their drinks.

Jimmy's eyes bulged when he saw Archer. "Hey, 'bout bloody time you got here. Where you been, man?" Jimmy filled another couple of glasses and held them up for Rosalina and Archer.

"It's a long story. Tell you tomorrow." Archer accepted the glass but had no intention of drinking just yet. He needed to return this lot to *Evangeline* first.

Rosalina sat beside Alessandro, and he leaned into her ear. "I really like Ginger." He was loud enough they all heard.

Rosalina giggled. "That's great, Alessandro."

He raised his bushy eyebrows. "You're not mad?"

"No, I'm happy for you."

"Oh." He swayed towards Ginger and she caught him before he fell off the chair.

"Have you guys eaten?" Archer asked.

"Nope. We were waitin' for you," Jimmy said.

"I think we better order before you all pass out." Archer reached for Rosalina's hand and they went inside to order. When they were out of earshot, he said, "I'll wait till tomorrow to tell them everything."

"Good idea. I don't think they'll remember much of tonight, anyway."

Back at the table, Archer fended off Jimmy's enquiries about his afternoon by topping up his drink and relaying stories of their days back in Australia. The pizzas arrived and were devoured in minutes.

The moon was high in the sky when Archer called it a night.

Alessandro tried to stand, staggered sideways and fell into a seat at a different table.

Ginger giggled, and the Italian burst out laughing.

It was going to be a long walk back to the jetty.

Alessandro had trouble putting one foot in front of the other, and Ginger wasn't much better. Between the two of them, they spent as much time on the path as they did in the sand. But their infectious laughter confirmed they were having fun, and it was impossible not to laugh with them.

They were only halfway back to the yacht when Jimmy must have had enough, as he tossed Alessandro over his shoulder and marched ahead. Alessandro's meagre attempt to fight him off was short-lived, and he either fell asleep or passed out. He looked like a sack of potatoes over Jimmy's shoulder and Ginger trailed behind them like a little lost puppy.

Once they were aboard *Evangeline*, Archer placed the floral bag beside the sofa, away from view, and Jimmy carried Alessandro to his room. Archer and Rosalina were seated at the bar when Jimmy returned.

"Don't think we'll see much of him tomorrow." Jimmy looked as if he could flop into bed, too.

"You guys seemed to have fun," Rosalina said.

Jimmy nodded. "Yeah, they're good people. Where'd you go? The way you shot outta there, thought you must've shit your pants."

Archer huffed. "Just some business to attend to. I'll tell you about it in the morning."

"Afternoon!" Jimmy snorted. "I'll be sleeping in tomorrow, so don't even think about waking me early."

Archer chuckled. "Right. Got it."

"Did you see where Ginger went?" Jimmy asked.

Rosalina shrugged. "To her room, I guess."

"She's got the hots for Alex." There was no malice in Jimmy's comment.

"I'd say it's mutual," Rosalina said.

"Lucky bastard." Jimmy knew when his match was met. "Right. See you tomorrow."

"Night, Jimmy."

Jimmy left and Rosalina pointed at the floral bag. "Do you want to have a look?"

"Not tonight. I'm exhausted."

She placed her hand on his leg and let her fingers trail down his inner thigh. "Not too exhausted, I hope." She ran her tongue over her bottom lip.

Her breasts rose and fell with each breath, and when her gaze fell to his lips, his desire to kiss her took over. Their lips touched, and she returned the kiss so tenderly that when a groan tumbled from her throat, it took all his might not to make love to her right there.

Her lips parted and their tongues met in a delicious dance. He absorbed her scent, her touch, her sounds. It was a kiss that said a thousand words.

Archer surrendered to the desire burning through him. He scooped Rosalina off her chair and she wrapped her arms around his neck, squeezing tight. Her hot breath brushed his ear and the throb in his groin pounded like a jackhammer.

He switched off the lights as they left each room. Archer paused outside his room and pulled back. "Your room or mine?"

Her eyes were a seductive haze. "Mine."

In four long strides, he was at her door. After closing the door behind him, he reached for the control panel and with the tap of a few buttons, the blinds lowered and the lights dimmed.

He placed one knee on the bed and gently eased her onto the covers. Her dress fell to the side, revealing her long, golden legs. Every thumping heartbeat made Archer want her more.

Placing his palm on the bed on either side of her legs, he lowered to clutch the soft fabric of her dress in his hand. As he crawled up her body, tugging the dress from her, her breathing deepened and she wriggled beneath him, allowing the dress to be free and he flung it aside.

When he was directly above her, his face mere inches from hers, their eyes locked. Her lips pouted as if plump with desire and when her lips parted a fraction, heat surged to every part of his body.

"Kiss me, baby," she said.

He didn't need to be asked twice. When their lips met, he inhaled her familiar scent of vanilla and citrus and tasted the sweetness of her tongue. Her throaty moans mingled with his, convincing him she wanted this as much as he did.

She was ready.

He slid off her to one side, and she reached behind her back to unclip her bra. It was off in a flash and cast aside.

He cupped her full breast, welcoming the weight into his palm, and her sigh of pleasure had his groin hardening more. He eased down to sample her nipple, and she ran her fingers through his hair, pulling him upon her, arching her back to meet him, urging him on.

Knowing she wanted him drove him crazy with lust.

Caressing her breast after all these months was like capturing a slice of heaven. Everything about her was heaven. . . her touch, her smell, her luscious body. He wanted to ravish Rosalina, to satisfy her pleasures.

Her hands glided beneath his T-shirt and were warm on his chest and soft against his hardened nipples. He gasped when she pinched his nipple and the look in her eyes matched the deep passion burning within him. He tore off his shirt and she sucked his nipple, first one, then the other.

She fell backward and a lock of her hair curled upon her right breast, tantalizingly hiding it. But Rosalina hid nothing. She was an open book, every emotion was expressed and now, finally, he was ready to show her his raw feelings, too.

He stood, tugged his jeans off, and tossed them aside. Then, resisting the urge to tear her knickers from her body, he instead tugged them down inch by inch. As her eyes followed his movements, desire shimmered in her pale blue irises.

She threw her arms back, and her breasts wobbled their own luscious dance. Her pants released and his breath hitched when she wrapped her long legs around him, skin to skin. He'd waited far too long for this moment and he pulled back, savoring her gloriousness.

She whispered his name as if he were an apparition, and her voice was seductive velvet that nearly drove him over the edge again. He drew her closer, but she winced when his hand passed over her bruise.

He'd completely forgotten about that. "Oh, babe." He eased back to look.

But she cupped his cheek, drawing his eyes to hers. "It's okay, don't worry." She planted kisses along his shoulder, making the hairs on his neck rise to meet her.

He guided his hand down her flat stomach, pausing for a moment at her perfect navel before he plunged his finger inside her.

A hot breath tumbled from her lips as her eyes glazed over, lost in the moment.

Archer had to concentrate to contain himself as he brought out her sweet arousal. "Come on, baby."

"Oh, Archer." Rosalina climaxed with a primal gasp, and her body shuddered with release.

She was still gasping for breath when he cupped her breast again and rolled his tongue over her peaked bud.

Rosalina pulled him onto the bed, and he flopped onto his back to face her. She kneeled at the end of the bed between his spread legs. Her body glistened in the dim lights, glowing golden. Her hair fell in cascading auburn locks that tickled his skin as she moved down his body with a combination of nibbling, sucking and kissing.

She sat back and glided her hands in slow sweeping movements up his thighs. The sensation was incredible. Every nerve ending followed the tips of her fingers. "Do you have a condom?"

He did a double take. *Do I?*

It'd been so long since he'd needed one. Dashing out the door naked, he ran to his room and commando rolled over his bed to the nightstand. He returned to Rosalina with a row of foil packets dangling from his hand. He tore one open with his teeth and rolled the condom on with trembling fingers.

She did that to him. She drove him wild.

"Make love to me, Archer." Her words were a throaty whisper.

Archer climbed on top of her and guided himself into her hot zone. Savoring every inch, he went slowing at first, until he filled her completely. He wanted this moment to last forever, and it took momentous self-control to keep it slow.

She cupped his cheek and when her finger slipped into his mouth, he lost all his willpower. Archer thrust into her over and over, making love to the woman who captured his soul.

When Rosalina orgasmed again, he reached the moment of no return. He thrust into her, riding a climax that was nearly a year in the making.

She took him to the moon and back.

His arms trembled when he collapsed onto her chest and rolled to the side. As his breathing returned to normal, he ran his hands over her body, exploring every luxurious curve.

Her body was perfection.

But she was more than that; she was the woman he loved, the woman he wanted to spend the rest of his life with. She was everything, and she deserved everything from him. His heart. His soul. His love.

All the jumbled pieces of his life were finally in their rightful place. . . a treasured luxury that had escaped him for a very long time.

As tiny waves lapped at the side of the yacht, he draped his arm over Rosalina's waist. "I love you." It was wonderful to say it aloud.

But she was already breathing deeply, and for the second time, he couldn't tell if she'd heard him.

Or maybe she had heard him, but she wasn't ready to repeat it back to him yet.

Chapter Thirty-Six

Rosalina woke nestled within the crook of Archer's arm. His steady breathing was reassurance that he'd made it through the night without a nightmare.

Had the recent events finally cured him?

Only time would tell.

Waking up next to him, inhaling his unique scent, listening to the therapeutic beat of his heart and feeling the smoothness of his skin was like waking up in a perfect dream.

It was raining outside. She couldn't remember the last time it had rained, and nature's soothing melody combined with waking up in Archer's arms made her sigh with content.

The last thing she wanted to do was move, but she couldn't ignore the pins and needles in her arm any longer. She carefully tried to ease out of Archer's embrace.

"Where do you think you're going?" His voice was a sexy baritone.

"Sorry, I didn't mean to wake you."

"I've been awake for a while. It was nice listening to you sleeping beside me."

"What time is it?"

"Nearly eight o'clock."

"Do you think anyone else is up?"

"I don't think we'll see anyone until after lunch." He rolled onto his side to face her and placed his hand just under her breast. "Did you know the sound of rain makes me horny?"

"Really?" She kissed him, just a sweet brush of their lips. "You've never mentioned that before."

A cute grin curled on his lips. "I like to keep some things up my sleeve."

"No more secrets, remember?"

"Never again." He gathered her into his arms, and they made love to the therapeutic harmony of the morning rain.

Afterward, as Rosalina showered, her mind drifted to their love-making. Ever since their reunion in Tuscany, she'd fought to contain her lust for him. She had hoped to resist him for longer.

But after she'd watched him completely unravel emotionally yesterday, she couldn't control herself. She wanted him more than ever. Their lovemaking was magical, as usual, but there was something even more special about last night.

It was like he'd finally let her have a piece of his heart.

She toweled off, tied her hair in a quick bun and tossed on a maxi dress. Her choice of earrings for today were a pair of dangling pink shells that Archer had bought her from a beach seller in Thailand. It had been a magical day on the beach, filled with fun and laughter, and they'd purchased as many cocktails in coconuts as they did cheap trinkets. The earrings were the perfect match for how she was feeling right now.

She walked towards the kitchen with thoughts of preparing breakfast, but stopped short. Archer was at the dining table. His back was straight with his left hand on the floral bag. Severe contemplation was etched on his face.

The silent stillness was unnatural; even the boat had stopped rocking. With everything else that happened yesterday, she'd forgotten about that bag.

What it contained could shatter the reverie she'd experienced just moments ago, and her choice of earrings now felt foolish. But

Archer was counting on her to help him get through this. So, the only way to deal with it was to keep with her upbeat vibes. Her dress billowed around her legs as she strode into the room.

She kissed Archer on the forehead. "Before you get stuck into that, how about a breakfast to die for?" She cringed at her choice of words and tried to mask it by kissing his forehead again.

"That'd be nice."

"Is there something special you'd like?"

"Are there any blueberries? We could have pancakes."

"Pancakes it is then." She set about making a fresh pot of coffee, and as she rummaged about the cupboards for the pancake ingredients, she kept an eye on Archer. He didn't seem sad. He looked more bewildered. Rosalina made the pancake batter and set it aside to rest, then filled two mugs with steaming coffee and sidled up next to him.

"Do you want help?"

He drove his fingers through his unruly curls, that were more haphazard than usual today. She recalled running her fingers through his hair during this morning's lovemaking and had to force back a smile.

Finally, Archer released a sigh and nodded.

She tried to ignore his forlorn look and, determined to remain positive, placed the bag on the table and reached in. First, she removed several leather-bound black diaries, each wrapped with a thin leather strap. She stacked them, counting them as she went. Eight diaries in total.

Rosalina expected Archer to reach for them. Any movement right now would be good, but he didn't move.

A brass object was the next item she removed. A compass; the kind with two pointed ends and a scalloped knob at the top. She placed it on the table and, to her relief, Archer reached for it. He planted one point on the table and slowly spun it around.

Finally, he spoke. "I wonder if this was Dad's."

"I bet it was."

The next item was a small pair of Olympus binoculars that Archer adjusted to his face, and then scanned out the kitchen window. He huffed and then dangled the binoculars around his neck by the strap.

Rosalina removed a series of notepads. The quality of these notebooks paled in comparison to the leather-bound diaries. The edges were ragged as if from repeated handling, the corners curled up, and pages had been ripped out.

Archer picked one up and flicked through it. The writing was erratic, childish even. "These are Dad's notes. His writing was this crazy scrawl." He chuckled. "Mom used to complain about his notes, and she constantly joked that he should've been a doctor."

Rosalina smiled. Archer was remembering good times for a change.

She reached for a different notepad, flicked the pages over, and paused on a hand-drawn map. In the right-hand corner was a directional compass indicating the north. The rest of the page had drawings of islands with lines linking them together.

"What are these lines all over the map?"

Archer ran his finger over one line. "They're shipping lanes." He turned to the preceding pages. "Says here, it's a map of the Cyclades Islands. Oh, look, here are the first three islands we visited, Andros, Tinos and Mykonos."

"Why did he draw them? Surely, he could've downloaded a picture off the web."

Archer lowered his eyes, frowning, as if searching deep within his memory. "It was the early nineties. The Internet wasn't really around then. Actually, I can't recall Dad ever having a computer."

"Oh, right. So strange to think about."

Archer nodded. "He recorded everything he researched in these notebooks. I don't think these are all of them. He kept dozens of these pads on our boat. I wonder if the others are lying around somewhere."

"Maybe your mother thought these were the most important."

Archer flicked over a couple more pages and came across a drawing of an ancient ship. "Holy shit!"

"What?"

"He's drawn a boat. Look, he's written *Flying Seahorse* under it." He turned the book towards Rosalina.

"The same one Yanis mentioned? Oh, wow. Look at how much detail is in the drawing."

The ship was penciled with light strokes that pulled the details of the intricate sketch together. Two enormous sails filled most of the page. Ropes linked the sails to the large wooden hull. Large oars, manhandled by detailed little men, touched the water with small penciled-in splashes. The aft was adorned with a platform that looked like a miniature castle.

The writing beneath the ship described it as a *thirteenth century cog*.

"What would this have been for?" Rosalina pointed at the castle-like structure.

"They used them as a lookout point, watching for pirates and warships."

Rosalina cocked her head, debating over whether he made that up. But his serious look gave her the impression he knew what he was talking about.

"His drawings are elaborate. Your father was quite an artist."

"Huh, I don't remember that about him. I recall him as a fearless, muscular man who never sat still. He drove Mom crazy with his energy. Yet when he was onto something, he'd spend hours in these books, writing every detail. Look at how he drew the oar plowing through the water, the detail in the splashes. You can really picture the boat powering along."

"It's amazing."

Below the drawing was a series of facts about the boat: its length, tonnage and how it was built with oak caulked with tarred moss and wooden laths secured by metal staples.

Archer turned the page to another drawing of the ship. This one was an examination of its interior. It showed a cross-section of the hull, detailing the flush-laid flat bottom of the midship crammed with crates of cargo.

"Do you have any photos of your dad?" Rosalina would love to know what Wade looked like.

"No. None." He sighed loudly. "Hey, keep looking. Maybe there are some in there."

She reached into the bag and removed a stack of envelopes bundled together with a white satin ribbon. Somehow, she knew these would be the letters Mother Maria had mentioned.

Archer eyed the bundle as she placed them on the table, but didn't reach for them.

He breathed in deeply and let his breath out slowly. "I'll look at those later. What else is in the bag?"

Rosalina was grateful for this decision. Going through the items in the bag was difficult enough, but the idea of reading through his mother's grief-stricken letters sliced another layer of sorrow from her heart.

She delved back into the bag. The next item she removed was a sheet of paper that had been folded down to A4 size. She handed it to Archer and he unraveled it to reveal another hand-drawn map. "It's a map of the Greek Islands." He slid his finger along a line. "I wonder if this was the path the *Flying Seahorse* took?"

Rosalina reached into the bag and sucked in her breath at the sight of the next item.

"What?" Archer had seen her reaction.

She tried to ignore her trembling fingers as she removed a silver frame. It reflected the bright morning sun as she passed it to Archer. Inside the frame was a picture of Wade and Helen. The photo was in pristine condition for its age, not a hint of yellowing or fading. Being sealed in this bag for all those years had preserved it well.

In the photo, Wade wore all white, his trousers were rolled up, and he stood ankle deep in crystal-clear water. Helen was in his arms, also in white. Her long, flowing dress almost touched the water. Sand on the exotic, deserted beach in the background glowed with the pure energy of the setting sun, and palm trees stood majestic and proud along the length of the foreshore.

The picture was enchanting, but it was the look on their faces that captured Rosalina's interest. They were in love. The photo could have been taken on their wedding day.

Archer stared open-mouthed at the picture. With his thumb, he wiped a fine layer of dust from the glass.

Rosalina battled the knot in her throat. "They're a beautiful couple. Have you seen this photo before?"

"No. Well, I guess I may have. But I don't remember. They look so happy." Archer clipped out a stand at the back of the frame and sat the picture on the table. Helen and Wade smiled at them with naïve matrimonial bliss. "What else is in there?"

Rosalina needed a minute to compose herself. "How about I get our pancakes on the go?"

"I'm not hungry anymore." He reached for her forearm, urging her to stay seated. Her chin dimpled and she tugged on her lip attempting to stop it quivering.

"Oh, babe." He pulled her to his chest, and her tears flowed. "It's okay. This is good. Actually. . . it's incredible. My parents were dead, both physically and in my memory. Now, not only is my mother still alive, but Dad is coming alive through these things. I can't believe how much I forgot."

"It's still so sad."

"Yes, but it's also wonderful. It's like Dad is speaking to me from the grave, telling me to keep his legacy alive." He gathered one of Wade's notebooks. "He's practically pointing the way to the *Flying Seahorse*."

Rosalina choked back tears and dried her eyes with the back of her finger. "I'll get more coffee." She picked up their mugs and headed to the galley.

At the sink, she rinsed the cups and dabbed cool water on her face. Her entire childhood and well into her adulthood, she'd had the luxury of being surrounded by an abundance of family. Four generations of the Calucci family had always lived within walking distance of each other.

Imagining the emptiness Archer must've felt after the loss of his parents tied a heavy knot in her stomach. Guilt-ridden, she vowed to ring her family later and tell them how much she loved them. With that positive notion, she topped up the coffees and placed a couple of yesterday's pistachio and white chocolate cookies on a plate.

But each step she took back to the dining table added another layer of anxiety. She put the brimming coffee mugs on the table, placed the cookies to the side and took up her seat again.

Archer was focused on the floral bag but his eyes were laced with anxiety.

After an awkward silence, she sighed loudly and reached into the bag. She removed several more notepads, a couple more maps, a random collection of bar coasters, an assortment of paperwork and two hardcover books, which, judging by the number of sticky notes plastered through them, were well read.

She read out the titles. "*Treasure Hunt: Shipwreck, Diving, and the Quest for Treasure in an Age of Heroes*, and *Ships & Guns*."

Archer fingered the covers but didn't reach for either of them.

When it became obvious Archer wasn't interested in opening them, Rosalina looked back into the bag. The last item crushed her heart. It was a photo album, maroon, leather-bound, with gold-trimmed corners and a picture centered in the middle of a classic style motor yacht with polished teak trimming. Archer swallowed loudly when she placed it on the table.

"Was that your dad's boat?"

All Archer did was nod.

Rosalina gripped onto her coffee mug with both hands, hoping the warm liquid would ease the chill in her stomach. It was almost a full minute before Archer reached for the album and turned the front cover. The first page was a large photo of a baby in a crib.

Rosalina gasped. "Is that you?"

Archer shrugged. "I guess so."

As he turned each leaf, the baby in the first photo grew a little older. The album was dedicated to Archer's childhood — photos of him as a baby, a toddler, a small child and a grown boy. Pictures of him enjoying life like any seafaring child did, playing in the sand, swimming at the beach, chasing soldier crabs with a stick, fishing, kayaking, snorkeling, scuba diving, and many more.

Just about every photo included either his mother or father, always bursting with pride.

Archer stopped at a picture of himself fishing with his mom and began wringing his hands, practically strangling his fingers. Rosalina's heart crushed when he sucked back a sob. She wrapped her arms around his shoulders in an attempt to absorb his trembling.

"Mom must've made this for me." He could barely speak, fighting back the tears. "She wanted me to remember what our life was like."

"It's wonderful, Archer. You finally know how fantastic your parents and your childhood were."

"I'm an idiot. I wasted all those years hating Mom."

"No, you didn't. You had no idea."

"Of course I did. How could I have forgotten all this?"

"You saw a shark attack your father. How you recovered from that is a miracle. You probably suffered post-traumatic stress. And after what they did, telling you your mother was dead. . . they should be punished for not getting you the proper help you needed. Nobody should go through what you did."

Archer ran his finger over a photo of him and his father wearing scuba diving gear. His father's arm was draped over his shoulder and he was grinning like an excited thrill seeker. "I remember this." He let out a long, slow breath. "It's. . . it's the day Dad died." A tear slid down his cheek and Rosalina wiped it away. "I bet him I'd find the treasure first."

"You can make up for lost time by getting to know your mother."

"I know. It's so strange. I feel like I've been given a second chance."

Rosalina curled her hand across the back of his neck. "I guess in a way you have."

"*Buongiorno*." Alessandro stepped into the room and both Rosalina and Archer jumped.

"Good morning," Rosalina said.

Archer flipped the photo album closed and pushed it away. "I didn't think you'd be up until after lunch."

Alessandro still wore his clothes from last night and his sickly pale skin was a hint that he might throw up at any moment. He squinted against the bright morning sun as he approached the table.

"I don't feel very well."

"You look like shit too," Archer said.

"*Grazie*. Is Jimmy up yet?"

"We haven't seen Jimmy or Ginger," Rosalina said. "But they were just as happy as you were last night."

Alessandro crumbled into a seat next to Archer and dropped his forehead on the table. Rosalina laughed as she moved to the kitchen to make another coffee.

"I've seen Ginger." Alessandro sat his chin on the back of his hands.

"Where?" Rosalina asked.

He groaned. "She was in my bed when I woke up."

Archer slapped him on the shoulder. "You old devil."

"I'm sorry, Rosa." He turned to her, his eyes the picture of an apology.

Rosalina waved her hand. "You don't need to apologize. You told me last night how much you liked her."

Alessandro deflated even more. "I did? Did Jimmy hear?"

"I'm sure he did. You were very loud." She'd never seen Alessandro that drunk before; he'd always remained in control. Maybe it was a good thing that he'd let loose last night. Even if he was paying for it now. It was as if he was discovering himself, too. Maybe this trip was what everyone needed.

Alessandro grumbled. "Jimmy's not going to be happy."

"Jimmy's all right, Alessandro," Rosalina said. "It's pretty clear Ginger feels the same way about you."

"Really? You think so?"

"I know so." Rosalina placed the steaming mug before him and ruffled his hair. "She was all over you last night."

Alessandro grinned sheepishly, and when a flush of red washed over his cheeks, he looked even more ill. He sat back and reached for the mug. "What are you doing?" His eyes were on the large map on the table.

"It's a long story. Why don't you have a shower and freshen up?" Rosalina said. "When Ginger and Jimmy wake up, we'll tell you all together."

Alessandro seemed to have a mental fight with himself, but eventually he stood and with shaking fingers, gripped his coffee and shuffled from the room.

Once Alessandro had gone, Archer opened the photo album again. At the last page, his frown grew even deeper. The final photo was of a small baby in a long pink christening gown.

"They christened you in pink?" But she realized this wasn't a photo of Archer. This little baby, with plump lips and wisps of blonde hair, looked like a girl.

Archer peeled back the clear plastic protective sheet and removed the photo. He turned it over and gasped. On the back of the photo was written *"Evangeline Anne Mahoney, 9 August 1978–18 August 1978"*.

"I had a sister?" A frown drilled across Archer's forehead.

"She only lived for nine days."

"That was a year before I was born. They never spoke of her."

"Maybe they did." She touched his arm. "It can't be a coincidence that you named your yacht *Evangeline*."

Archer rubbed his chin, scratching at his one-day growth and she saw the trouble brewing just beneath his usually smiling eyes.

She just hoped this treasure hunt ended the way Archer wanted it to.

If not, they were destined for some very emotional times.

Chapter Thirty-Seven

S everal hours, and several batches of blueberry pancakes later, Archer and everyone else, sat around the cleared table. Yet Archer was struggling with the overload of information from the items in the floral bag. It was surreal to enjoy breakfast and rehash their fun last night, when he was trying to piece together how to tell them about his bullshit childhood.

Rosalina was the only one who knew everything. Jimmy had heard bits and pieces over the years, but not anything of significance.

His father's things were now back in the floral bag at his feet. Archer reached for the photo album on the top and flicked the pages over to the photo taken just hours before his life turned to crap.

"See this photo?" He turned the album and held it so they could all see. "This was taken 14th of June, 1992, about an hour before my dad was killed."

Alessandro's eyes bulged, then he looked at Rosalina as if expecting her to say Archer was joking.

Archer ignored it. "How he died and what happened after that is something I've been hiding from my whole life."

"Not all of it's your fault," Rosalina said.

"Shhh, Rosa." He scowled. "Do you want me to tell this or not?"

"Yes. But don't be so damn harsh on yourself, Archer Mahoney." Her smile was sassy and damn sexy.

He cocked his head at her and waited for her smile to cut back a notch before he continued. "Dad was convinced we were diving in the location of an ancient wreck. We'd already spent weeks scouring the area, but his confidence was unwavering. The water that morning was crystal clear, flat as a bathtub and as warm as one too."

He tried to organize his thoughts, making sure he told the story exactly as it happened. The others silently sipped their coffee. Their calmness suggested they had no idea of the shitstorm he was about to tell them.

"We jumped overboard and followed the anchor line down to the ocean bottom, then along a coral shelf. We were in an area coated in coral, and Dad's belief was that an old shipwreck was the catalyst for the growth."

Archer laughed. "God, if I believed that, I'd be dropping overboard every twenty minutes, expecting to find shipwrecks."

Jimmy chuckled with him.

"Anyway, we scoured the area for forty minutes and found nothing. But I was convinced we were onto something." He shook his head. "I was an eleven-year-old kid sold on the idea of finding treasure. Giving up wasn't an option. I knew we were running out of time, but I deliberately swam away from Dad, poking and prodding everything. Dad had warned me about the dangers of doing that, but I didn't stop."

"The visibility was amazing, about fifty yards. We came across a mountain of coral, hundreds of years old, and I broke off a piece. But when I pulled it away, it was attached to a chunk of wood. The shipwreck was right in front of us and we couldn't see it."

"Oh, wow. That'd be awesome." Ginger rubbed her hands and inched forward.

"Dad and I celebrated a little, but he then signaled it was time to surface. But after finding that wood, I wanted to keep going, and I swam away from him, forcing him to follow. I found a hole and pushed my arm in up to my shoulder. Dad just about choked on his regulator when he saw me. But then I came up with this." He reached for the pendant.

Jimmy huffed. "I always wondered where you got that ugly thing from."

Archer huffed right back at him. "But after that, everything went to shit."

Archer sucked a breath through his teeth. "Dad put this pendant into his buoyancy vest and we were high-fiving and stuff when a shark came along and ruined our day."

He was going to make light of it, but couldn't stop himself from delving into every gory detail. It was like it'd happened yesterday. He remembered everything from before the attack and what had happened after. Parts of his life that he'd completely wiped from his memory were suddenly completely vivid.

Ginger and Rosalina flicked away tears, Alessandro looked on the verge of throwing up and Jimmy kept swallowing hard. Archer paused to let them all settle and grabbed a couple of beers from the fridge.

He returned with a six-pack and Jimmy reached for it like it was a life-saving device. The big fella snapped a bottle from the pack and handed one to Archer. Archer twisted the top off his Corona and sipped at the bitter nectar. It tasted good. Too bloody good for this time of the morning. By the look on Jimmy's face, he thought so too.

"I have a question." Alessandro scrunched his nose, like he didn't want to ask, but couldn't help himself. "How did you reclaim the pendant if it was in your dad's buoyancy vest?"

Rosalina shot Alessandro a death stare.

"They recovered some of Dad's. . . remains. Including half of his vest."

Alessandro's face paled. "Oh God, sorry. I didn't mean—"

"Good one, numbnuts." Jimmy grunted.

"It's okay. Ask me anything. I'd blocked out everything from my childhood, but after yesterday's events, I'm beginning to remember so much."

Jimmy cocked his head. "What happened yesterday?"

"I'm getting to that." For the next hour Archer detailed everything from his mother's death, to being shunted around orphanages until he was eighteen, and finally to Rosalina finding the pendant in the stained-glass window in the church.

Archer then told them about what had happened yesterday.

"Your mother's alive!" Jimmy bellowed.

Archer nodded.

Jimmy plonked his beer on the table. "Holy shit, man. Why the hell didn't she get in contact with you?"

Archer explained his mom's condition. Then he lifted the floral bag and spilled the contents onto the table. "The nuns gave me this bag full of Dad's things."

Archer shoved the envelope stack back into the bag as everyone else reached for something.

Jimmy spread out the large map of the islands and pointed out the shipping lines. "He was certainly trying to work out something."

"He was looking for the *Flying Seahorse* and as I just told you. . . we found it. But I can't for the life of me remember where we were. Somewhere in all of this are the clues to its whereabouts. And the treasure."

The energy in the room increased. Alessandro flipped through the notebooks as if a big *X* would mark the spot. Jimmy pored over the maps, Rosalina revisited the photo album, and Archer went through one of his mother's diaries.

"Can I ask a question?" Ginger said to nobody in particular. "I understand the maps, books, diaries, and drawings. But what I don't get is all these beer coasters. Why would he keep those?"

Archer flipped through the coasters, each one from a different taverna on a different island, and the answer hit him like a swinging boom on a racing yacht. "Give me that map. . . I need tape. Alessandro, grab a laptop. I need a pen, too."

After a flurry of activity, Archer had taped the large map to the window and Alessandro and Rosalina were ready with a laptop each.

"Here's what I think. Dad was tracing the path of the *Flying Seahorse*. He probably hopped from island to island, just like we did. He loved a cold beer at the end of the day. So, I'm guessing the coasters are souvenirs from each of the pubs he visited along the way. If we trace the pubs, we may find the path he took and, more importantly, which one was the last stop. That may be where we'll find the *Seahorse*."

"Brilliant." Ginger grinned like a drunk teenager.

"Okay, the first one is. . ." Rosalina selected a coaster at random. "Emborion Seaside Tavern on Milos Island."

By the time they finished, they had a line running from Kythira to Milos to Santorini to Anafi, with many smaller islands in between.

"We know the treasure came from Italy, so we can assume the ship's path was most likely this way." Archer ran his finger from the left to the right-hand side of the paper. "Which means. . . Dad's final pub was Captain Nikolas Taverna on Anafi Island."

It was a sobering thing to point at the small island to the right of Santorini, and wonder if that was the last island his dad ever enjoyed a beer on. "What do we know about Anafi?" He looked to Alessandro for the answer.

Alessandro's fingers attacked the keyboard. The Italian paused his typing to read. "Anafi has an area of only twenty-five miles squared. Current population, about five hundred people. Its history is fairly unknown as there has been a lack of archeological finds, although it's assumed this island was under Minoan and Cretan rule in the second millennium BC." He read in silence for a while. "Ahhh, this is interesting. In the thirteenth century, the Venetians arrived, and they ruled the island and its surroundings until the sixteenth century."

"That's promising," said Rosalina.

"I don't understand." Alessandro shook his head. "If your father wrote everything in these books, why didn't he write down where the *Seahorse* was?"

Everybody looked at Archer for the answer.

"Dad was paranoid about people finding out what he was doing. He was constantly telling me how important it was to keep everything a secret. Actually, it sort of explains one thing. . . his notebooks aren't written in any order. The notes are all over the place. It's like he chose any book or any page to begin writing. That's why there are loads of blank pages."

A silence fell over everyone.

"Anafi seems like a good place to start." Archer looked at Rosalina. She'd have an opinion; she always did. Not that he was complaining; he missed that when she wasn't around.

She nodded.

Jimmy raised his beer. "Anafi it is."

"Anafi." They cheered in unison with raised glasses.

Jimmy drained his beer. "So, we head there tomorrow. Then what?"

"I guess we start with the locals and see if they have any info that may help."

"Can I make a suggestion?" Ginger twisted her ponytail around her hand.

Archer nodded. "Of course."

"In that photo of you and your father?" She lowered her eyes. "You know, the one just before you dived."

"Yes, I know the one." Archer kept his tone neutral.

"Well, behind you and your dad, there's a weird formation of rocks. Maybe we could find them."

Archer reached for the album and flicked to the photo. He looked past the smiling faces to the background. Four large, rectangular rocks appeared to have been stacked on top of each other as if they'd once formed part of a wall.

Archer stood and kissed Ginger's forehead. "You're a genius."

Ginger grinned at Alessandro like a woman who'd just been proposed to. "I always did have a good eye for detail."

The distance between Patmos and Anafi was one hundred and fifty nautical miles, and it took nearly five hours to get there. The sun was slipping into the horizon when Archer released the anchor in an alcove west of the main port.

There was no point going ashore tonight. A sleepy little island like this one wasn't likely to have anything open at night anyway. Archer declared they would go ashore at first light.

Archer joined Jimmy and Alessandro at the table and each of them went through one of Wade's notebooks.

The notes in the book Archer flicked through were interesting and confusing at the same time. His father's scrawl deviated from rational thoughts to random scribble. Judging by Jimmy's grunts, he was experiencing the same with the book he had.

Alessandro, however, was as intense as a bulldog with a fresh bone, devouring every page like it was a stick of marrow.

From his position, Archer watched Rosalina and Ginger prepare dinner. They seemed to be working together like they'd been doing it for years.

That was a connection Archer never thought he'd see. Rosalina was pretty damn protective of her kitchen.

Dinner was served, and as soon as Ginger sat, she turned to Archer. "Archer, I know how you learned about the treasure and the *Flying Seahorse*, but how did your father figure it out?"

Archer shook his head. "I have no idea."

"I believe I can answer that." Alessandro rummaged through Wade's ragged notebooks. He flicked through the first one he picked up, then the second, and finally a third. "I know it's in here somewhere." He progressed through two more before he found what he was looking for.

"I came across this drawing of the *Seahorse* and your father has made this notation that he's underlined several times. It appears the captain of *Flying Seahorse* questioned why cotton bales weighed so much. Then he charged a priest extra to take the cargo on board."

Jimmy slapped his palm on the table, and everyone jumped. "The captain figured there wasn't just cotton in them bales."

Rosalina clicked her fingers. "Oh, I found a letter that may help. It was from a woman whose husband was a crew member of the *Seahorse*. Let me find it." Rosalina flicked through the loose sheets of paper until she came across a photocopy of a handwritten letter. The black and white copy had yellowed slightly, highlighting its age. The elegant handwriting filled most of the page.

"It reads:

MY DARLING ANASTASI, OUR BABY GROWS WITH THE STRENGTH OF AN ox, every day increasing the size of my belly. But my mind cannot ease. I know the extra coin is God given, however the priest you talked about haunts my dreams. I pray the wind is swift so the Seahorse *can complete her mission before our baby takes his first breath."*

ALESSANDRO'S EYES BULGED. "AGAIN, THERE'S MENTION OF A PRIEST aboard the *Seahorse.*"

Archer suppressed a laugh. The Italian scholar was as excited as a three-year-old in a sandpit.

"But wait. There's another letter." Rosalina took a minute to find the next letter.

"Here we go."

"MY DARLING ANASTASI, IT IS NOW FOUR MONTHS SINCE THE BIRTH OF our first son, and I have not named him yet in the hope that you would choose a good, strong name. But your delay has me fearful that our son may never see his father. I pray every day the Seahorse's *sails bring you to me."*

"THIS IS HOW YOUR FATHER KNEW THE *SEAHORSE* WAS MISSING AT sea." Alessandro's jaw dropped, showing his amazement.

Archer wasn't surprised, though. His father was a clever man and tenacious as hell. Once he got a whiff of something, he'd pursue it until he ran out of leads.

Ginger tried to stifle a yawn. "Sorry."

Archer looked at Rosalina. She, too, was struggling to keep her eyes open. "How about we get an early night?" he said. "Because tomorrow we're going treasure hunting."

"*Mi scusi*." Alessandro ran his hand down his neck. "I don't really want to mention this, but. . . aren't you worried about sharks?"

Everyone shot their gaze at Archer.

Archer had done extensive research about shark attacks in that region, and based on that research, he concluded that his dad was just plain unlucky.

He shook his head. "There are sharks in the Mediterranean. Forty-six different species. But shark attacks here are incredibly rare, less than one per year. Dad was the only person to have died of a shark attack in this region in the last thirty years. You've got more chance of being killed by a toaster."

"*Va bene*." Alessandro huffed. "I think I'll take my chances with a toaster."

As everyone chuckled, Archer couldn't shake the rotten feeling that sharks were the least of their worries.

Chapter Thirty-Eight

Nox stepped out of the grocery store and gazed across the Patmos marina toward Archer's yacht. It wasn't there. His heart jumped to his throat as he scanned the ocean, searching for the yacht he'd been following for days.

He spotted the *Evangeline* just past the last jetty.

Christ! I nearly missed them.

They took off fast. They must be onto something.

He ditched his parcels and raced back into the store. Brother Bonito was at the freezer, staring in a daze at tubs of gelato. Nox dug his fingers into the priest's thin arm. "Let's go." He yanked him towards the door.

Bonito looked at him with horror etched on his face. "What? Hey. You're hurting me."

"They're leaving. If we don't get to the boat now, we'll never find them."

Nox yanked Bonito outside, and forcing the pathetic priest in front of him, he ran as fast as he could down the steep hill.

Brother Bonito panted with heart-attack heaviness behind him as he ran along the foreshore. Ignoring the curious glances from everyone, he kept his eyes on the escaping *Evangeline*.

Nox was so lucky he'd come out of the grocery store when he did, otherwise Archer and the rest of those bastards would have vanished without a trace.

Even though the larger yacht could outpace his small speedboat, its enormous size also made it highly visible. If he lost sight of *Evangeline* again, he'd have to island hop until they located them again. Last time it had taken a week. It was time he didn't have.

As soon as he was on board his rented boat, he reached for the high-powered binoculars he'd also rented and scanned the horizon. *Evangeline* was a white dot in the distance. He noted her position and started the engine.

Brother Bonito scrambled onto the boat like an old cripple, and Nox shoved him forward "Untie us, you fool."

"Don't push me." Bonito's eyes flared with anger.

Nox didn't have time for this. "If we don't get after them right now, we'll never find them." He spoke through clenched teeth; it was all he could do to resist yelling at the pathetic man.

Brother Bonito didn't move.

"Did you see the way they took off? They're onto something. Which means we're *this* close to the treasure." He held his fingers an inch apart.

Brother Bonito still didn't move and Nox could almost see the debate raging in his mind.

Nox pushed past him. "Move! They're getting away."

The Lamberti fishing boat he'd hired provided camouflage amongst the other fishing vessels, but he regretted his choice. A faster speed boat would have been much more useful.

It was too late to lament on that now. He unhooked the ropes that attached them to the jetty, raced back to the cabin, started the engine, and slammed the throttle to full speed.

In his race to depart, he nearly plowed over a couple of fishermen in a small boat, and they hurled abuse as he motored past.

Seated beside him, Bonito's knuckles were bone white as he clutched at the railing. He looked like the trapped man he was. But his sudden bout of defiance was very untimely.

Nox reached for the binoculars again. The horizon was dotted with dozens of boats.

But *Evangeline* was gone.

"Shit!" He grabbed his dirty coffee mug from this morning and hurled it at the back of the boat. It shattered to pieces, pitching shards all over the place.

Brother Bonito blinked at him with wide darting eyes that proved he was petrified.

He should be. Nox was furious enough that he could kill him with his bare hands.

Instead, Nox fought that urge by gripping onto the steering wheel until his fingers ached. He couldn't eliminate Bonito. Not yet.

Hopefully, he wouldn't need the sniveling priest much longer.

But as the nautical miles cruised beneath his boat and he raised the binoculars over and over, Nox took a long time to admit defeat.

Archer was gone.

"Son of a bitch!" Nox screamed at the heavens until his throat burned.

He leveled his eyes at Bonito and a sob burst from the priest's throat as he crumbled into his chair.

Nox clenched and unclenched his fists, conceding he would have to put up with Bonito and his whining a bit longer.

Provided he could resist gripping the scrawny bastard around the neck and strangling him to death, that is.

Chapter Thirty-Nine

A rcher and Rosalina were the first to make their way to the saloon that morning. But Archer's plan to go through his father's books before everyone else joined them was obliterated within minutes. It seemed everyone was excited about today's plan and not one of them was showing any of the apprehension Archer had flowing through him.

They had a lot riding on that twenty-year-old photo of him and his father. Most of it being his memory, which, given the number of things he'd forgotten from his childhood, seemed like a damn stupid idea.

Rosalina made everyone a simple breakfast of coffee and toast and as they sat around the table together, the conversation flitted from what they hoped to find, to how long it would take to find the treasure.

Not once did anyone suggest they wouldn't be successful. Especially Jimmy. He was talking like they'd find gold on their first dive. Archer had to resist reminding them that finding treasure took time and patience. Both of which were not high on Jimmy's skill list.

Jimmy slathered his toast with Vegemite. "Mmm, tastes like home," he said with a mouthful of bread.

"Looks *disgustoso*." Alessandro screwed up his nose.

"Yep." Jimmy rolled his eyes as he swallowed, showing how much he was enjoying the vegemite. "But not as *disgustoso* as them pickled artichokes you Italians eat."

Alessandro's heavy frown suggested he was ticking over a witty response, but he had nothing.

Archer decided to save him. "It's time to pull up the anchor and get going. Ginger, you and your eagle eyes are on rock-hunting duty."

He handed his father's binoculars to her, and she grabbed them in one hand and reached for Alessandro with the other. Together, they raced towards the stairs.

Alessandro flashed a smug grin at Jimmy as they passed. But Jimmy wouldn't care. He wasn't naïve enough to think he had a chance with Ginger. Not when her eyes had been almost fixed on Alessandro since he'd stepped aboard.

Jimmy worked the anchor engine and within minutes, the entire chain and its heavy burden were secured on *Evangeline* and they set sail.

Rosalina stayed by Archer's side as he hugged the boat close to Anafi Island's shoreline. With Rosalina's delightful scent and tantalizingly low-cut top, he struggled to focus on both the depth sounder and the craggy island.

For seven hours, they cruised the crystal-blue waters that lapped at the deserted beaches dotted around the island with no success.

Archer needed to get some air. He left Jimmy at the wheel, grabbed Rosalina's hand and led her up to the top deck where Ginger was still scrutinizing the island through the binoculars.

An enormous bluff rose out of the ocean on the south-eastern end of the island. On top of the cliff stood the abandoned monastery of Panaghia Kalamiotissa. Most of it was in ruins, but Alessandro was quick to point out its architectural significance.

Archer was doubting their choice of island, and threads of disillusion drifted into his thoughts. He fought to curb the negativity and began reviewing his father's clues in his head.

"I found it!" Ginger's squeal catapulted Archer from his negative rabbit hole. She jumped into Alessandro's arms, wrapping her arms and legs around him, and the unprepared Italian just about toppled overboard.

"Do you see it, Archer?" she yelled.

Ginger climbed off Alessandro and proudly pointed midway up the island cliff. She handed the binoculars over and Archer scanned the scraggy landscape.

The four rectangular blocks stood out like a lobster on a buffet table.

"*X* marks the spot." Archer fought back a flood of emotions by kissing Rosalina.

Can I really do this? Can I return to the spot where Dad was killed?

Rosalina looked at him, probably trying to read his mind.

Scared that she really could, he put on a fake smile. "This is it, babe." He hugged her to his chest so she couldn't see him.

"Are you okay?" She said it anyway. Damn, she was good.

"Of course. This is closure. I've been waiting a bloody long time for this."

That seemed to placate her as she snuggled deeper into his arms. He looked over her head at the island. Other than the deserted monastery high on the right, there were no other buildings or signs of civilization.

Archer reached for the pendant.

I'm going to make things right again, Dad.

The last time he'd been in this spot was an hour before his father died.

A long, pebble beach met the water's edge at the base of the cliff and there were no obvious access points to it. Hopefully that meant no one visited the secluded beach.

Their diving spot was completely isolated and looked safe from prying eyes.

Yet he couldn't shake the feeling that someone was watching them.

But for the sake of Rosalina and everyone else, Archer had to pretend there was nothing wrong.

Scuba diving was dangerous enough, but with additional fear in the mix, it was deadly.

And Archer knew that fear all too well.

Chapter Forty

Rosalina's emotions were a tangle of both excitement and trepidation as she tightened the knot on her bikini bottoms, then tugged her sleeveless wetsuit shirt down to her hips. For six days they'd been diving off the shore of Anafi Island and so far, they'd come up with nothing.

Each night, Archer's mood had darkened just a fraction more. And although she had a strong feeling they were diving in the right place, she also feared they weren't. And that was a reality that would challenge Archer in ways she hadn't experienced before.

Before each dive, he had the energy and playfulness of a teenager. After the dive, not so much.

Archer's sassy grin lit up his face as he helped her into the buoyancy vest. As he took his time gliding the zipper over her breasts, he devoured her with his gaze and her insides tingled at their intensity. It was incredible how much power he held in those chocolate irises of his, especially when the golden halo around the outside sparkled as much as the surrounding ocean.

His wavy hair was longer than he normally wore it and in the blazing sunshine, the tips shimmered like gold. It was moments like these that made all the stress she'd had when they'd separated fade into oblivion and she felt like they'd been together forever.

She clipped on her fins and adjusted her stance to hold the weight of the air cylinder. "Okay, I'm ready."

Archer loaded her buoyancy vest and tank onto her back, and the weight nearly had her knees buckling. Preferring not to wait on board for Archer to get his gear on, she put her regulator in her mouth and took a giant step overboard into the warm Mediterranean Sea.

Archer smiled at her from the dive deck when she popped to the surface. She formed a circle with her thumb and index finger indicating she was okay, and adjusted the air in her buoyancy vest so she could float without kicking at the surface.

Now that they were treasure hunting, Jimmy and Archer's competitive spirits had them pitted against one another. Each morning started with some creative wagering. Yesterday's wager and the subsequent lack of success had Jimmy and Archer cooking dinner together.

Archer could cook, but last night's meal choice might've been deliberate sabotage.

The two men combined some interesting flavors. But it was all just a bit of fun, and she'd loved every minute watching Archer and Jimmy and their impromptu cooking show.

Archer had been buzzing all morning, and after Jimmy and Ginger came up empty-handed on their first dive, he'd bragged that this dive was the one that would find the *Flying Seahorse*.

Rosalina was swept up in Archer's excitement and she had a good feeling about this dive, too. She selfishly wanted to be with Archer when he rediscovered the ancient wreck.

Archer jumped into the ocean beside her, and after signaling they were okay to Jimmy, they released the air in their vests and descended down the anchor line together.

Between the two diving teams of Jimmy and Ginger, and Rosalina and Archer, they had already covered an area about the size of a football field. A large map taped to the dining room wall was divided into sections, and as they searched each section, they marked it off the map.

Nine sections now had large crosses through them.

They had started closer towards shore and gradually progressed further out to sea, all the time keeping the four unusually shaped white rocks at the same angle from the upper deck to replicate the view in the photo.

Fifty-foot visibility allowed her to see the ocean floor as a brilliant display of color and movement. It was good diving, lots to see, and as usual, a peaceful sense of being at one with nature enveloped her. She wanted to explore wherever her eyes took her, but instead, she followed her compass to the designated area. With the portable metal detector gripped in her gloved hand, she swept it over the ocean floor in wide arcs. Archer was slightly ahead of her, doing exactly the same.

Giant sea turtles cruised overhead, creating large shadows as they floated above her on the warm current. The underwater scene was picture perfect, with hundreds of fish that danced about in a kaleidoscope of neon colors and an abundance of coral of all shapes and sizes, each one showing off its unique design. Some were bigger than Rosalina.

A large school of trevally swam close to the surface, their bodies flashing occasionally in the afternoon sun. Her metal detector beeped and she tracked the signal into a large mound of pink coral. Using her gloved hand, she dug around the sand to locate the source of the sound. With a sigh, she removed a rusted fishing reel and dropped it into a netted bag hooked to her hip.

A slight movement caught her eye, and when she studied the coral near her cheek, she found a seahorse camouflaged within the soft coral. Laughing at the irony, she caught Archer's attention by banging on her tank with her metal signal rod.

But when he reached her side, he rolled his eyes and indicated to her to keep swimming. The small creature hovered in place as if held by an invisible string. It was impossible to see how it propelled itself forward, but it did, and soon disappeared amongst the plant life.

Rosalina pushed off the sand and kicked to catch up to Archer. His white shorts looked luminescent against the rest of his tanned body. She caught up to him and tugged on his fin. He spun towards her and she placed her index fingers side by side, a signal that translated to them sticking together.

He gestured 'okay', but she thumped his shoulder anyway. One of the first rules of diving was to swim with your buddy. His impatience was reckless. Separating could be dangerous.

He removed his regulator and mouthed, *sorry*.

She removed hers and mouthed back, *you will be*.

He gripped her hand and they swam along, moving the metal detectors ahead of them in a synchronized swing. Both scanners beeped at the same time and they released hands, slowed down and panned the equipment back and forward. The beeping grew in intensity as they glided towards a large coral outcrop.

Archer paused at the base of the coral and lowered onto the ocean floor; Rosalina kneeled beside him. Their detectors emitted a high-pitched squeal and Rosalina joined Archer in digging away the coarse sand.

Rosalina touched something hard and pulled it from the sand. It looked like a large metal spike and when she held it up, Archer produced an almost identical item. He hollered through his regulator and his eyes glimmered with obvious delight.

But, not understanding the significance, she shrugged.

Archer imitated hammering.

They were nails. Giant nails. The type used in ancient ships.

Archer hugged her, and they spun in the water. She removed her regulator and tugged his from his mouth to kiss him. But she had to give in to his impatience to keep looking and put her mouthpiece back in.

Rosalina put her rusty nail into her net bag and checked her dive watch.

They still had thirteen more minutes at this depth before they had to begin their ascent. She put her watch right in front of Archer's face-mask and pointed at the time. He responded with the 'okay' signal.

They began digging. Within minutes, they'd extracted dozens of giant nails from the sand. Rosalina was itching to reveal something of value, and, determined to beat Archer to the first significant find, she dug up to the wrist of her glove and scooped back the loose sand.

She continued to dig in a frenzied race against Archer who, based on his frantic digging, recognized the challenge. Sand particles dispersed into a cloud that floated away in the current.

Rosalina nudged something with her fingers and as she tugged on it, she brushed away the sand that secured it. She fingered the curved outer rim of the item and her heart pounded.

This was not another nail or abandoned fishing gear.

The outer rim gradually revealed itself from beneath the sand like a sunrise on a frosty morning. As each inch unfolded, the golden metal reflected a warm glow, as if delighted by its final discovery.

It released in a cloud of sand that spoiled the visibility, and Rosalina anxiously waved it away. When the water cleared, her breath caught at the brilliant piece reclaimed from its sandy grave. The artwork around the edge of the large gold plate was like nothing she'd seen before: beautiful, bold, and its elaborate decorations told a story.

She held it up like a trophy, and Archer's eyes nearly popped out of his mask. His reach for the plate was in slow motion, as if he were dreaming, but as soon as he felt the weight of the piece, his eyes lit up.

Rosalina almost burst with pride. This moment was twenty years in the making and she was so humbled to be sharing it with him.

She checked her watch. Time was up. She showed him her watch. He nodded and held the plate towards her, but she indicated he should carry it.

Archer hugged it to his chest before tucking it into his net bag. He motioned for her to wait one minute and she frowned as he undid the zippered pocket of his buoyancy vest. Once open, he removed a reel and tugged thin white cord from the device. Using his dive knife, he cut the cord at a length of about two yards and handed it to Rosalina. He then signaled for her to tie one end down.

Now understanding what he was doing, she kneeled on the sand to tie it to a lump of hard coral. When completed, she turned to Archer, who was removing his board shorts. He struggled to get the shorts over his fins, and she giggled as he wrestled in the water. She spread her arms and shrugged her shoulders in a *What the hell are you doing?* silent question.

She gasped at a flash of movement at her side and snapped her hand back, but she was too late. An eel as large as her arm plunged its teeth through her glove and into the fleshy part of her hand. She shrieked, and the eel released and disappeared back into a hole in the coral.

Rosalina yanked off her glove, and a crimson cloud blossomed into the water.

Despite the amount of blood, she was lucky. Eels can bite fingers right off. She only had six puncture wounds. But the salt water made the sting excruciating. The wounds were in the fleshy part of her palm between her wrist and little finger.

Archer kneeled beside her and reached for her arm, cupping her elbow and palm as he examined the bite. She made the sign for *eel* and his frown deepened.

She dreaded what would be going through his mind. The last time he was in that location, a cloud of blood had resulted in one of the most horrific things a person could see.

Rosalina fought the sting, determined to play down the injury. She gave Archer the okay symbol and put her glove back on.

She signaled *boat* with her hands and pushed off the sand towards the anchor line, but Archer tugged her back. He pulled his emergency safety sausage from his vest and did the thumbs up signal, indicating that he wanted to ascend there and draw the attention of the boat to them.

They rose to five yards from the surface and Rosalina checked her watch. They would need to hover at this level for five minutes before they continued their ascent.

Archer's usually calm, almost angelic diving pose was gone. Instead, he spun from side to side, checking their surroundings with frantic movements.

Rosalina refused to get swept into his paranoia, so with forced determination, she tried to relax. She pointed at the gold plate to change his focus. Archer reached for his net bag and wriggled the plate free. Hovering at the decompression depth, Rosalina eased in beside him and they studied its intricate designs.

If this plate was a piece from the thirteenth century Florence Calimala collection, then it was in remarkable condition, with minimal signs of aging. The outer edge was decorated with pictures of castles, knights, and horses pulling chariots. An emblem embossed in the center displayed three lily flowers connected by a dotted line. Beneath that was the word *Thopia*.

Rosalina tried to guess what a piece like this would be worth and had to remind herself to keep her breathing steady. One of the most dangerous things to do while scuba diving was to hold your breath.

She checked her dive watch and was surprised to see four minutes had already passed. Archer tucked the plate back into the net bag and they inflated their buoyancy vests to float gracefully to the surface.

They popped above the waterline, and after a quick cheer, Archer filled the safety sausage with air from his regulator while Rosalina blew on her whistle. Once the fluorescent orange sausage was fully inflated, it stood six feet above the surface and should attract the attention of the spotters on the boat fairly quickly.

To Rosalina's relief, a couple of flashes from *Evangeline* confirmed they'd been found and she could imagine Jimmy would be frantically pulling up the anchor to cruise toward them. Jimmy was an impatient bugger.

Rosalina struggled not to wave at the approaching yacht, as they could misconstrue her excitement as a sign of distress in the water.

The yacht stopped and Rosalina and Archer swam to the back dive platform.

"We found her," Archer blurted as Alessandro and Ginger helped him and Rosalina onboard.

"I knew it," Jimmy cried out. "I knew we'd fucking find it." Jimmy clapped Archer's back.

"How do you know?" Alessandro asked.

Archer tugged the plate from the net bag and offered it to Jimmy.

"Holy hell." Jimmy beamed like a grandfather presented with his first grandson as he examined the plate.

Alessandro pointed at the three lilies. "That looks like a family emblem. *Magnifico*. I'll look up *Thopia*. Hopefully, it'll help us establish the age of the plate."

"You should also check the diary we found in the tomb, see if it's mentioned there," Rosalina said.

"Agreed." Alessandro dashed off so fast, Rosalina giggled at his urgency.

"I'll go help him." Ginger skipped after him.

"Well, I reckon it's beer time." Jimmy's smile was so big, his gold tooth flashed in the sun.

"I reckon it is, old man, but we need the first-aid kit before that." He nodded at Rosalina.

She cringed when she removed the glove, shocked at how gruesome the wound was. With fresh blood oozing from the six deep puncture holes, it looked much worse.

"Fucking hell! What happened?" Jimmy's brows slammed together in a deep scowl.

"An eel."

"Shit! I'll get the first-aid kit." Jimmy marched away.

When Jimmy disappeared inside, Rosalina allowed Archer to look after her.

He draped a plush towel over her shoulders and, despite her objections, he carried her inside and positioned her on the leather sofa with an abundance of pillows.

Jimmy returned with the first aid kit, and his tenderness surprised her as he bathed her hand in antiseptic ointment.

Her injury didn't undermine the upbeat banter of the group though, and Rosalina didn't want to dampen anyone's spirits either, so she downplayed the agony. "Do you think it's the *Flying Seahorse?*"

"Absolutely!" Jimmy's eyes twinkled as he nodded with conviction.

Rosalina laughed. "In that case, I think we should celebrate."

"This calls for champagne," said Alessandro.

"I'll get something to eat." Ginger raced off towards the galley.

"I'm getting the rum." Jimmy disappeared behind the bar.

And suddenly Rosalina and Archer were alone. She reached for his hand. "Happy?"

"Are you kidding? I feel like I've waited my whole life for this moment." He kneeled beside her and kissed her forehead. "It wouldn't have been the same if you hadn't been here with me."

The intensity in his eyes was like the facets of an expensive diamond, brilliant and precious. "Do you realize what this means, Rosa?" His warm palm cupped her cheek. "We've found a treasure that's been missing for over seven hundred years."

Rosalina leaned into his hand. "Your father would be proud."

He melted a fraction and opened his mouth to say something, but Jimmy stomped into the room carrying a rum bottle and two glasses.

As the celebration kicked off around them, Rosalina didn't miss the worry in Archer's eyes. It was strange. After what she'd found, she thought he'd be nothing but happy.

Chapter Forty-One

Rosalina had to fight the disappointment raging through her when it was decided that Archer and Jimmy would do the first dive of the day. Their plan was to mark out the final resting place of *Flying Seahorse*, and then start digging for the treasure that, of course, they were certain had to be there.

She wanted to be with them. She wanted to share the joy of removing precious pieces from the soft sand. But the choice was no longer hers. The bloody eel bite meant she had to keep her wounds out of the water for at least twenty-four hours. And after her golden discovery yesterday, the timing could not have been worse.

The day was perfect for diving. . . clear blue sky, gentle breezes, and the warm weather kept the water temperature at a pleasant seventy-five degrees. And all that only added to Rosalina's depression.

Ginger and Alessandro leaned over the railing from the deck above, watching Jimmy and Archer get ready to jump in. By the frown rippling Alessandro's forehead, Rosalina guessed his hangover was still giving him grief. They had partied until late into the night, and with every fresh detail Alessandro had revealed about the ancient golden relic she had found yesterday, Ginger and Alessandro had sipped more wine.

By the time the pair of them had staggered to his cabin, it was after midnight.

Archer slipped his scuba mask around his neck and leaned in to kiss Rosalina. "I wish you were coming." Maybe he sensed her frustration.

Sticking out her bottom lip, she pulled a sad face.

He cupped her cheek. "There'll be plenty more to find, babe. I promise to leave some for you."

"Ha. You better." She slapped his chest. "Be careful you two, and Jimmy, make sure you stick together."

Jimmy grunted his response as he tugged his mask into position.

Archer jumped overboard first and popped up to give the 'okay' signal. Jimmy followed, and they slipped below the waterline.

Rosalina sighed and turned to Ginger. "Might as well work on my tan."

"Not me." Ginger shook her head. "Five minutes in the sun and I'll be as red as a lobster."

"Will you be all right by yourself out here?" Alessandro asked.

"Sure. You kids head on inside. I'll watch out for Archer and Jimmy."

Ginger gripped Alessandro's hand, and they disappeared through the doorway.

Rosalina couldn't believe how quickly they'd become a couple. She just hoped Ginger was legitimate in her affections. It was pretty easy to get caught up with the fancy yacht and the exotic travel. Yet even with the doubts she had swirling through her mind, she couldn't deny how lovely they seemed together.

She was pleased for Alessandro. He deserved to find happiness in love.

With nothing more to do for the next forty minutes, she put her sunglasses on, removed her T-shirt, adjusted her bikini, and flopped onto a deck chair. Making herself comfortable, she placed her good hand behind her head as a pillow.

Her bite wounds throbbed. Despite the amount of champagne

she'd consumed last night, it had failed to mask the pain which had kept her awake for hours.

They'd all had a lot to drink last night, and she was surprised Jimmy even woke this morning after the amount of rum he'd consumed. But before she'd even finished preparing breakfast, he'd bounded into the kitchen like a puppy at mealtime.

Jimmy was a good man. He'd look out for Archer down there.

She was still jealous, though.

Sounds of tiny waves lapping at the sides of *Evangeline* were relaxing, as was the slight breeze that took the edge off the warm sun. She checked her watch. Five minutes had passed, and she pictured Archer and Jimmy already kneeling on the bottom of the ocean, digging in the soft sand.

A shout over water had her sitting upright and peering over the railing. A small boat was speeding towards them and the driver was waving madly for her attention.

She stood and tugged her T-shirt back on. Looking over her shoulder, she hoped to see Alessandro or Ginger, but she was alone.

"Help!" A man in a black peak cap waved like crazy.

She clutched the railing as the small boat pulled up to the dive platform.

"Please. Help. My friend is hurt really bad."

Rosalina gasped. The second man in the back of the boat was covered in blood and barely moving. "What happened?"

"He was trying to fix the propellers and. . . and I think he's nearly lost his arm." His high-pitched voice was barely decipherable.

Rosalina peered over her shoulder, but still no Ginger or Alessandro. "Let me get help." She raced up the steps, taking them two at a time.

"Alessandro! Ginger!" She sprinted through the yacht and found them in the kitchen. "Quick, I need the first-aid kit."

"What happened? Is it Archer? Jimmy?" Alessandro strode toward her.

"No. A couple of guys have come over in a boat. One of them is covered in blood." Rosalina grabbed the first-aid kit and dashed along the passageway, out the back and down the stairs to the dive deck.

Alessandro and Ginger were right behind her.

A bloody trail led them to the injured man, who was alone on the dive deck. He was on his back and had blood all over his arm and stomach.

She kneeled at the wounded man's side, and Ginger and Alessandro joined her.

"Don't move!"

The booming voice made her blood freeze.

Fear shot up her spine as she turned around.

The creep who had occupied her nightmares was on the deck above them. Nox. His stance screamed authority. His bald head was an angry red dome.

The barrel of his gun pointed straight at her.

Rosalina's mind screamed. *How the hell did this happen?*

The wounded man jumped up from the floor and waved a large knife as he backed away from them.

Alessandro stepped in front of the two women. "What do you want?"

"I want what is rightfully mine." Nox's face contorted into a hideous smirk.

Fear prickled Rosalina's skin.

"You!" The gunman pointed at Ginger. "Tie them to the railing." He tossed a rope towards her.

Ginger's wide eyes darted from Rosalina to Alessandro. Fear riddled her features.

Rosalina's brain scrambled to catch up as she stepped her back against the railing. She didn't want to look at the ugly priest, but couldn't resist. Her stomach twisted at his evil glare.

Ginger's fingers trembled as she looped the rope around Rosalina's wrists and tugged it into a knot.

Ginger moved to Alessandro to tie his wrists, but he shoved off the railing and released a primal roar as he lunged at the knife-wielding man.

He was fast. Faster than Rosalina had ever seen him move. But he missed and stumbled sideways.

Rosalina screamed. Ginger did too.

Alessandro swung his fists. The man dodged left and right.

The blade flashed in the sun, and then it disappeared.

Alessandro howled a sickening cry. He clutched his stomach. Blood oozed through his fingers.

"No!" The ropes bit into Rosalina's wrists.

"Alessandro. Alessandro!" His name broke in her throat as Alessandro's haunting eyes drifted from his bloody hands toward her.

Oh my God. Is he going to die?

Chapter Forty-Two

Tears blurred Rosalina's vision as she fought the restraints on her wrists.

Alessandro fell to his knees and groaned as he toppled sideways. The bloody knife clanged to the floor.

"No!" Ginger raced to his side. "Alex!"

The attacker backed away; his bloodied fingers trembled as he shook his head. The whites of his eyes were wide, crazy. "I'm sorry, it was an accident."

"You bastard!" Ginger shot to her feet and lunged at him.

He dodged backwards, but she rammed her fists into his chest, shoving him overboard.

But he clutched to the railing of the smaller boat and with brute strength, he pulled himself onto that boat.

Anger rose in Rosalina like a demon. Wrestling against the ropes, she shot her gaze from the blood spilling from Alessandro, to the ocean where Archer and Jimmy had disappeared, to the evil bastard on the upper deck.

A sickening noise gargled from Alessandro's throat.

"Alessandro." Ginger fell at his side and clutched his hand.

The man who'd stabbed Alessandro started the boat engine.

"No!" The bald priest shrieked from the deck above.

The front of the boat pulled out of the water as it roared away.

"Come back here!" Nox fired at the departing boat. *Boom. Boom. Boom.*

The noise was louder than anything Rosalina had ever heard.

Did he shoot him? Or the boat? When the boat changed course and accelerated away, she decided the creep must have missed.

"Alessandro! Stay with me, honey." Tears streamed down Ginger's cheeks as she pressed her hands over his bloody wound.

"I'm okay." His agonized tone belied his words.

Rosalina clenched her jaw and glared up at the madman. "You bastard! Look what you did."

Nox ran his hand over his barren scalp. His eyes were pure evil. "Get him up. You three get up here. Now!"

"We can't move him." Rosalina darted her gaze to the first-aid kit, just three feet away. "He needs—"

"Get him up now or I'll push him overboard for the sharks." His grin was more menacing than the barrel of the gun.

With trembling fingers, Ginger untied Rosalina, and they helped Alessandro to his feet. He was heavy with unsteady steps as the three of them staggered up the stairs.

A wave of nausea wobbled through Rosalina at the amount of Alessandro's blood that had spilled onto the polished wooden deck.

At the top of the stairs, Nox moved behind them.

The barrel of the gun was shoved into the small of her back. Rosalina gasped. "Please. Don't shoot."

"Move."

His foul stench should've carried away with the breeze. *But it didn't.* It hung in the air, cloying and nasty.

Bile lacerated her throat. Acid churned in her stomach.

It was only a handful of steps to the first sunlounge, but each one came with a brutal groan from Alessandro. At the lounge, she and Ginger struggled to lower him as gently as possible. Wincing, he flopped back and when Ginger lifted his feet onto the bed, a howl of pure agony burst from his throat.

"I'm here, Alex." Ginger shoved the other lounge out of the way and kneeled at his side. Her white-knuckled fingers entwined with his.

Rosalina turned to the bastard, and it took all her might not to charge at him.

He stood back from the furniture; the gun aimed at her.

It would take at least six large steps to get to him. *I'm fast. But a bullet is faster.*

Unclenching her jaw, she glared at him. "What now?"

"We wait."

Rosalina glanced at her watch. In about ten minutes, Archer and Jimmy would resurface — straight into a trap.

Sweat trickled down her temple as her mind raced for a way to warn Archer. But there was nothing. Seconds whizzed by; minutes flew. Her heart thundered in her ears.

I'm running out of time. I have to do something. But what?

Alessandro groaned, and she shot her gaze at him. His blood pooled beneath the sunlounge. *Drip. Drip. Bloody drip.*

He needed help. And fast. "He needs a doctor."

"He can wait." The creep grinned.

She'd been too close to those putrid teeth once before. A shudder raced up her neck at that rotten memory.

He waved the gun at her. "Sit."

As she sat on the edge of another sunlounge, Ginger looked at her with pleading eyes. . . but the situation was hopeless.

Rosalina searched for a solution. Behind Ginger was the sporting goods cupboard. She mentally summarized what was in that compartment. Fishing rods, water skiing equipment, dive gear, spear-fishing gear. *Yes!*

A glimmer of hope washed through her. But without a way to get into that cupboard, the hope crumbled away before it even began to crystallize.

"I need to get the first-aid kit." Rosalina rose without waiting for an answer.

"No. Don't move!" He raised the gun at her. Then turned it toward Alessandro.

This is insane. "He needs help, for God's sake. What kind of priest are you?"

He cocked his head. "I am the divine Nox."

Rosalina sat down and glared at the devil. His skin was insidious. His lips were thin and nearly non-existent. And his eyes. . . they had no soul. "You're a freak."

"I have searched for this treasure my whole life. Nothing will stop me. It is my destiny."

"You're still a freak."

"Shut up." He launched at her and whipped the gun across her temple.

The assault was so fast she didn't have time to react. The blow knocked her off her chair. Stars flashed across her eyes as she slumped to the floor. Rosalina blinked, trying to shake the fog from her brain.

This is my opportunity!

Groaning, she closed her eyes and, determined to convince Nox she'd passed out, she froze.

"Jesus! What did you do?" Ginger raced to Rosalina's side. Her hand was gentle on her shoulder. Ginger's position would block Nox's view of her and Rosalina risked opening her eyes to quickly wink.

Ginger's eyes widened, and she winked back, then she shook Rosalina's shoulder. "Rosa. . . wake up, Rosa."

"Now it's just you and me," Nox said.

"What do you want?" Fear quivered Ginger's words.

"I want it all."

A chair scraped over the polished deck.

"Stand here, bitch."

"Please don't hurt them," Ginger pleaded.

"Oh, I won't hurt them. Yet."

Rosalina understood what that meant. He needed Archer and Jimmy to keep diving. They were how he was going to get his hands on the treasure.

Archer and Jimmy would surface at any moment. Right into Nox's trap.

Moving as little as possible, she adjusted her hand to check her watch. Forty-seven minutes had passed.

"Woo hoo!" Jimmy's excited cry carved through the silence.

A dagger of despair drove into Rosalina's heart.

"Jesus, man. There's so much down there. It's like plunderin' Aladdin's cave." Jimmy cheered.

"I told you, buddy," Archer's tone was so upbeat she could imagine him smiling.

Rosalina swallowed bile, and squeezing her eyes shut, she waiting for the perfect moment to make her move. She chanced a peek. But Nox had moved out of her line of sight.

Where is he? And where's Ginger?

Oh Jesus! He's going to use Ginger as a shield.

That's how he'll get Archer and Jimmy to continue diving.

"Hey, where is everyone?" Archer called out.

"Keep your mouth shut," Nox whispered, obviously talking to Ginger.

Rosalina held her breath as she risked a glance over her shoulder.

Nox had the gun wedged into Ginger's back. His eyes were aimed below, probably on the step at the top of the dive deck.

Both Nox and Ginger had their backs to her. With a breath trapped in her throat and maintaining the same body position, she inched towards the cupboard.

Her mind was on the edge of hysteria as she risked being shot or, worse, Ginger being shot because of her. But she had to get to the dive cupboard. Everyone was counting on her.

A heavy clunk banged on the deck below and she assumed one of the men had removed his tank and dropped it onto the dive deck.

"I thought everyone would be. . . oh fuck!" Jimmy boomed. "Is that blood?"

Footsteps pounded across the dive deck. Then they raced up the stairs.

"Don't move." Nox's calm voice showed how much he owned the situation.

"Rosalina!" Archer's voice was shrill. From the top of the stairs, all Archer would be able to see of her was the lower half of her body. The rest was hidden behind Alessandro's sunlounge.

"Stop! Or I'll shoot her."

Rosalina wanted to show Archer she was okay, but couldn't risk Nox seeing it. She held her breath and waited. Her heart pounded like a battle drum. *Boom. Boom. Boom.* The cupboard was just four feet away. Nox would be distracted with three people to watch; two of them were angry enough to kill him with their bare hands.

Inch by inch, teeth clenched, body frozen in position, she clawed her way towards the cupboard.

"Alex! Did you shoot him? You son of a bitch!" Jimmy growled. "I'm going to kill you."

"I'll put a bullet through her brain if you take one more step."

Alessandro groaned and Rosalina couldn't decide if that was a good or bad thing.

"Let her go!" Archer demanded.

"That treasure is mine."

"You can have it. Just let them all go." Archer sounded calm, but Rosalina pictured pure rage drilled onto his face.

"Not until I have it all."

"It's all there."

Rosalina's heart raced.

Would Nox fall for Archer's lie?

Or did he hear Jimmy say how much was down there?

The cupboard was hidden behind Alessandro's chair. She could make a run for it.

But would he shoot Ginger?

Rosalina was holding her breath and she slowly let it out, then took another.

"I know there's more. Much more. And I'm not leaving until you get it all. Now show me what you have!"

Heavy footfalls thumped down the steps and across the dive deck. Then there was a tinkling sound as someone picked up what she assumed was a net bag. Footsteps stomped across the deck, followed by a loud clattering noise as the treasures spilled out.

Confident all eyes would be watching the treasures, she used the opportunity to raise her hand and wave, but she had no way of knowing if Archer saw her movement.

"Back away. Let me see," Nox barked.

"Ow! Let go of me!" Ginger squealed.

Rosalina tried not to visualize what Nox had done to make Ginger shriek like that. Instead, she wriggled towards the cupboard, then froze again, ensuring she was in the same body position as she'd been when she fell.

"How many pieces?"

"You count 'em, dickhead." Jimmy's voice boomed with anger.

Ginger shrieked, and Rosalina cringed. *What is Nox doing to her?*

"Spread them out so I can see what's there."

"There's more on the lower deck," Archer said.

"You. . . go get them. You spread these out."

As footsteps retreated, Rosalina crawled another inch and hated how big the sun deck was. Two feet to go. But she had a new dilemma. To move any further would put her completely behind Alessandro's sunlounge and make it obvious she was moving. She had to wait for the perfect moment.

Braced like a cobra set to attack, she readied to move. Mentally, she tried to recall the cupboard interior.

She inhaled a long, shaky breath. And waited.

Each second was another second Alessandro didn't have. It wasn't right that no one was with him, holding his hand, reassuring him he was going to be okay.

Damn it, I have to do something…

Everyone was so quiet; she had no idea what was going on. She desperately wanted to look over her shoulder. But she had to focus. . . to wait for the right moment, and when it came, she had to commit fully, no matter what the outcome.

The tinkering sounds continued, and Nox was murmuring something unintelligible. He must be looking at the treasure. *Good, that means he's not watching me.*

But what's Archer doing?

He's taking a long time on the lower deck.

Her stomach twisted into angry knots.

"You okay, Ginger?" Jimmy's gruff voice was surprisingly calm.

"Yes, but Alessandro. . . he's been stabbed. . . he needs a doctor." Ginger's voice was shrill.

"You stabbed him," Jimmy barked. "You fucking bastard."

"No, I didn't. Now shut up or I'll shoot you."

"No, you won't." Jimmy spat the words; full of defiance.

There was a pause. "Why won't I?"

"You need me to dive."

"I don't need all of you."

A weird silence filled the void.

Oh Shit. Nox has been watching us. He knows everyone but Alessandro could scuba dive.

Oh my God! He doesn't need all of us. We're in serious trouble.

"Where is Archer? Get over here."

Ginger shrieked. "That hurts, you bastard."

"Archer!" Nox yelled like a demon.

His calm façade was gone. He was now a madman.

A loud crash shattered the silence, and Rosalina sprang into action. A gun exploded, but she didn't falter.

Bullets slammed into timber. Glass shattered. Ginger screamed. Furniture crashed.

But Rosalina blocked out the bedlam and lunged at the door. Her trembling fingers made unhooking the spear gun harder than it should be. It tumbled off the rail, and she grabbed a spear from the rack.

Ginger screamed, and a man released a horrific cry of pain.

Shit! Was that Archer? Or Jimmy? *Oh God. Oh God!*

Rosalina jumped out of the cupboard with the weapon, and ducked under the cover of Alessandro's chair to load the spear into the gun. Unsteady fingers made drawing back the rubber trigger hard and clamping her teeth, she pulled with all her might. It snapped into position.

Then she looked toward the chaos.

Shit! Jimmy was on the floor holding his stomach and his feet were splayed out before him. His face was deathly pale, and his hands were jammed onto his stomach and covered in blood.

No! Jimmy was shot.

Golden trinkets were spread out at his feet.

Ginger was on her knees, sobbing with her hands over her face.

Nox stood over them with the gun lowered at his side and his chest heaving.

Rosalina aimed the spear gun at him. "Drop the gun."

Nox spun toward her. His eyes locked in. He grinned and raised his weapon.

Archer appeared at her left with his dive knife drawn.

Rosalina was an excellent shot with the spear gun, but with her trembling fingers and the people she loved within range, she couldn't risk firing it.

Nox snapped the gun towards Archer.

Her anger hit overload.

Rosalina pulled the trigger.

A flash of steel crossed the distance in a millisecond.

The spear pierced Nox's belly. The gun fired with a deafening boom.

Nox cried out and stumbled backwards, clutching the spear.

He tripped over Jimmy's feet, fell overboard, and splashed into the ocean.

Chapter Forty-Three

The emergency helicopter took an agonizing forty minutes to arrive, and during every one of those minutes, while they tried to help Jimmy and Alessandro with their horrific wounds, a profound sense of utter uselessness crippled Rosalina.

Alessandro and Jimmy had similar injuries. Jimmy had been shot in almost the same place Alessandro had been stabbed. Their wounds were horrific and scary and Rosalina grew more petrified with each drop of blood that spilled onto the polished wooden deck.

Despite Jimmy's injuries, he'd pulled Archer down to his level and as he'd voiced his opinion on keeping the treasure they'd found a secret, the veins had bulged along his forehead.

While they waited for the medical evacuation, the five of them had discussed what they would tell the police. Information in the media about the treasure would have relic hunters from across the globe descending on their location. Archer was determined to keep it a secret for as long as possible and Jimmy made Archer promise to do exactly that several times before he relaxed.

They had no reason to hide any details about the attack, though, and Rosalina intended to tell them every single thing. It was time to get that insane bastard out of their lives for good.

If he wasn't already dead, that is.

They hadn't seen him since he went overboard. Not that they had really tried. Their focus was on Jimmy and Alessandro, and to placate Jimmy, they also had to hide the treasure.

Jimmy was lucid when the helicopter landed on *Evangeline's* helipad and Archer had to beat the stubbornness out of him when he wouldn't lie down on the stretcher.

Alessandro was the opposite, and with Ginger fussing over him, he was first into the helicopter.

Rosalina released a huge sigh of relief when Alessandro and Jimmy were finally in the hands of the paramedics. The helicopter could only accommodate one other person, and she was pleased Ginger had pleaded for the coveted place.

Rosalina wanted to stay with Archer. She shielded her eyes against the setting sun as the helicopter flew towards the horizon. Archer held her to his chest, and she drew on his steady beating heart for reassurance.

Within half an hour of the medical helicopter leaving, the water police arrived. Together Rosalina and Archer detailed the assault, relaying as much information as possible about Nox.

But the attack had been so swift, Rosalina barely remembered anything about the second man, let alone the boat they had arrived on.

By the time they had finished, they had portrayed Nox as a crazy stalker, which wasn't hard given his first attacks in Florence and at the Maritime Museum.

Her stomach had done sickening twists as she detailed firing her speargun. And how the spear had gone right through Nox's stomach. And his sickening howl of agony as he'd gripped the spear.

Once she informed the police that the crazy priest had fallen overboard and that they hadn't seen him since, their focus turned towards searching for him.

The knots in Rosalina's stomach only released when the police returned to their boat and raced towards the marina.

She turned to Archer, wrapped her arms around his waist and tried not to look at the pools of blood drying at her feet.

It was nearly twelve hours before the doctors advised that Jimmy and Alessandro had made it through their surgeries and that they should both make a full recovery.

It was another twelve hours before they were allowed visitors.

Rosalina clutched Archer's hand and guided him along the hospital corridor. He was as stiff as a board and had barely said anything since they'd stepped through the sliding glass doors. The last time he'd been at Athens hospital, Archer had been an eleven-year-old boy recovering from decompression sickness, who had just seen his father get killed by a shark.

His reluctance to visit the hospital was justified. But Rosalina had put her foot down and made him come with her. That's what friends did. Looked out for each other.

This time, however, when they left the hospital, it would be with good news. At least, that's what she prayed for.

Jimmy and Alessandro's recovery was what she needed to focus on, not Archer's stony look.

She tugged his hand. "Hey. . . relax. They're going to be okay." For Archer's sake, she pretended that his anxiousness was for his friends.

He nodded and clenched his jaw further.

She had imagined the hospital would be a hive of activity, but it wasn't. Even the air was still and the only sound was Archer's ragged breathing. They arrived at Jimmy's room and Archer stiffened again.

She knocked, pushed the door open, and stepped into the room.

Jimmy's face was deathly pale. Usually, his skin was recovering from a hard day in the sun, but now it looked as if his color had drained.

It was a shocking sight and proved how close he'd come to dying. A machine beeped at his side, sounding out his steady heartbeat.

Archer stood at the end of the bed while Rosalina slipped into a chair beside Jimmy and reached for his hand. The calluses on his palm were a reminder of how Jimmy liked to live his life. Hard, and fast, and full of gusto. She hoped nothing was going to change.

Jimmy opened his eyes and turned to her. His quick smile had a wave of relief washing through her.

"'Bout time you got here." His voice was a ragged croak.

Rosalina giggled. "Hey, Jimmy. How are you?"

"I'll live. You gotta get me outta here. Them nurses are about as gentle as pit bulls."

Archer laughed and came around the other side of the bed.

"Hey, Archer." Jimmy glanced at the door as if checking for privacy. "Tell me they didn't get their hands on that treasure."

Archer placed his palm on Jimmy's shoulder and smiled. "No, buddy, it's all tucked away in the Heron Suite."

"Good. 'Cause the second I get outta here, we're going diving."

"Hold your horses there, buddy. It's been down there seven hundred years; it can wait a little more."

"You don't understand. You know how I said I don't do cemeteries? Well, I don't do hospitals either."

"What? No sponge baths?"

"Are you kidding? Have you seen those nurses? They look like they'd rather sumo wrestle with me."

Despite how poorly he looked; Jimmy put on a brave show. If Rosalina closed her eyes or ignored all the tubes and equipment around the bed and attached to him, Jimmy sounded just like he did every day. Like a man in his prime. It made her believe that he really was going to be fine.

When his eyes drooped with exhaustion, they said their good-byes and promised to return tomorrow.

They made their way to Alessandro's room a couple of doors down from Jimmy's and were halfway there when Ginger's laughter drifted to them.

It was a good sign.

Archer knocked once, and they entered hand in hand.

Ginger sat on the edge of Alessandro's bed and her smile would have any man's health improving by the second.

"Hey Alessandro, how are you feeling?" Rosalina kissed his forehead.

He didn't look as pale as Jimmy did. In fact, it was hard to believe he was recovering from surgery at all.

As Ginger fussed over him, Alessandro detailed his operation and how well he was doing.

Alessandro looked both exhausted and besotted.

With Ginger's help, he would recover just fine.

In the following days, Rosalina and Archer juggled their time between the hospital and *Evangeline*, which they had returned to a berth at Fliszos Marina in Athens.

The days and nights blurred into one and time slipped away like leaves on an outgoing tide.

Four days after the attack, the water police returned to *Evangeline* and Archer welcomed them into the saloon and called for her to join them.

With every step Rosalina took from her cabin to the waiting police, her mind flashed to images of Nox lying dead somewhere with a spear sticking out of his belly.

She had to force her feet to carry her along the passageway and it was a metal battle to sit facing them, rather than run away.

"How can I help you, officers?" Archer tugged out a seat at the dining table for her and placed his hand on her shoulder, possibly trying to instill some assurance that everything was going to be okay.

Rosalina tried to draw on Archer's relaxed demeanor, because there was a very real possibility that the police were there to arrest her for killing a man.

She fought to hold down the twisted knot in her stomach.

It didn't matter how many times Archer told her what she did was justified, the memory of firing that spear gun and watching the weapon pierce the body of the creep, no matter how crazy he was, had the effect of an acid milkshake on her insides.

"We want to show you some photos." The taller of the two police officers reached into his coat pocket. His accent was strong, suggesting that English was his second language.

He placed a series of color photos on the table, and gasping, Rosalina covered her mouth.

The man in the photo was dead. His skin was white and his open eyes were ghostly blue.

"Do you recognize him?"

Rosalina snapped her gaze from the photos and met with the police officer's glare. He was studying her, watching for her reaction.

She nodded and swallowed the lump in the back of her throat.

Archer cocked his head at her, confused.

That's right. . . he never saw the other priest.

She tapped the photo. "He's the other priest who attacked us. What happened to him?"

The second police officer shuffled a photo from the bottom of the pile and slid it towards her. "Was this his boat?"

The boat in the photo was sitting on top of jagged rocks. It leaned over at a brutal angle and it was a miracle it hadn't toppled right over. As the photo had been taken, a large wave had crashed over the stern and into the cabin.

"I think it was the boat. I didn't really get a good look at it. What happened?"

"We're still trying to piece it together. But we believe he ran the boat aground, and either fell overboard or tried to swim ashore. His body washed up on a beach yesterday. We are waiting for the autopsy results, but our preliminary investigation indicates he drowned. So unless anything changes, we will rule this as death by accident."

Despite her relief, nausea still wobbled up her throat at the horrific photo of the dead man.

"What about Nox?" Archer said.

"There have been no reports of him being found. Bust based on your accounts of the attack, we assume he is dead." The police officer shrugged. "His body may never be found, and we have called off the search."

By the time the police left, Rosalina's mind was a tornado of swirling questions that had no answers.

Is Nox really dead?

If he is, does that make me a murderer?

If he's not dead, will he come after us again?

The answer to that last question was an absolute yes. Nox was crazy. A lunatic. Blind determination to get his hands on that treasure made him a ruthless madman.

He would never give up.

When Archer had invited her to come treasure hunting with him, he never suggested that their lives could be in danger.

But they'd nearly lost two of her closest friends because of that ancient gold.

And none of the men seemed to have any of the trepidation that she felt. Not Archer, or Jimmy, or Alessandro. And Alessandro was the sensible one.

Neither did Ginger. She was like a giddy school girl distracted by all the shiny objects.

They were all focusing on the treasure.

Maybe searching for gold made everyone crazy.

Rosalina couldn't settle her thoughts and turned her attention to cooking. She made caramelized onion jam. And garlic aioli. And cookies and cupcakes for Jimmy and Alessandro. She made dinner for her and Archer, too. One that reminded her of Nonna and the comforts of the kitchen she loved in Villa Pandolfini. . . traditional pasta carbonara.

While she spent hours flitting around the kitchen, Archer turned to his other love. . . *Evangeline*. A few days ago, they had scrubbed the bloody evidence off the wooden decks together. But Archer wanted to do it all again.

Maybe he *was* analyzing the danger after all.

Later that night, as they ate dinner, she couldn't stop the turmoil crashing through her. Even with a glass of Villa Pandolfini's chianti and the perfect pasta, and Archer, who smelled incredible after he'd showered.

He slipped his hand onto her thigh. "Babe, what's wrong?"

She twisted the stem of her wine glass. "What if he's not dead, Archer? Nox will never stop chasing us."

He tugged her chair around so they faced each other, knees to knees. "He is dead. Nobody could survive that."

"But they never found—"

Archer cupped her cheek. "He's dead, honey. He will never bother us again."

She relaxed her posture and let his positivity wash through her negative thoughts. "You think so?"

"I know so. Come here." His eyes were dark with desire as he swooped Rosalina into his arms.

Clasping her hands behind his neck, she pressed herself against him and allowed him to carry her to the Hamilton Suite.

This was the moment she'd been waiting for. She'd promised herself when she came back aboard *Evangeline* weeks ago that she wouldn't return to the Hamilton Suite until everything was perfect. And with Jimmy and Alessandro getting better every day. And Nox dead. And the police investigation closed. And with Archer's arms around her and his eyes penetrating right into her soul, everything was absolutely perfect.

He carried her through the bedroom doorway and flicked a few switches to dim the lights. Gentle notes of music filled the room, and the blinds glided shut with a soft hum.

Archer sat her on the bed. His gold pendant dangled from his neck, almost touching her breasts as it swung back and forward. She rode a wave of desire as Archer eased her legs apart and dropped to his knees to meet her at eye level.

Her heart pounded as she saw love in his stunning, soulful eyes.

He caressed her cheek, and she pressed into his hand. The musky scent of his cologne drifted faintly from his skin. It triggered memories of past nights spent in this cabin. She looked into his eyes and ran her tongue over her lip.

Archer's breathing deepened, and the gold flecks in his dark irises shimmered.

Rosalina couldn't wait a second longer. She wanted to ravish him, to steal every bit of his measured control and take him into salacious bliss. When their lips met, her insides clenched with the thrill of his fingers caressing her neck.

He eased back from her, holding his palm forward.

Her heart skipped a beat at the small black box in his hand.

Gasping, she studied his glistening eyes and tugged her lip into her mouth.

He squeezed her hand in his. "Rosalina, I can't live without you. When I thought I'd lost you, something died inside me."

Rosalina couldn't breathe. Her pounding heart thumped out an excited beat as Archer opened the box. An enormous single diamond glimmered in the subtle lighting. "Will you marry me?"

"Yes." Tears pooled in her eyes. "Yes, yes, yes."

He tugged the ring from the box and her hand trembled as he slipped the stunning diamond onto her finger.

"I love you." He locked his eyes on her and she felt like she truly was looking into his soul.

"I love you too." She wrapped her arms around him and every worry in her world vanished as she squeezed her body to the man of her dreams.

Chapter Forty-Four

Rosalina didn't realize how hollow the yacht would be without Alessandro and Jimmy and Ginger onboard with them. Although she had enjoyed having Archer all to herself for a change, *Evangeline* was way too big for just the two of them. It had her thinking of her home in Tuscany and Nonna. She missed their conversations that could go on forever.

How long will it be before I see Nonna again?

Now that they had located the treasure, they would need to bring it up before anyone else found out about the priceless relics. She had no idea how long that would take.

Much quicker than Rosalina had expected, Jimmy and Alessandro were released from the hospital and returned back aboard *Evangeline*. Archer had pulled some strings, and paid a lot of money, to have them released early. He had arranged for a doctor to visit them every second day, and a full-time nurse had a new lodging in the Daydream Suite.

For the moment, anyway. Jimmy quickly recovered from his life-saving surgery and didn't waste any time inventing ways to harass the nurse. The way Jimmy was complaining, she'd probably quit in a day or so. Alessandro, on the other hand, played the injured patient just a little too well for the overzealous Ginger.

Having Jimmy and Alessandro back aboard was like having her family back, especially now that Archer's mother had moved aboard too. Helen had barely spoken a word in decades and her transition from ancient nunnery to luxury yacht had made little difference. She had accepted her room on *Evangeline* as if it were an everyday occurrence and so far, it was impossible to tell if she was happy with the move.

Helen's silence made Rosalina miss Nonna even more.

Their first night together, a storm cloud as black as chimney soot rolled over the horizon. Enjoying the spectacle from the lounge on the top deck, Rosalina hugged herself as flashes of lightning blazed across the darkened sky.

Beside her, Helen stared trance-like at the burgeoning clouds. Her mouth was ajar, poised between voicing an opinion and numb confusion. *Evangeline* rocked gently under the ebb and flow of the waves curling into the Anafi shoreline.

"I think we're in for a storm," Rosalina said, not expecting a reply.

Helen placed her knobby fingers over Rosalina's arm. "The storm has already passed." Her voice was a brittle whisper.

Rosalina blinked at the frail old woman and wondered if she'd heard correctly. But as she rolled the words around in her head, she was certain Helen had indeed spoken. Rosalina didn't want to ruin the magical moment, so instead of making any comment, she simply turned her palm over and gripped Helen's delicate hand within her own. Her heart fluttered when Helen squeezed back.

Rosalina caught Archer's approach out of the corner of her eye, but he stopped and turned around. Rosalina frowned. *Maybe he didn't want to disturb us.* But Archer returned a short time later with a bowl of soup. He pulled up a chair beside his mother and spoon-fed the broth into her mouth.

"Your mom was just telling me that the storm has passed." Rosalina chose her words carefully.

Archer cocked his head, and she nodded, willing her eyes to

convey her excitement. His eyes lit up. He looked at his mother and his lips formed a question, but then he grinned as he fed her another spoonful. "Mom always was good at predicting the weather."

Helen squeezed her hand again. Archer caught the movement and Rosalina forced back tears of joy. After only a few mouthfuls, his mother refused to eat any more, but Rosalina was happy. Helen was eating a little more with every meal.

Within fifteen minutes, Helen had drifted off to sleep. Archer gathered her into his arms and carried his mom to her room. Rosalina dressed her in her nightgown and together they tucked her into bed and said goodnight. After they turned off the light and closed the door, Archer reached for Rosalina's hand. "Did she really speak?"

Archer's eyes held hers, and when she nodded, he picked her up and spun her around in the hall. "Fantastic."

He lowered her and his lips met hers for a brief, chaste kiss that had her wishing for more. But now wasn't the time. Jimmy, Alessandro and Ginger would be waiting for them in the saloon, no doubt with drinks in hand.

The distant storm created an electric buzz in the air that enhanced the excited banter at the table. Jimmy was his usual gruff self, cracking jokes and picking on everyone's small idiosyncrasies. It was hard to believe that he'd nearly died just ten days ago.

Ginger helped Rosalina in the kitchen and together they made a delicious fettuccine marinara with the fresh fish Alessandro and Ginger had caught that day. It had been Ginger's turn to teach Alessandro something for a change and Alessandro's fishing *faux pas*, especially as he could barely move at the moment, provided excellent fodder for Jimmy's jokes.

"Has there been any news about Nox?" Alessandro asked during dinner. "Do you think he's alive?"

Archer shook his head. "Rescuing someone with a spear sticking through their body would've made front-page news. So no, I don't think he made it. Let's just assume that a wound like that would've attracted an abundance of predators."

A bloody image snapped into Rosalina's mind, and as she reached for her glass, she stared at the bubbles gliding to the top and tried to swing her focus back to something more pleasant.

After a moment of silence, Alessandro grinned. "Not toasters, I assume."

"You're getting funnier every day, numbnuts." Jimmy clapped Alessandro on the back and for once, Alessandro didn't react to Jimmy's nickname for him.

"What's our plan, boss?" Jimmy asked, and with almost identical timing, both Jimmy and Alessandro leaned forward on their elbows.

"It's obvious, isn't it?" Archer said. "We can't leave the Calimala treasure down there. It's time to haul it up. Unless you fellas want to go back to your old jobs."

"No fucking way." Jimmy glanced at Rosalina with a sheepish grin. "Sorry, ladies."

"It's okay, Jimmy." Rosalina knew that deep down Jimmy was a gentleman.

"I couldn't leave you guys. You'd flounder out here without me." Alessandro puffed out his chest. "You need me."

"Yeah, like a hole in the head." Jimmy smirked and swigged his beer.

Alessandro clutched his chest in mock hurt, and Ginger placed her hand on his leg.

"So, we're treasure hunting?" Jimmy's grin was that of a man who had won the lotto.

Archer held up his drink, and Rosalina chinked her glass to his.

Smiling at the family around her, she raised her glass. "To treasure hunting."

But even as she laughed and cheered with everyone, Rosalina couldn't shake the dreadful feeling that the hell they'd been through to find this treasure was only the beginning of their horror.

Epilogue

Nox expected to die.

To close his eyes and block out the pain would be heaven. But pure agony kept him awake. The spear protruded from his stomach like a mast without a sail.

Fish slithered all around him. Over his hands. Against his cheeks. At first, he cringed against it, but as the hours passed, he no longer cared.

Islands slipped by and he tried to paddle towards them, but each movement sent excruciating pain down his legs. Fearing he might pass out; he gave up trying to swim. As he drifted out to sea on the warm current, he waited to be rescued, expecting to see helicopters overhead. Or boats pulling up alongside. But they didn't come.

Having never swum before, he marveled at his ability to float.

It was a miracle.

As was his survival.

His blood spilled into the ocean, and yet the fish failed to bite. He wondered if his disease was saving him from being eaten alive. Once again, the hand of God saved him.

He was surrounded by ocean, nothing but blue water, dotted

with small white caps and blue sky marred by the occasional cloud. He could do nothing but wait.

Wait to be eaten by sharks.

Wait to die of dehydration.

Wait to be rescued.

Wait. Wait. Wait.

Night came, and the blackness enveloped him. The stars were as brilliant as the jewels he'd seen on the Calimala treasure. Anger welled within him. The treasure had been within his grasp. He'd absorbed the power of the ancient gold.

He punched the water and screamed until he could scream no more.

Nox closed his eyes and dreamed of owning the treasure. Once he'd treated his disease and bought himself a perfect set of shiny white teeth like he'd seen on television, people would look at him with pride, marvel at his success and admire his wealth. They'd all be jealous of him.

Day merged into night. Yet he continued to drift.

Enormous cruise ships passed close by. So close, he called out to them, but they couldn't hear him. *How could they?* His parched throat ensured his voice was barely a whisper.

Night became day so swiftly he believed he'd slept through some of it.

The morning rays burned his face.

The midday sun burned his scalp. Blisters became large, festering welts. He tasted blood when his lips cracked and he sucked on the thick liquid as if it were an elixir.

Late on the second day, the sun's fierce heat burned him like laser beams. He couldn't bear it anymore. As he tore his shirt from his body, each touch of the spear sent driving pain down his legs. Reaching behind his back to rip the fabric apart, drove him to the point of delirium.

The shirt finally broke free of the spear and he pulled it over his head. His stomach would now succumb to the same burning fate as his face, but the reprieve would be worth it.

He considered the vial of mushroom powder in his ring.

He was just one mouthful away from ending it all.

The sun passed in a great arc above him, and the heat penetrated the flannel material, creating a suffocating sauna. His hot breath was steady as he waited for the end.

Whenever that would be. However, it would come.

But the fact that he was still alive was a miracle.

He pulled the cloth off his face and stared at the heavens.

I'm being kept alive for a reason.

And I know exactly what it is.

To kill Rosalina and Archer and the rest of those bastards and then the Calimala Treasure will be all mine.

THE END. . . for now.

DEAR FABULOUS READER, THANK YOU FOR FOLLOWING ARCHER AND Rosalina on this crazy journey.

But the adventure isn't over. Turn the page to discover a whole new treasure hunting adventure in Treasured Lies.

OR KEEP TURNING THE PAGES FOR MORE ACTION-PACKED ROMANTIC **suspense books by Kendall Talbot.**

Made in the USA
Middletown, DE
16 August 2022

71500521R00196